HARLEM MOON

BROADWAY

Gold Diggers

Gold Diggers

TRACIE HOWARD

HARLEM MOON
Broadway Books / New York

[Handwritten inscription across page:] To an Victor-Wise with Smmmless Love!: All that glitters Gold!. Happy Reading!!

PUBLISHED BY HARLEM MOON

Copyright © 2007 by Tracie Howard

All Rights Reserved

Published in the United States by Harlem Moon, an imprint of The Doubleday Broadway Publishing Group, a division of Random House, Inc., New York. www.harlemmoon.com

HARLEM MOON, BROADWAY BOOKS, and the HARLEM MOON logo, depicting a moon and a woman, are trademarks of Random House, Inc. The figure in the Harlem Moon logo is inspired by a graphic design by Aaron Douglas (1899–1979).

This book is a work of fiction. Names, characters, businesses, organizations, places, events, and incidents either are the product of the author's imagination or are used fictitiously. Any resemblance to actual persons, living or dead, events, or locales is entirely coincidental.

Book design by Casey Hampton

LIBRARY OF CONGRESS CATALOGING-IN-PUBLICATION DATA

Howard, Tracie.
    Gold diggers / by Tracie Howard.—1st ed.
      p. cm.
    1. African American women—Fiction.   2. Public relations consultants—
Fiction. 3. Manhattan (New York, N.Y.)—Fiction. I. Title.
  PS3608.O94G65 2007
  813'.6—dc22
                                         2006025269

ISBN: 978-0-385-51798-0

PRINTED IN THE UNITED STATES OF AMERICA

10 9 8 7 6 5 4 3 2 1

FIRST EDITION

I dedicate this novel to my beautiful family for their unconditional love and support; to my friends for their inspiration
and never-ending generosity of spirit; and to God our
Father, for his divine wisdom, of which I hope I've lived
long enough to begin to scratch the surface.

ACKNOWLEDGMENTS

I would like to acknowledge those few companies in the publishing industry (including retailers) that help bring stories to readers without first editing the integrity of the work or infringing upon it misconceived racial notions (and you know who you are!). We all have stories to tell, and often—regardless of race—those stories are a lot more similar than they are different. Like many problems that we face in today's world, if race could just be set aside, it would be easier for us all to understand and appreciate one another.

As for me personally, there are many people whose help, support, and encouragement I deeply appreciate. First and foremost, at a time when I'd decided to put away my pen and paper forever, my agent and attorney, Denise Brown, forced my hand, encouraging me to finish writing *Gold Diggers* (which I started over four years ago, two years before Kanye's hot song!). But it wasn't until I met Janet Hill at Random House/Broadway/Harlem Moon Books that I felt totally comfortable bringing this wonderful book to life; I knew that she would "get it." It's a painful and heart-wrenching experience for a creative person who puts his or her work up for public scrutiny to realize that those who are supposed to support the process don't "get it" at all.

Next, I'd like to thank my family for reading and helping to promote *everything* I write (this includes Katherine Wimbley and Margaret Mroz!); my mother, Gloria Freeman, for passing on such creative DNA, and my sisters for sharing it (Alison Howard-Smith is a renowned contemporary African quilt maker: www.Quiltograph.com, and Jennifer Freeman is a very popular vocalist in Atlanta: www.JenniferFree.com). My nieces Chelsea Smith and Korian Young have inherited great genes and have much to look forward to! I was also smart enough to marry great genes—my husband, Scott Folks, is one of the most brilliant (and sweetest) men I've ever met (though my sister could argue the same for my brother-in-law, Donny Smith).

I also have to thank my crazy friends. I must say that I have the most eclectic assortment of friends, who are constantly feeding my fertile imagination. I'm often asked by some if they represent a character in my novels. Just for the record, the answer is almost always yes! It's rarely (except in the case of CoAnne Wilshire in *Why Sleeping Dogs Lie*) a one-to-one comparison, but more often, quirky idiosyncrasies are filed away and dredged up to add additional flavor and spice to the characters in my books. This cast of characters include: Karen, my partner in our fashion company Ethos (ExperienceEthos.com), and her husband Oswald Morgan, Sharon Bowen and Larry Morse, Alicia and Danny Bythewood, Vikki Palmer, Baidy Agne, Omar Sow, Imara Canady, Judith and Juan Montier, Jocelyn Taylor, Vanessa and Bill Johnson, Lorri King and Edbert Morales, Pam Frederick and Monroe Bowden, Julie Borders, Len Burnett, my cousins April and Ted Phillips, Mario Rinaldi, Ken Taylor, OJ Simpson (no, not that one!), and Anne Simmons. There are others, like Eric Omores, Harold Dawson, and Michael Dortch, who also offer their friendship and support, both of which I appreciate greatly. I'm happy to say that I don't count any gold diggers among my friends, though there are *many* among my acquaintances (and you know who you are, too!). After all, this is New York! For an incomplete list of famous and infamous gold diggers, both contemporary and the more legendary (provided by readers), please visit www.GoldDiggersTheNovel.com.

I also owe major thanks to Carol Mackey at Black Expressions for her continued support of my work, and to the hundreds of African American bookstores that we *must* support, lest our stories become *his*tory!

Furthermore, and above the rest, I thank God for all things large and small, and for each additional day I'm given to experience them all.

Gold Diggers

Book One

ONE

Paulette's bedsheets had barely cooled down when her telephone rang, erasing the lazy smile that curled the corners of her mouth, and interrupting the fresh memory of her lover's recent visit. Though he'd been gone fifteen minutes now, she still smelled a trace of his Hermès cologne on her pillow.

The phone's shrill ring was like *someone else's* wailing child—a complete annoyance. When she saw the name displayed on caller ID, Paulette smirked and rolled her eyes. It occurred to her not to answer it, but her curiosity got the best of her, so she reached over to the nightstand and picked up the receiver.

"Hello." She was careful to cover the irritation she felt. Paulette was the owner of one of New York's premier boutique public relations firms, and thus was a pro at covering a multitude of things she didn't want exposed. She was a master of positioning, whether it was between the sheets or in the gossip pages.

"Are you still up?" the caller asked.

Paulette's alarm clock said it was a quarter past midnight. She twisted her lips into a tight, pinched sneer, sighing lightly out of earshot of the phone's receiver. "Yeah, girl, I'm still up. What's going on?" It was her cousin Lauren, the absolute last person on earth she wanted to talk to. Only the spoiled-rotten Lauren would feel no compunction whatsoever for calling this late at night. Paulette, unlike Lauren, the pampered princess, had to work for a living.

"I'm sorry to call so late, but I didn't have anyone else to talk to." Lauren was choking back tears. She'd always worn her emotions on her designer sleeves, a luxury not possible for Paulette, who'd grown up always fending for herself.

Gillian must be out of town, Paulette thought as she pulled herself up in bed, resting on one elbow while cradling the phone between her ear and shoulder. Those prima donnas were like two peas in a pod. "What's wrong? You sound awful." Instantly, a perfect pitch of concern and sympathy warmed Paulette's voice. Working actresses in Hollywood—Ms. Berry included—had nothing on her; Paulette could summon fake emotion the way other people drew a breath.

"It's Max," Lauren croaked. "I think he's having an affair." Just saying those dreadful words out loud somehow made Lauren's sneaking suspicions feel even more real than seconds before, bringing life to thoughts she hadn't dared to speak.

"Calm down, Lauren," Paulette cooed, though she was actually unmoved by the tears and sat idly drumming her fingers on the nightstand through the chorus of sobs as she processed Lauren's alarming—if not surprising—revelation.

When Lauren finally calmed down enough to speak, she said, "I'm sorry; I just don't know what to do."

"Are you positive he's having an affair?"

"Definitely."

"How can you be so sure?" Paulette asked. She needed as much information from Lauren as possible to properly deal with this sticky situation.

What little strength Lauren had returned to her voice, her anger supplanting her hurt feelings. "Well, for example, tonight he told me he was having dinner with Rob, one of his business partners, but Rob just called and left a message for Max saying that he's still out of town and has to reschedule their *breakfast* meeting."

Oops. "Maybe there's a reasonable explanation," Paulette offered.

"A wife knows these things." Lauren made her proclamation sound intuitive, as though she'd read mystic marital tea leaves, when in fact the clues were as concrete and tangible as Mount Everest. For starters there were his countless late nights, the pungent aroma of another woman's essence on his shirts and soiled boxers, and the cavernous gulf that had spread between Lauren and her husband when they lay in bed. Lauren and Max hadn't made love in over two months, and whenever they did, the act was about as passionate as two cells merging in a petri dish. Though he always had a handy excuse ready to serve up, she realized—as any wife should—that he had to be getting it somewhere else, since celibacy was not a part of Maximillian Neuman's DNA.

Paulette took Lauren's all-knowing proclamation and her familiar haughty tone as personal digs devised to mock her own perpetual-bridesmaid status. By comparison, Paulette felt like such a loser for not having the fairy-tale life that Lauren had been handed on a platinum platter: wealthy and successful parents, natural beauty, a handsome and successful husband, and a grand town house on the Upper East Side. Even worse than all of these unforgivable sins was the fact that Lauren was completely impervious to the ill effect her life had had on Paulette's.

Paulette managed to hide her simmering hatred for her cousin under another layer of fake concern. "So, who is it?"

Lauren took a deep breath, searching bravely for composure. "That I don't know. At least, not yet."

There was a soft beep on Paulette's line, indicating that another call was waiting. "Hold on a minute." Paulette pressed the flash button after scanning the LCD to identify the waiting caller. "Hey, baby," she purred after switching calls.

"Are you still naked?" a husky voice oozed into her ear. He was ready for a round of phone sex, even though he'd been gone only twenty-five minutes. His insatiable appetite for her was one of the many things that she loved about him.

"Do you miss me?" she cooed.

"Of course I do," he answered. At the very least there were certainly *parts* of her that he missed.

"I miss you, too," she crooned back at him. "And so does your wife." A sly smile crept across her face as she dropped this bombshell.

"My wife?" Maximillian's deep, sexy bedroom voice quickly scaled an octave higher.

"Lauren's on the other line," Paulette announced offhandedly. She managed to keep the coyness from her voice, realizing he wouldn't find the situation nearly as amusing as she did.

"What does she want? And why did she call you?" Panic flashed a shade of red over his high-yellow complexion like high tide washing up at sunset.

"Let's just say she called to tell me something I already know." Paulette twirled a lock of her thick, coarse hair. Its brittleness and frayed ends were the result of the constant perming and coloring it took for her to achieve the light brown Barbie-doll look that she preferred. It had also taken a nose job, skin bleaching, and a lifetime gym membership, the latter needed to fight off those pesky pounds that were always one french fry away.

"What's that?"

"That you're having an affair." She barely stifled a giggle. The irony of the situation was rich as whipped cream; her lover's wife was calling in the middle of the night for sympathy, when his wet spot on her sheets had barely begun to dry.

"Oh, shit! She knows?"

Paulette heard the panic well up in his voice. It was nauseating. "She at least suspects," she offered him.

"Wh-what did you tell her?"

Of course, his only concern was for himself, and worse, his tone seemed to imply that Paulette had done something wrong. Hell, she wasn't the one married! She chose to ignore all of this for now. She'd deal with him later. "I didn't tell her anything. I'm just listening." Paulette got up from the bed with her bedsheet wrapped around her naked body, letting it trail the floor. She soon calculated the best position to assume while in the tight spot wedged between husband and wife.

"You have to convince her that I'm *not* having an affair," he pleaded.

Yeah, right. "Okay," she said. *What nerve!*

"Call me when you're off the other line." He didn't even wait for a good-bye before he hung up.

She thought for a second, then clicked back over to Lauren's call. "I'm back. Sorry about that." She sat on the side of the bed and resumed twirling her hair, a sure sign that a scheme was moving from concept to implementation. "It was a client who needed consoling."

"It's okay. I appreciate your listening. I'm just so upset." Lauren sounded close to releasing another tide of tears.

"And you should be. If my husband were having an affair, I would be too. In fact, I wouldn't stand for that shit! Have you confronted him?" Paulette was working Lauren up, building the head of steam needed to blow the lid off of her sad little domestic problem.

"No," Lauren admitted. In fact, the thought had never even occurred to her.

"Girl, if you don't put that Negro in check he'll walk all over you."

Lauren was quiet for a moment. "You really think I should?" As was her way, Lauren would rather ignore the problem and hope that it went away. Besides, what if she confronted him and he admitted to an affair? Then what? Or worse, what if he left her? Her mother would have a fit!

"Lauren, if you want to save your marriage, you're going to have to nip this situation in the bud," Paulette counseled.

Ten minutes later, Lauren was more than sure that her husband was a lying, cheating son of a bitch who had to be dealt with accordingly. Though she would have preferred to talk to her best friend, Gillian, who was out of the country, there was still nothing like a conversation with her no-nonsense cousin to help clarify things. The girls had practically grown up together, albeit on different sides of the same track.

After Paulette was finished working Lauren into a frothy lather, she ended the call and dialed Max back. By now he was parked a block from his house, anxiously awaiting her call so he could sufficiently arm himself before walking into the waiting ambush.

"What happened?" he asked anxiously.

"Nothing, really. I did what you asked. I told her there was no way you could be having an affair. That you loved her way too much, and that it was all in her mind." Paulette lied like the seasoned pro she was.

"Did she believe you?" He was already breathing a bit easier.

"Of course she did."

"Good. I'll call you tomorrow."

"Good night." She placed the phone back on the hook and reclined on the four-poster bed, cradling the masculine-scented pillow while vividly imagining the drama that would soon unfold in the Neuman household.

Paulette only wished that she had an orchestra seat and a bag of popcorn.

L auren paced the floor in her bedroom suite, nearly wearing a circular swath into the rich, plush carpeting. She was glad that she'd called Paulette, who always made her feel so much stronger. Her cousin's gritty survival skills had somehow magically rubbed off on Lauren and empowered her, at least momentarily. Paulette, unlike Lauren, had been forced to hone such skills her entire life, because her mother, Lauren's mother's sister, had married poorly and been promptly disinherited by the Baines family matriarch, Priscilla Baines-Reynolds.

The esteemed Baines family had been wealthy and powerful for generations, back when Negroes were property themselves. The Baineses were fiercely proud of their auspicious heritage—slave-rape beginnings and all—and considered it their responsibility to breed only into families of similar status. When June married a poor, dark-skinned man with no pedigree, the unblessed union sullied their pristine gene pool, and, unfortunately, Paulette was the by-product.

If Paulette could handle all she'd been through, Lauren reminded herself, surely she could handle Max. But before she could adequately shore herself up, she heard the chirping of the door's alarm sensor. Her wayward husband had returned home. Lauren was as nervous as if *she* were the one caught having an illicit affair. She took a deep breath to calm her shaky nerves, straightened her back, and held her head high as she marched through the spacious brownstone to confront him in his den, the first place he always stopped whenever he entered the house. Every evening Max walked in and compulsively checked his computer screen for the status of the world financial markets, keeping a wary eye out for any changes that might affect their overall net worth, as though his own blood, sweat, and tears had earned every dime. In truth, those seven zeros behind the comma were the result of his ability to woo Lauren, thus leading her, her mother, and a chunk of their money right down the aisle. Even though there were ropes tied to the hefty sum—namely remaining married to Lauren—it was worth every penny to be able to go to bed comforted by the presence of so much dough.

Soothed by Paulette's report of how well her conversation with Lauren had gone, Max was no longer worried. In fact, he didn't even bother to look up from the computer monitor when he heard Lauren walk through the door.

"Max, where were you?" Lauren demanded, trying to remain calm and not give her hand away too quickly.

He was taken aback. Based on Paulette's recounting, he hadn't thought Lauren would question him at all. "Out to dinner. Why?" Nonetheless, he was wily enough to know not to offer any details while under inquisition. He remembered telling Lauren the lie about having dinner with his business partner, and instinctively knew he'd better leave room to wiggle out of it if necessary.

"With whom?" she asked. Normally she wouldn't dream of questioning him, but emboldened by her knowledge of his lie, she went for it.

Max saw red flags whipping in the wind. She somehow knew that he hadn't been at dinner with Rob, so he'd have to sidestep across a land mine of his own lies. He looked up from the computer and decided that the best offense was always a good defense, especially where Lauren was concerned. "Why are you questioning me?"

She stood her ground. "Why don't you *answer* me?"

"To be honest, I'm a little upset. I've been working since seven o'clock this morning, and it's unsettling to be greeted with a Spanish inquisition when I enter my own home twelve long hours later," he retorted, with more than a dose of outraged indignation.

His tone and anger caught Lauren off guard. She'd expected to hold all the cards and easily trap him in a twist of lies. But she wouldn't give up that easily; she still held her ace of spades. "For your information, I know that you didn't have dinner with Rob. He called and said he was still out of town." Her tone was icy as she stood over him with her arms folded across her chest.

Max swallowed the sigh of relief he felt for not leaning on the shaky lie he'd set up that morning. "So?"

Lauren looked as though she'd been jabbed with a left. "So? You told me you were having dinner with Rob *tonight*."

"I was until his secretary called to cancel earlier today." He stood up and towered over her, using his six-foot-one height to his full advantage.

She hadn't thought of that possibility. Of course Rob's secretary would have managed his schedule more efficiently than he had, but that still didn't explain where Max had been. "So where were you?"

He grabbed the newspaper from the desk and faced her again. "If you must know, Danny and I met to prepare for next week's board meeting. Is that all right with you?" he asked snidely. When she didn't have a ready comeback, Max sidestepped Lauren and walked out of the room, leaving her standing there with her foot lodged firmly in her mouth.

TWO

Paulette's mouth was fixed in a snarly pout as she lay on her now-empty bed, remembering the day four years earlier when their unwitting ménage à trois had begun.

As usual, Lauren had shown up at Paulette's office finely turned out on that early summer afternoon: Hermès khaki pantsuit, a tasteful bag from Gucci's new summer collection, and fresh but subtle makeup. Her unaffected air of superiority was worn as casually as a second layer of skin. She wasn't necessarily arrogant, just supremely comfortable in her uncontested role as the most beautiful, best-bred, and wealthiest well-connected girl in most social circles. Thanks to ancestors with good DNA, astute social-climbing skills, and a legacy of trust funds, Lauren's life had been carefully crafted, paid for in full, and neatly wrapped in Tiffany blue.

"Hi, I'm Lauren. I'm here for lunch with Paulette."

"Miss Dolliver is just wrapping up a meeting and should be with you momentarily," Paulette's assistant chirped with an ultrabright smile plastered across her face. "Have a seat; it shouldn't be too long."

While Lauren cooled her four-inch Chanel sling-backs, she

picked up the latest copy of *Uptown* magazine. The hot publication was the uncontested barometer for hip social movers and shakers. Leafing through the glossy pages, Lauren saw several pictures of friends and acquaintances she'd met over the years in Boston, Martha's Vineyard, and Manhattan, all smiling broadly at various New York social events. There was even a photo of one of her college roommates grinning like a Cheshire cat on crack, alongside the handsome bachelor, Maximillian Neuman III, at the Studio Museum's spring gala. After spying the same photo days earlier, her mother, Mildred, had speed-dialed Lauren, fully armed with the man's bio. In short order she'd proclaimed him acceptable "son-in-law material." Sometimes Lauren rightfully wondered whether it ever mattered to her mother if a prospect were "husband" material. She strongly (and correctly) guessed that it did not.

Mildred Baines-Dawson epitomized the second generation Jack-and-Jiller; she was someone who was capable of measuring her own success only by executing a direct comparison to the Joneses, the Smiths, the Hunnicutts, et al. Since Lauren was her only daughter, and by extension a direct reflection on and of her, Lauren's script called for a handsome and successful leading man to be guided, with great grand fanfare, down the wedding aisle. The "blessed" union was then to quickly produce two kids, preferably a boy and a girl—in that order. Later, if Lauren so chose, she could work outside of the home, perhaps volunteering on occasion for an of-the-moment charitable board, since it was considered (at least by Mildred) to be *très* gauche for a woman of her status to ever actually *need* to make money—but spending it was another matter entirely.

In fact, Lauren's script was just an updated, brushed-off reenactment of Mildred's own, which had been—for the most part—flawlessly executed decades ago. She had her $8 million Westchester mansion, a pied-à-terre in the city, a five-bedroom beach house in Martha's Vineyard, a brand-new Jaguar XL, a wood-paneled boudoir full of designer clothes, and all the other necessary accoutrements that bespoke wealth and fine living. Never mind the intermittent bouts of clinical depression, the countless sleepless nights, or her increasing reliance on vodka gimlets, starting the moment the clock struck five. Those little trifles aside, Mildred's life was perfect!

The only unscripted scene was when her son, Gregory, abruptly yet flamboyantly exited the closet at the age of twenty-one, leaving a serious legacy issue for Mildred. There would be no male bloodline to carry on the illustrious family heritage. After months of intense therapy, outright bribery, and high-scale histrionics, Mildred finally gave up claim to her son's sperm supply, which meant that all procreation obligations were left squarely in Lauren's lap. Unfortunately, Lauren graduated from Harvard undergrad without an engagement ring, so plan B was swiftly called into action.

Lauren was going to law school. Mildred reasoned that this was an acceptable way to pass more time until Mr. Just Right showed up. Mildred even adjusted a few of her previously ironclad requirements. Before, only another blue-chip black would be considered, but time was ticking, so Mildred deigned—to herself—to consider young men who were merely accomplished and attractive, since her family was already well stocked with a lofty pedigree from which to look down on the rest of the world.

Ever the strategist, Mildred chose Columbia to keep Lauren visible in the most lucrative breeding ground in the country: Manhattan. As she pointed out on more than one occasion, it was only in New York City that Lauren would have access to Wall Street tycoons, media moguls, and heads of business, all on one ten-mile island. Of course, athletes and entertainers were also plentiful, but, regardless of bank accounts, as far as Mildred was concerned they need not apply.

"Hey, girl. Sorry I'm late, but a couple of meetings ran over; you know how it is," Paulette said.

Lauren stood and gave her cousin a hug and an air kiss. "No problem. I'm just glad you could find time in your busy schedule," she teased, nudging Paulette with her elbow.

Paulette blushed unconsciously, enjoying, for once in her life, that she had something her wealthy cousin didn't. Since opening About Time Publicity two years ago, Paulette had made quite a splash in the choppy waters of celebrity publicity. Just last week she'd been featured in *Essence* magazine, and was a party-page regular in publications ranging from *Town and Country* to *Gotham*.

Fifteen minutes later they were settled at a prime outdoor table at Pastis, watching the nonstop parade of fashionistas, metrosexuals, and others drift by. It was one of those incredible afternoons that made living in New York—regardless of the ups and downs—fully worth the high price of admission.

"So, what's the big news?" Paulette asked after placing their drink orders. She relished playing the wise older cousin. For Paulette, theirs truly was a love/hate relationship, whose balance teetered precariously from one moment to the next.

"I've decided to go to law school," Lauren announced, wearing a look that begged for Paulette's approval. And for that reason alone, she'd never get it.

"You decided, or your mother decided?" Paulette gave her an appraising look. She knew her aunt all too well. The woman lived her daughter's life as if it were her second act—Lauren was simply Mildred's body double.

Lauren gave Paulette a tight smile. "Well, she suggested it, but what else am I supposed to do?"

"God forbid, you could do what hundreds of thousands of other college graduates do—you could get a job." She gave Lauren a wide-eyed did-you-think-of-that look. "It's not like you've got a degree from Podunk Community College. You went to Harvard, for Christ's sake!"

"Mom said—"

"Enough about what your mom said. You sound like a four-year-old. What do *you* want?"

Lauren bristled at Paulette's sharp tone. Slinging her straight auburn hair over one shoulder, she brusquely retorted, "If I didn't *want* to go to law school, certainly I wouldn't do it. After all, it is my decision."

"Glad to hear *that*," Paulette snapped back. Fortunately the waitress appeared with their drinks, helping to take the edge off of the brusque exchange. Lauren had ordered a French rose, and Paulette requested her favorite summer drink, a mojito. She took a sip, savoring the mint-infused rum concoction, and bracing herself for the rest of the inane conversation that was sure to follow. "So where are you going?"

"To Columbia."

Suddenly a frightening thought torpedoed Paulette's composure: Instead of being tucked away in Boston, or anywhere else on the planet, Lauren would now be encroaching on her territory, the isle of Manhattan. She wasn't sure she liked the idea. Truth be told, she *was* sure: She hated it! Having Lauren stuck up in Boston the last four years, while Paulette was making her mark in New York, had been great. It was one thing to be the poor relative from the other side of the tracks when her family was hundreds of miles away, but facing that indignity in her own city was something else altogether. Paulette tried to swallow her concern along with her cocktail. "So, when are you moving?"

"I figured I'd get an early start on finding and decorating an apartment. So, rather than wait until the fall, I've decided to stay for the rest of the summer." She practically glowed with excitement.

Paulette wasn't nearly as excited. She had been sure—and happy to know—that her cousin was leaving the city for Martha's Vineyard this very weekend.

"Oh, that's great!" Paulette lied, chasing her lie down with another long sip of her cocktail.

"I'm really looking forward to hanging out in New York." Though, growing up in Westchester, Lauren had spent time in the city her whole life, living here was an entirely different matter. "Speaking of hanging out, what are you doing later?" It was Thursday, the best party night in the city.

"Nothing, girl. I've gotta work." This was partially true. Paulette attended most of the hottest parties in town, but as a publicist, she did it under the guise of work.

Lauren gave her the little pout that had worked like a snake charm on her father for years. "I really wanted to hang out."

There was no way that Paulette would willingly assist Lauren in scaling Manhattan's social ladder. She had enough of a head start already, with her family money and famous (at least in the "right" circles) Baines-Dawson surname. Besides, who needed the extra competition? It was hard enough to get noticed among all of the Gucci-clad, size-four-wearing females constantly prowling the streets, so why add another? Especially a beautiful, rich cousin?

After settling the tab—which, as usual, Lauren picked up compliments of the Baines-Dawson family credit card—they were heading up Ninth Avenue. "Paulette!" They turned to find a statuesque, buttery-complexioned beauty with long, dark, wavy hair that flowed over her shoulder caressing full but perky breasts. She looked like Thandie Newton with J.Lo's body and Nicole Kidman's height. "I thought that was you."

"Oh, hey, girl." Paulette looked a tad uncomfortable.

"I saw that your assistant RSVP'd for you to attend tonight's party. That's great! You know it's gonna be hot. Everybody will be there. Oh, and of course you'll have VIP access." Mystery Girl was obviously very excited about this little soiree that Paulette had conveniently forgotten.

"Oh, yes." Paulette bumped the heel of her hand to the side of her forehead, as though all thoughts of this hot party had escaped her. "I'd forgotten about it."

The dark-haired diva turned to Lauren and extended a beautifully manicured hand. "Hi, I'm Reese. Reese Hutton."

"I'm Paulette's cousin, Lauren Baines-Dawson."

Reese lit up. "It's great to meet you, Lauren." Turning to Paulette, she asked, "Is Lauren joining us tonight?" Reese was an assistant co-ordinator for *Uptown* magazine. Though she'd been hired to assist Jocelyn Taylor, the associate publisher, what she did best was make sure that she attended every entertainment-related party in the city, often by tossing around the magazine's name as though it were free currency. The party tonight was being given by the magazine in honor of the sexy Oscar-winning actor Denzel Washington.

Before Paulette could conjure up a plausible excuse as to why her cousin couldn't join them, Lauren answered the question herself. "I'd love to!"

"Great! Gillian, my roommate—she just finished *Jelly's Last Jam* on Broadway," Reese explained to Lauren, "will also be hanging out with us. It'll be fun—plus I'll have a car and driver, so I'll pick you guys up, say, around nine? We'll have dinner first."

Continuing up Ninth Avenue, Lauren excitedly pulled out her cell phone, calling Joseph's Hair Salon, insisting that Joseph Junior squeeze her in for an emergency visit. As far as she was concerned, tonight could serve as her adult entrée to the fabulous social scene in New York. Now she need only look her best—which was never diffi-cult for her to do.

Paulette had walked beside her, feeling like a lamb being led to slaughter. Somehow she had known that that night would be a turn-ing point for them both, but not necessarily in a good direction.

Now, four years later, as Paulette sat in bed simmering in Lau-ren's husband's wet spot while he raced off home to appease his sim-pering wife, she was surer than ever that that night had been the beginning of a bad accident waiting to happen.

THREE

Later that fateful night, after Lauren inserted herself into Paulette's carefully crafted life, their course, along with their friends, became set for the next five years.

"Heeey, boo," Reese crooned into her cell phone, which she had cradled between her diamond-studded ear and shoulder. She tossed a sly smile to Paulette, Gillian, and her new friend, Lauren. Their stiletto heels were kicked back in a sleek Mercedes limo on the way to the hip New York nightclub Nikki Beach. "I know; I miss you already, too, baby cakes," she lied smoothly. She winked at her partners in crime, who were barely able to stifle a rousing case of the giggles. Earlier, at Nobu, "baby cakes" had picked up a hefty tab for a fabulous dinner, so they'd had the pleasure of meeting the disheveled but sinfully rich older Jewish man whose money Reese spent on a regular basis. He was her plan B in case her NBA-playing boyfriend, Chris, dropped the ball. She'd had Chris on the hook for three years now, but so far he'd eluded her clutches.

"I'll be careful, baby cakes. I promise. And thanks for dinner and the car tonight." His response elicited a loud smacking/puckering sound from Reese into the phone's receiver; she was sending him a kiss, one that he'd have squeezed through the receiver to get, if possible. "I love you, too," she purred before hanging up the phone, then doubled over in a fit of laughter.

"I don't know how you do it," Gillian said, shaking her head. She was a dark, bronze-skinned beauty with wild, warm brown hair and an elegantly tousled look.

Reese regained her composure and pushed the button to close the privacy panel between them and the driver. Tossing her long, flowing hair she said, "It's very easy. The man is loaded." To her, no other explanation was necessary.

Gillian rolled her eyes. "To sleep with him I'd have to be loaded too. And I don't mean with money." She and Lauren, who was seated beside her, exchanged disapproving glances. The man was old enough to be their grandfather.

Paulette looked on admiringly. She had full appreciation for Reese's ability to get what she wanted out of whoever had it, whenever she saw fit. The two women had met when Paulette was schmoozing Chris to sign him to her public relations agency. Reese had pulled Paulette aside and done some schmoozing of her own. She agreed to convince Chris to sign with Paulette as long as Paulette agreed to get free press for Reese as well. It had been a match made in tabloid heaven. After that Reese's name popped up in the right places with such regularity that she was transformed seamlessly into a New York "it girl."

"The man's got skills, okay?" Reese pulled out her compact to blot her collagen-enhanced lips. Though they hadn't needed injections, she'd been influenced by Angelina Jolie's seductive bee-stung kisser, and all of the attention it received.

"Somehow I find that hard to believe." Gillian frowned, turning up her nose. "He looks like he should be on Medicare." She and Lauren shook their heads, joined in mutual disgust over the distasteful lengths to which Reese would go to get to a man's wallet.

"That just means that he's been fucking a lot longer than most of us." Satisfied that her appearance was showstopping, Reese snapped the mirror closed.

By now the sex talk had Lauren blushing. Listening to Reese was like driving by a bad accident on the side of the highway: You knew that what you were about to see would be ugly, but somehow you still couldn't resist looking anyway.

Gillian, an artsy type, was bored already. She was a moderately successful model and an emerging actress who had seen it all. On the other hand, Paulette seemed to be transfixed, and taking detailed mental notes. Maybe Reese was onto something with the rich-older-man thing. Trading sex for cash didn't seem like such a bad idea to her; after all she—and countless other women—had had bad sex that had cost *them* money, or worse, heartache. The way Paulette saw things, there was a winner and a loser in every transaction, and she was tired of carrying a deficit.

"How long have you been seeing him?" Paulette asked. She tried to appear nonchalant, knowing that Lauren found Reese's behavior abominable.

"My friend Kira and I met him at the Four Seasons bar a couple of months ago—a place I strongly advise you to frequent if you really want your pick of rich old men," she advised. "As soon as we met he pulled out his American Express Black Centurion card, and he hasn't put it back in his wallet yet." She raised her palm in the air for a high five, which Paulette gave, but Gillian and Lauren ignored.

"You go, girl," Paulette said.

Reese tossed a nonexistent strand of hair from her face. "He'll do until I reel in the big one." She planned to get a wedding ring out of Chris by hook, crook, or—her last resort—an "unplanned" pregnancy.

"Then you'll just toss him aside, huh?" Gillian reached for the bottle of champagne that chilled in the bucket on the seat between them. She and Lauren sat on one side of the limo, while Reese and Paulette shared the other. She refilled all of their glasses with Champagne Paul Goerg—also courtesy of Reese's current sugar daddy.

Since childhood Reese had recognized the power of good looks, but she had taken manipulation to another level when she discovered the untapped power between her long, shapely legs. It all started with a cute young PE teacher who had threatened to fail her because she rarely attended his class. When she realized the full calamity of the situation—which included not graduating from high school and forfeiting her acceptance to the University of North Carolina—she turned up the charm, and before you could say, "Let's make a deal," she'd exchanged an A for a blow job in the PE teacher's office.

"Actually, I'll just toss him back to his wife." With that, Reese raised her glass for a toast. "Here's to catching the big one."

As their glasses clinked—Lauren's and Gillian's reluctantly—Lauren thought about how little she had in common with Reese.

Gillian, who actually liked her roommate, Reese, but disagreed with her lifestyle, was a bit more pragmatic. Her bohemian model's lifestyle would require a benefactor of some kind as she aged, unless her acting really took off soon. She realized that her looks would eventually play out, which for models happened sooner than you could bat a fake eyelash. It was a depressing yet realistic thought that had begun to creep along the edges of her consciousness.

Paulette toasted without reservation. She welcomed the opportunity to marry well, at any cost. It would be worth it to redeem her family's honor. More than any of them, Paulette felt entitled to the wealth and lifestyle that her mother's poor choice in matrimony had deprived her of.

"To the big catch!" Paulette said.

Reese pumped her fist. "To Mr. Moneybags."

Expensive champagne–filled flutes met between them, and the

ensuing chime resonated throughout the plush environs of the expensive car. That special crystal-on-crystal ping was the universal sound of a good time about to be had.

As the car rolled to a stop in front of the packed nightclub, the driver ceremoniously opened the back door of the car, helping each girl out. The line behind the velvet rope was long and chock-full of skimpily clad females vying for the hunky doorman's attention to get in, and guys hoping to get in to then vie for the girls' attention. When the foursome stepped out of the stretch Mercedes, every head in the line turned to see who'd emerge from behind the darkly tinted windows.

The first to appear was Reese, who'd already mastered the art of exiting a limo in front of a red carpet. She'd practiced getting out of her Honda in front of her parents' modest Queens home at the age of thirteen, and was now fairly efficient at executing the leg-revealing exit while simultaneously flinging her hair over one shoulder. Everyone watching would have to assume that she was someone, even if they had no idea who.

Next out was Paulette—or should it be said, Paulette's boobs. She often thanked God for those two huge blessings. She might not have the family money that Lauren did, or the natural good looks, but the set of can't-miss knockers were all hers, and she'd learned very early just how to use her two biggest assets. Tonight she wore a dangerously low-cut halter top that barely covered her nipples, so of course the rest of her pillowy bosom was on full display. When she stepped out of the car men openly ogled, and women jealously assessed whether they were real or purchased.

Gillian stepped out behind her. In sharp contrast, she was very tall and model thin, all chiseled features, wild, exotic hair, and dark glowing skin. Her complexion couldn't be bought in a bottle. Stepping out of the expensive car, she looked like a Parisian runway model on a high-profile photo shoot. A few cameras manned by celebrity-hungry paparazzi flashed in appreciation, which Reese dourly noted before slinging her hair dismissively. The effect that Gillian had on the crowd was the very impact Reese strived so hard to achieve. Reese sighed quietly, and resolved to practice her entrance that much harder. Such was the downside of hanging out with girls who were also attractive, but the benefit of more bait with which to lure a catch did offset the negatives.

Last to exit was Lauren, who was as different from the rest as humanly possible. While the other three were all versions of the same glamour-puss, Lauren was elegant, poised, and tasteful by comparison. She gave the impression of not trying hard, and of being completely nonplussed by the events around her. In other words, she was the perfect socialite in training. Rather than the trashy club clothes the others had on, Lauren stood out for the simplicity of a sleek melon-colored Michael Kors sundress that complemented her fresh-from-the-Vineyard tan, and a pair of strappy cream Ron Donovan stilettos.

Side by side the girls marched to the door and were met immediately by an Armani suit–wearing Italian with the demeanor of an undercover FBI agent. He wore all black, including dark shades, and a wireless headset in his left ear. "Follow me, ladies," he said, also wearing a serious expression. Though his task was simple, it was executed amid cloak-and-dagger theatrics, all for show. He proceeded to part those left on the wrong side of the velvet rope like the Red Sea, as the four divas were ushered by.

"You can always tell the gold diggers," one jealous, plain-looking young woman sneered. It pissed her off that being beautiful and stylish seemed to be the prerequisites for admission into life itself in New York City. The unattractive need not bother even to show up. Here she was, as usual, one of the unlucky ones who would happily pay extra just to get in, while these skinny bitches not only got in free, but had an escort as if they were important or something. Who were they, anyway?

The girls were swiftly led past the throngs of everyday people

into the pulsating nightclub as if they were rock royalty, all because they looked good. Each knew the power she possessed, and
was intent on a making the most of it while it lasted. When they
came to the private section for the *Uptown* party, the I'm-too-hot
for-this-job gatekeeper clutched her clipboarded guest list as
though it were the Holy Grail. She took the girls in all at once. She
didn't like what she saw. "Who are they?" she inquired of the escort with much attitude.

"They're with me," Paulette stepped forward and announced.
As a publicist, she was accustomed to taking charge.

This was too tempting for any serviceperson who thought she
was too good to actually perform the job for which she'd been
hired. "And who are *you*?"

Paulette bristled with all of the authority of a celebrity publicist, even though her agency had only two B-list rappers, a C-list
actor, a few athletes, and an assortment of other wannabes with
enough dough to buy some publicity. None of this stood in the way
of her attitude as she came toe-to-toe—or as close as her mammoth
breasts would allow—to the nobody gatekeeper. "If you don't know,
I suggest you ask your boss." She slung her weave and pushed past
the now-timid woman. The others followed without pause, leaving
her even more pissed off than before and poised to take it out on the
next customer.

The private party for *Uptown* magazine was a see-and-be-seen
fishbowl for hip urban African Americans and those who wanted to
be like them.

While cool Afro-Euro music set the tone, free-flowing champagne fueled it. The party was sponsored by the French Champagne Paul Goerg and its bon vivant U.S. representative, Mario
Rinaldi. It was the type of party where you could be declined access simply because of the hang of your trouser or the quality of
your weave; fashion victims were not allowed. Though the audience was varied, including those from the media, fashion, and

banking, as well as athletes and entertainers, they all had a few things in common: They were upwardly mobile, socially aggressive, and, without question, stylish.

As promised, the magazine reserved special seating for Paulette, so she and her crew commanded a power booth, complete with its own overhead light to showcase them for all to see, in the event anyone should have missed their grand entrance. As soon as their well-toned derrieres touched the velvet seats, two servers appeared with three perfectly chilled bottles of Champagne Paul Goerg nestled in sterling-silver signature buckets.

The champagne was loudly uncorked, competing with pings of laughter and the incessant buzz of light social chatter. Unable simply to sit, Paulette was soon up parading around with a glass of champagne in her hand and witty repartee ready for any takers—preferably male and attractive, though she was just as capable of working anyone in the crowd who might be able to help her or her clients make it to the next rung of the ladder. Just as she was taking in the scene, deciding where best to fit, in waltzed the finest, most self-assured man she'd ever seen in person.

His entrance was tantamount to the sudden appearance of a black panther prowling a cage. He was six-one, with a tight build, one made for the fine drape of an Italian-cut suit. It hung well in every place that counted, and he had a silent swagger that suggested a better-than-average muscle *there*, too. His complexion was buttery, his hair dark and thick. It was clear that if it grew longer it might curl, but the man had enough panache to know that curls on brothers went out with bell-bottoms, so he wore it nice and low.

Paulette put her flute to her mouth to catch the drool, stuck her chest out farther than need be—her girls looked like two buoys at high tide—and made her approach. "I'm Paulette Dolliver, the publicist for this event. And you are . . . ?" She extended her hand for a feel of his.

He reached out to shake it, but his eyes never left her chest. Many women might have found that Pavlovian-breast-effect look offensive, but Paulette was of the mind that any attention was better than none at all—the perfect disposition for a publicist.

"I'm Maximillian. Maximillian Neuman the Third." He flashed a smile that said it all: sexy, confident, and primal. A man on the prowl.

His voice was a melodic tone of smooth masculinity. And he was beyond handsome; Paulette was convinced that the word for him had yet to appear in Webster's. She now knew the meaning of *weak in the knees*. Even though he hadn't touched her in a meaningful way, she could feel her insides melt like heated butter. An orgasm was only a well-placed stroke away. "Are you alone tonight?" By now her chest was heaving up and down, bobbing seductively with each breath she took.

His eyes never left them. For her, it was as if time stood still; nothing else in the room mattered except for the potent chemistry that was set to explode between them.

"Oh, there you are." Reese's chirpy voice was like a shard of glass, quickly piercing the sexy spell that Paulette had cast.

Reese was smiling like she'd won the Miss America pageant, and worst of all, Paulette knew those pearly whites weren't being displayed for her benefit. Couldn't she be satisfied with an NBA star and a filthy-rich sugar daddy?

"Who do we have here?" Reese finally got around to asking. She appraised Maximillian the way a hungry butcher might look over a tender side of beef.

Maximillian seemed entertained by the brash show of feminine wiles. Certainly he was accustomed to undue female attention, and was even turned off by it at times, but given the extraordinary mammary glands on display, and the glistening fangs bared by the man-eater, it was hard for him to turn away.

"Maximillian, this is Reese. Reese, Maximillian." Once the hes-

itant introductions were over, Paulette repositioned herself between the two. "So, where were we?"

Reese sidestepped her. "Would you care to join us?" She mo-
tioned toward their table. "We have plenty of room, and lots of
champagne."

He glanced at the table that Reese had gestured to, and saw
Lauren and Gillian watching the melodrama unfold. "What kind
of man would turn down champagne and the company of four
beautiful women?"

"Not the kind I know." Reese shook her hair out and sauntered
away, briefly looking back over her shoulder to witness his eyes slip
and land on the rhythmic motions of her ass. *Got him,* she thought.

When Lauren grew tired of watching the predictable drama
between the two divas, she turned to Gillian, who had also grown
bored with the scene, and said, "Weren't you in *Raisin in the Sun*
last year?"

"Yes, I was." Gillian immediately brightened. While many of
her girlfriends were impressed that she was an actress, not many
ever actually bothered to come to the theater.

"You were great! I loved that last scene. You were brilliant!"

"Thank you."

"What are you doing now?"

"I just finished a run of *Jelly's Last Jam.*"

"I saw the original, with Debbie Allen, and I loved it, too."

"Do you go to the theater often?"

"Every chance I get. I love the arts." Lauren smiled for the first
time all night, and then shrugged. "Although I have no artistic
ability myself, I've always admired those who do."

"I do love my work." Gillian sighed. "Though it can be so hard
for actors that sometimes I wonder if I'm doing the right thing."
She was not the open type, and rarely bonded with other women,
but there was something genuine about Lauren that she immediately liked.

"You're so talented that I'm sure your big break will come."

Before Gillian could respond, Paulette, Reese, and the catch of the day were headed in their direction, led by Reese, who was tailed by Max. Paulette brought up the rear, deeply pained by the slick maneuver Reese had used to lure this prime catch from her well-set net.

"Gillian, Lauren, meet Maximillian," Reese announced. She introduced him as though he were already her property, leaving Paulette feeling like a wobbly third wheel.

"Ladies." As smooth as silk, Maximillian slid into the booth next to Lauren. Reese sat to his left, and Paulette to hers, so in record time he was happily sandwiched between the four women.

"Have some champagne?" Paulette strategically leaned over Reese to pour bubbly into an empty glass, causing her boobs to nearly pop from the tight confines of her top. It had just the effect she'd counted on. All bets were off. Paulette realized that she'd have to play hardball to stay in this game.

"Sure." Maximillian was like a spectator at Wimbledon: He didn't know which way to look, to his left or to his right.

"So, tell us all about yourself." Gillian leaned back and pulled a brown European cigarette from her bag. It didn't matter that it was illegal to smoke in New York bars; Gillian never abided by normal rules. She lit the cigarette as it dangled from her highly glossed lips.

"What do you want to know?" He leaned back, too, quite the cool customer.

"What do you do, for starters?" Gillian wasn't interested in him at all. He wasn't her type—too pretty. She simply felt like stirring the pot a little bit to see what spice she could add to the brew simmering before her.

"I'm an attorney."

"Where are you from?" Paulette jumped in now.

He swiveled in her direction. "D.C."

Maximillian took a sip of his champagne, not at all affected by the bare bulb dangling just overhead. "Is it okay if I ask a couple of questions?" He directed this question to Paulette, who leaned back, boobs propped up, waiting for anything he had to say. "Shoot."

Unfortunately, she'd have to wait a little longer. He turned to Lauren. "You've been awfully quiet. Tell me about yourself."

"What do you want to know?" Lauren asked, coolly.

"Anything you want to tell." A coy smile toyed with the corners of his mouth. He'd just turned his game up a notch.

"I think you have enough to deal with already." Lauren was not about to volley on the same court as everyone else; mixed doubles weren't her sport. She preferred playing center court, all alone. She recognized the handsome man from the *Uptown* magazine photograph, and remembered his name because her mother had made such a big deal of him when she called after seeing his picture, so the least she could do was get to know him. But sitting around with three other women all vying for his attention was not the way to do it.

"Excuse me." Gillian slid out of the booth, allowing Lauren to exit. She walked away and never looked back. If she had, she'd have noticed that his eyes never left her, leaving Reese and Paulette speechless. He also took the opportunity to excuse himself, then joined Lauren at the bar.

"That bitch," Paulette and Reese both said in unison. Innocent Lauren had just executed *The Italian Job*, the title of the brilliant movie about a double-crossing thief who stole the loot from fellow thieves.

Gillian took a leisurely puff of her filterless cigarette swallowing an amused smile, then expelling a whirl of smoke toward the ceiling, making two perfectly formed smoke rings. "It takes two to know one," she noted.

Reese sucked in her cheeks and flipped her hair dismissively, and Paulette, following suit, flung her weave too. The hair tossing was followed by a look that would stop an African elephant. "Ain't that some shit?" Paulette muttered as she reached for her glass of champagne.

FOUR

Four years later, a lot had changed for each of them, with the exception of Gillian. Lauren and Reese were both married; Paulette had transformed About Time Publicity into a major force in PR; but Gillian was still scraping by on secondary roles on and off-Broadway, so there was no grand marquee beaming her name, and the prospects for one weren't looking so good.

"I'm moving to L.A.," she announced unceremoniously as she and Lauren sipped port downstairs at Pravda late one snowy February night.

"I realize that you don't like snow and cold weather, but don't you think that's a bit drastic?" Lauren teased.

When Gillian didn't laugh, Lauren sat her drink down, swallowing this sudden turn. Being an art connoisseur, she considered L.A. to be a cultural wasteland, and couldn't understand why anyone would willingly live there. "You can't be serious."

"It's not as if I'm setting New York on fire, and I'm not getting any younger." Now that she was twenty-seven her modeling days were over, and acting wasn't exactly working out the way she'd planned. This move to L.A. was her last-ditch effort to save her career.

"Maybe you just need a new agent," Lauren offered.

"I've been through three in the last two years." Just talking about her trials and tribulations made Gillian crave a cigarette. She'd kicked the nasty habit a year ago, but her cravings had intensified recently. "I've gotta try this, or else give up altogether. Maybe I should get a nine-to-five like everybody else," she said despondently.

Lauren hated to see Gillian so down. She knew that her friend had been concerned about her career, but had no idea that things were so desperate. It was so unfair for Gillian to have to struggle for parts; she was by far the best actress of their generation that Lauren had seen. The last thing she wanted was for her to give up, which meant that Lauren needed to support Gillian's decision and not just think about her own loss. "A nine-to-five is out of the question. But if you must go, we have to at least send you out in style, so why don't I arrange a little party with the girls?"

"There's not a lot to celebrate."

"Of course there is. We will celebrate your imminent success. You will take L.A. by storm!"

The next weekend they all gathered at Soho Spa, where Lauren had booked them all services for the entire day. In between manicures, pedicures, body exfoliations, deep-tissue massages, and facials, they had a specially catered champagne lunch and celebrated the new chapter of Gillian's life.

"Here's to the big screen!" Lauren said, raising her glass for a toast. Though she was sad to see Gillian go, she was also excited for the bright future that she was sure awaited her. Reese, on the other hand, couldn't understand why Gillian didn't just find a rich man and marry him, rather than wasting all this time on a career that seemed destined to fail.

Paulette toasted, with a smirk buried beneath her smile. What

made Gillian think that she was so special that Hollywood would fall
to its knees upon her arrival?

"I know you'll be a huge success," Reese lied.

"I hope so," Gillian said.

"You know I'll do anything I can to help," Paulette said. She'd recently opened an L.A. office, and had agreed to let Gillian stay at her
L.A. apartment until she got settled.

"I predict that the next time we all get together, it'll be in L.A. to
celebrate Gillian's first feature film," Lauren said.

"From your lips . . ." Gillian said, raising her glass to her own.

A week later Gillian sat ensconced in one of Delta's DC-10s, which
was packed with the worst kind of traveler: the tourist. She be-
grudgingly settled into her coach window seat, quietly praying that
the harried-looking woman next to her would have the strength to
control the rambunctious toddler who sat squirming to her left and the
infant in her lap for the five-and-a-half-hour transcontinental flight
from New York to L.A.

Gillian stuck her iPod's earpieces firmly into place, anxious to
block out the rest of the world, especially the rebel state next to her.
While listening to her neosoul and R & B play list, she questioned her
choice to abandon her fledgling Broadway career to go running off to
La-La Land in search of fame and fortune. The notion was such a
cliché—and a bad one at that. She tried convincing herself that she
hadn't just dropped everything to chase a fragmented dream. No question—on Broadway she had proven to be a rare talent, one of a few
young African American actresses who effortlessly communicated the
essence of a woman—any woman, not just a black woman. Her por-
trayals were free of color, intense, and profoundly moving. People
who'd seen her performances often likened her to a younger Angela
Bassett. After winning critical acclaim for her secondary role in *The
Color Purple*, Gillian had been convinced by the show's producer that

she should give Hollywood at least a year. Her mother's opinion was that the decision should be based solely on which move would lead her closer to marching down the aisle with a rich man. After all, the papers that had provided her mother, Imelda, with her millions were not diplomas, awards, stocks, or bonds, but marriage licenses—in fact, several of them.

Imelda von Glich, born Imogene Patterson, had made marrying up the food chain a profitable career. She was one of the original gold diggers, mining her fortune long before most black women were even aware of the term. Her first husband, Gillian's dad, Arthur Tillman, was a good deal for a poor, uneducated seventeen-year-old, because at least he had a steady job and the promise of a pension, albeit at the lumberyard in Waynesboro, North Carolina. Imogene was pregnant with Gillian before her eighteenth birthday, and named her daughter after the heroine in one of the many Harlequin paperback romance novels that Imogene passed the day reading whenever she wasn't spending Arthur's meager paycheck in the one dress and hat shop in town. He didn't complain too much, because she was by far the best-looking woman in the county, even after birthing a baby.

After becoming pregnant with a second child, one day Imogene just up and left. Arthur never saw her—or Gillian—again. Within a month of her unscheduled departure a prosperous local attorney also left town, headed for New York City, where Imogene met up with him soon after her abortion. From those shaky beginnings she never once looked back. Four husbands later, not only had she gone through many millions from increasingly larger divorce settlements, but her latest husband, a baron from Europe, had also contributed the title of baroness to her lengthy but impressive marital résumé.

After careful consideration, Imelda's advice to Gillian was simpler: *Go to L.A., quick and in a hurry.* Her rationale was even simpler: *If you're an actress you'll have a higher profile, and therefore find it easier to land a solid starter husband.* This sort of talk had always been unsettling to Gillian. Even as a child she was put off by her mother's ruthless pursuit of money and status, but as an adult Gillian was coming to realize that it was a dog-eat-dog world, and the only way she could ensure her own survival was also to pursue both money and power.

Though Imelda had made a nice run of it, her most recent husband was proving to be as tight as her latest face-lift with his money, and she'd used much of her own from previous husbands as seed capital to flit around Europe in search of her next one. Three years earlier, during one of her flush periods, Imelda had given Gillian fifty thousand dollars, telling her to not to spend it all in one place. So Gillian had no illusions of being taken care of by her mother or the woman's husband, and without siblings or family she was literally alone in the world and would have to fend for herself. Living in New York, even with roommates, and income from modeling and acting jobs, had sucked away most of her reserve. Only ten thousand dollars remained in her coffers, so it was time for drastic measures; hence the move to Los Angeles.

Gillian's other problem was that she hadn't dated seriously in years. It wasn't for lack of attention. She was a stunning woman, but not in the classic sense of the word. She was very tall at five-foot-ten, and had sharp, angular features covered by a smooth mocha complexion that was luminescent. Her hair was soft, curly shocks of dusty brown that she pretty much let grow wild, to her mother's dismay. Most men were intimidated either by her height, her avant-garde fashion sensibility, or her keen intellect. A blushing Barbie doll she was not.

The guys outside of the arts who approached her—the corporate types—were much too boring. The thought of being indoctrinated into the world of nine-to-five working stiffs, lumbering through life like a preprogrammed zombie, was too much for her to bear.

As for the creative types, the experience was always a crapshoot as to whether they were bi, gay, down-low, or simply sexually confused. It was way too much to think about. One conclusion she'd drawn from the dating game was that dumb women had a much easier time getting a man. Just look at Lauren, whom she had grown very close to over the last four years and loved like a sister. She had single-handedly won the Max contest that Paulette and Reese had also entered; sure, she wasn't dumb, but she was naive. Lauren had book sense, but when it came to life her brain was on remote control, and her mother was pushing all the buttons.

And then there was her former roommate, Reese, who was attractive and smart as a whip. She was the complete opposite of Lauren: She pushed her own buttons, and other people's too, all in an effort to get whatever it was she wanted. It wasn't beyond her to play stupid just to lock a man down. At the end of the day her victims rarely knew what hit them. Though it was touch-and-go for a while, she ended up maneuvering Chris down the aisle before he realized that she'd manipulated everything from their first meeting to her "accidental" pregnancy, which was by far the oldest trick in the gold digger handbook.

She was suddenly jarred from her meandering thoughts by the loud wailing of the infant who squirmed in her seatmate's lap. The woman shifted the child from shoulder to shoulder, patting his back in an effort to soothe him. The crying came to an abrupt stop when a thick mass of gooey spit-up projected from his mouth, landing with an unceremonious plop right onto Gillian's silk pullover.

By the time the plane bounced to a stop at LAX, Gillian was ready to jump out of it, and her own skin. The kids had cried, kicked, screamed, and squealed nonstop from one coast to the other, while their brain-dead mother displayed an uncanny ability to totally ignore the raging tornadoes that swirled around her. Gillian had been forced to hunker down in her coach seat and slowly simmer. When the perky flight attendant opened the door to the cabin, Gillian couldn't get off the plane quickly enough.

Standing at baggage claim waiting for her Louis Vuitton luggage to tumble down the conveyor belt, Gillian felt a fierce craving for a nicotine fix. She'd been trying to cut back for several months now, and so far had gone from ten cigarettes a day down to six, but after the unnerving flight and her general trepidation about the move to L.A., a serious backslide was on the horizon. When her bag finally appeared she snatched it up and headed for the door. The pricey luggage was a gift from her mother that had been purchased under duress. They had been traveling to Spain together recently, and Imelda couldn't stand the idea of Gillian's ratty duffel bags tagging alongside her spotless four-piece set.

Once outside in the bright Los Angeles sunshine, Gillian lit up a tar stick and sucked in the nicotine like a junkie taking a long-overdue hit of crack.

"Gil. Hey, Gil, over here."

She looked up to find Paulette yelling in her direction as she pulled her expensive convertible CLK 500 up to the curb. Gillian couldn't help but smile. In some ways things were so much more civilized here in L.A.—even for Paulette, who would never be confused as a poster child for civility. People actually came to the airport to meet you. In New York no one did. Whether you were arriving from Boise or Bangkok, you were usually sent a car service or forced to ride with a non-English-speaking cabdriver to your destination. She looked up to the sky and blew smoke toward the clouds before squashing the half-smoked cigarette onto the pavement. She'd make up the other half later.

After loading up the Mercedes's small trunk with Gillian's two bags, Paulette headed down Century Boulevard to the on ramp for the 405 with the top dropped and the wind whipping through their hair as she dodged in and out of lanes.

Gillian reached for her seat belt. "You should put yours on, too," she advised.

"And ruin a perfectly good outfit?" Paulette quipped. She wore a cream linen blouse that was opened one button too many, and a pair of black hip-hugger slacks that never should have been sold to a woman who wore size-twelve pants. Paulette had always fought—and usually lost—the battle of the bulge, so her weight fluctuated as erratically as the stock market. If she was extremely happy or extremely sad, she'd eat more and gain weight, so the only time she kept pounds off was when her life was a snore, which, thanks to her flair for drama, was almost never.

"Suit yourself." Gillian buckled up and glanced down at her own puke-smeared top, momentarily flashing back to her trip from hell.

The sky was movie-set blue with perfect special-effects wispy white clouds artfully arranged. As Paulette picked up speed, shifting with freshly manicured hands into fourth, the wind blew through Gillian's tangle of curls, tossing her hair like a salad, while the radio blasted Snoop and Paulette yapped on a mile a minute about the latest A-list actor signed to About Time Publicity. Paulette had caught her big break when Gillian referred her to an actress friend who blew up after being nominated for—and winning—an Oscar for best supporting actress. After that stroke of luck, business really took off, so Paulette opened her L.A. office and began shuttling back and forth between the two coasts.

Between manically shifting gears and erratically changing lanes, Paulette gave Gillian an earful of advice about how she could become the African American Jennifer Aniston, as if anyone with a valid black card would want to be. Gillian couldn't help but smile. There was something unreal and surreal about being in L.A. It was hard not to sip from the glass of happy juice that everyone seemed to share. The sun and silicone conspired to make any problem fixable; the solution always seemed as simple as another take or a different camera angle.

Gillian allowed herself to relax and succumb to the intoxicating drug that was La-La Land. By the time they pulled up to Paulette's building on Olympic Boulevard and entered her one-bedroom apartment, the irony of her friend's owning a car that cost a small fortune while renting a tiny apartment hadn't escaped her. In any case, she was grateful that Paulette had offered her the sleeper sofa at no charge until she could find a place of her own.

Paulette flitted about the bedroom, frantically changing clothes again and again, searching for something smashing enough to wear to a "must-attend" industry party they were invited to. Though a glass of wine and a heavy nap were more to Gillian's liking, Paulette convinced her that making it in L.A. was like a lesson in skydiving: You just had to close your eyes and jump in.

Gillian unzipped her bag, not sure what she'd find to wear. She'd shipped most of her things a couple of days ago, and was traveling with just enough to get by for a week or two, none of her flyest gear. When she opened the bag's zipper, to her horror she realized that she didn't have *any* gear!

"Oh, shit!"

Paulette stuck her head out the bedroom door. "What's wrong?" she asked.

"For starters, these are *not* my clothes," Gillian answered, holding up a pair of silk men's boxers with the tips of her fingers.

"What happened?"

"I must have grabbed the wrong bag." Gillian had been so anxious to get out of the airport after the hellacious flight that she snatched the first Louis Vuitton bag she saw. It looked exactly like hers, but the baggage tag, once she got around to looking at it, read, BRANDON RUSSELL. Upon further inspection she saw that Mr. Russell lived in L.A. and listed a 310 area code, which meant he lived in L.A proper. "This belongs to a Brandon Russell."

"That name sounds familiar." Paulette wrinkled her nose, and then snapped her fingers. "I got it. He runs Sunset Records!" she gushed. It was Paulette's business to know anybody who was anybody.

"I've got to get this back to the airport and hope that my bag is still there." Gillian couldn't care less who Brandon was; at that moment she could think only about her close friends Dolce & Gabbana, Calvin Klein, Gucci, and Prada.

"You should call him." Paulette appeared excited at the prospect. She was halfway to the phone already. She hadn't climbed to the pinnacle of the competitive PR field by being a shrinking violet.

"No, I should just take the bag back to the airport." Gillian didn't like the idea of calling up a stranger.

"He might actually have *your* bag. Have you thought about that? And if he does, getting it from him would be much quicker than sorting through red tape with the airline." By now Paulette had her arms crossed over her chest and her weight shifted to one leg, while the other foot tapped knowingly. She couldn't believe that Gillian hadn't made the leap and figured out that meeting Brandon Russell was a good move. She was just like Lauren, she thought; both had no idea of how to hustle and make things happen. They were both born into too much privilege, and therefore were accustomed to having things taken care of for them. While Gillian was flitting around the world with her glamorous mother, and Lauren was swaddled in luxury, Paulette had had to fend for herself *and* her not-too-bright mother.

"*He* was probably smart enough to read the name tag."

"Maybe, but once he saw that his was gone and yours was still there, he was also smart enough to figure out that you had his and would most likely call."

Excitedly, Paulette began flipping through the man's belongings as though she were at a rummage sale. When Gillian still didn't answer, she added, "Besides, he could be worth knowing; he's a powerful man in the music business. Get a look at these labels—Armani, Ferre, and Etro. He sure knows how to dress."

"Yeah, and . . . ?"

Paulette put both hands on her hips, giving Gillian a don't-you-get-it? look. "Are you crazy? In this business you meet powerful people however you can, and if they owe you a favor it's even better than gold.

Hey, I'm not suggesting you date him; I'm just saying call him. If he doesn't have your bag, you simply do what you would have done anyway and go to the airport. You have nothing to lose."

Don't remind me, Gillian thought as she slammed the luggage closed.

FIVE

Reese Nolan stepped out of her tricked-out champagne-colored Jaguar, dripping in money. A fleet of paparazzi swarmed her, capturing for Page Six and the other celebrity-hungry publications the more than a hundred thousand dollar's worth of jewelry, clothes, and accessories that she casually wore. On her left arm alone she sported seventy grand in merchandise, including her diamond-encrusted Rolex, an Ethos Art Collection necklace, her enormous engagement and wedding rings, and a fabulous diamond bracelet, a little something she'd picked up just this week from Cartier. Now that they were married, she had no reservations whatsoever about spending Chris's money. As far as she was concerned, the more personal property she amassed during the marriage the better, since her prenuptial agreement set a measly $2 million cap on what she could walk away with in the first five years, and based on her current lifestyle—which she wasn't about to give up—that wouldn't last a New York minute. Plus, for no specific reason, except for her own devious proclivities, Reese did not trust Chris. After the five-year mark, which was only a year and a half away, he'd have to pay her more money if they got divorced, so what would stop him from dumping her prior to her expiration date?

She tossed her Louis Vuitton key ring to the valet without a second glance. Thanks to Paulette, she was so cozy with the media that everybody knew Mrs. Reese Nolan. She was nearly as famous as her NBA superstar husband. Paulette made sure that Reese was invited to every red-carpet event in New York or L.A.; Reese even flew to Cannes and walked the carpet for the film festival every year, and in return she fed Paulette a constant stream of newly signed NBA stars who all looked up to her and Chris.

Reese hoisted her twelve-hundred-dollar Gucci bag up onto her shoulder, thrust her recently enhanced thirty-six-C cleavage out in front of her, tossed her hair back, and prepared to make her grand entrance. She was five-foot-nine, slim, but amply proportioned where it counted the most, and had just enough peanut butter in her complexion not to be considered high yellow. But her best feature was a full, thick mane of jet-black hair that flowed luxuriously down the middle of her back. From afar she was drop-dead gorgeous, but she wasn't nearly as pretty on closer inspection, which revealed eyes that were just a hair too close together, a nose that was a tad crooked, and skin that bore a coat of enlarged pores that weekly facials had done nothing so far to correct, but which coats of foundation did wonders covering.

There was a long, winding line that started at the velvet rope and snaked down the sidewalk and around the corner, away from Rush, the latest trendy hot spot for hip and fashionable New Yorkers. The New York Knicks had made it to the play-offs after a long drought, thanks in large part to Chris's three-pointers, and as a result a veritable who's who—and those who thought they were— descended on the club for a star-studded party to celebrate.

"Mrs. Nolan, right this way." A smartly dressed man wearing all black ushered Reese past the throng of groupies, wannabes, and hangers-on at the door. A gaggle of hoochies in skirts so short they needn't have bothered wearing anything sneered as she was whisked past them. As far as they were concerned she was the enemy; she had what they wanted: a baller. Reese was impervious to such women; they were like yesterday's news: They didn't matter to her at all.

Reese's escort glided her past the nobodies outside to enter the pulsing, dimly lit nightclub. The event promoter continued to guide her through another mostly female crowd who watched the door while sipping on the drink du jour, the Slam Dunk, a wicked concoction of Grey Goose and Red Bull.

New York's nightclubs were a study in class systems. Waiting outside placed you at the lowest rung on the shaky ladder, but even after flash, cash, or cleavage had appeased the doormen, once inside, unfortunately, the social hierarchy began anew.

At this tenuous point some women would do and promise whatever was necessary to make the cut; they were so close to being in the mix they could just about taste the cake. If only they could make it beyond this point, Mr. NBA would be there waiting to convert their ordinary nine-to-five lives into the world of money, power, and makeovers. All it took was dollars and sense to get the right boob job to add that extra bounce, buy a little Botox to smooth away the rent-worry lines, visit one of those celebrity dentists to whiten, brighten, and straighten a crooked or yellowing smile. And let's not forget a visit to Gucci, Prada, and Hermès to finish wrapping the end product in high style.

Seeing Reese sail by without a pause only fueled their burning desire to make it into the end zone, where instead of the Slam Dunk, those lucky enough to breathe the air would swill vintage Champagne Paul Goerg, or shots of Courvoisier.

Reese could hear the incessant chatter as she breezed by.

"That's Chris Nolan's wife. She thinks she so cute."

"I heard that he has over nine inches in those shorts, and I wanna see for myself."

"That's gotta be a weave she's got. Ain't no black girl got hair like that."

"My fake tits look better than hers."

"Don't let me get my hands on him. He ain't that cute, but I'd rock his world anyway."

And so it went. . . .

These women were either friends or girlfriends of players and their friends. They were in the mix, but still not a bona fide part of it. The endgame was the fiercely guarded section that rose high above the other two sections, where players, their wives, and other celebrities gathered to look down over the glass partition and reign supreme over the peons relegated to the depths below. This was Reese's domain. Though she'd been married to Chris for three and a half years now, that heady rush of superiority that followed such public displays of her position still gave her an incredible high, one that no twelve-step program could ever cure.

"Let me know if I can be of further assistance," the promoter said, nearly bowing as he opened the door for Reese to enter.

Scanning the room Reese saw a cluster of diamonds: a group of players' wives. The players hovered near the bar, surrounding André 3000, Jay-Z, and Russell Simmons. Most of the players were married and on a tight leash for the night, but a few of their single teammates were on the prowl, searching for the pick of tonight's litter. Assorted rappers were there with their posses, as well as a bevy of perpetually bored-looking models, a smattering of perky up-and-coming Hollywood actresses, and quite a few PR reps, some of whom confused themselves with their clients, so intent were they on their own fame.

Reese wasted no time diving right in. "My, my, my, don't you look trim. You've finally lost some of that baby fat," she said to Windy Latner, a rookie's wife who'd had a baby eight months ago and struggled mightily to return to a fighting size six. Until she did, the other wives would continue to treat her as though fat cells might actually be contagious. Reese was the worst, acting as though being fat and/or ugly were cardinal sins.

"You've certainly never had to worry about that," one of the rookie wives said, sucking up. The two women exchanged fake air kisses, not even bothering to touch each other's cheeks.

"And I never will." Reese tossed her impeccably maintained hair and proceeded to greet the other wives, and their inner circle, who stood as if to kneel and kiss her ring. The player's wives tended to follow the same pecking order established by the players. Those whose husbands made the most money or had the most fame lorded over the others. The rookie wives were at the bottom of the NBA-wife food chain, unless, of course, you'd managed to snag Lebron James or another bona fide rising superstar. Before taking her throne Reese greeted her old friend Kira, whom she'd personally invited to the party.

"Hey, girl. Glad you could make it," she said.

"As if I'd miss it," Kira replied.

Kira, who began her "career" as a video ho, was now simply a well-kept woman, or, more generically put, a high-class call girl. She lived in L.A., and because of her ferocious body, which she worked seven days a week to maintain, she was a regular on the celebrity circuit, often bedding one star or another, be they male or female, and sometimes in mixed groups. In exchange for her valuable services she got regular and substantial deposits into her many bank accounts, two of which were offshore. Hers was a cottage industry; the cottage just happened to be smack-dab in the middle of Beverly Hills.

After they'd all rearranged themselves so that Reese would be among their center, they resumed sipping champagne, gossiping, and looking fabulous for the photographers who milled about taking shot after shot of the beautiful people.

"Here comes your husband," said Kira. She nudged her in the side. "He had a great game tonight."

When Chris entered a room—particularly of women—a hush usually followed. He was tall, powerfully built, and though he was not necessarily handsome, his money made him very sexy; paper like his melted hearts and panties alike. All eyes followed him as he approached Reese, who beamed like a Cheshire cat. The other wives envied her, not just because her man was the star, but because he was faithful, at least as far as the busy NBA grapevine was concerned. One thing was certain: If a player was fooling around, everyone knew it; the grapevine usually took root in bed, and thus spread from pillow to pillow.

"Hey, baby." He leaned his six-five frame over to kiss her lips. After more than three years of marriage and a baby, he seemed to still be in love with her.

"Great game." She remained seated, but flashed him a smile, or at least one for the cameras, which were flashing right back.

"Can I get something for you?"

"I'll have another glass of Champagne Paul Goerg, please." It was the only champagne she drank.

"I'll be back."

After he left, Reese felt her cell phone vibrate, and checked the caller ID. It was Paulette, who'd just flown in from L.A. "I'm downstairs," she shouted. "One of the morons at the door, who doesn't have enough sense to know who I am, won't let me up. You have to come down to get me."

Reese wanted to tell her that it wasn't because he didn't know who she was that she couldn't get in, but because she was at least fifteen pounds overweight and her weave needed tightening up. In other words, she didn't look like a VIP. For a publicist she could be awfully dense, but then again, who knew what exactly Paulette saw when she looked at her own image in the mirror? "I'll be right down," Reese said. She got up and pushed her way through the thickening crowd to rescue her friend.

Out of nowhere a hand grabbed her arm, stopping her in her

tracks. She whipped around, ready to snatch it away and sling indignant outrage at whoever it was who had the nerve to touch her. She turned to face a man who had *danger* written across his handsome forehead, down his lean but muscular arms, and across his deep, broad chest. The man who stood unfazed by her glare was dark and ruggedly handsome, with a smile that Tyrese would envy. There was nothing pretty about him; he was sexy in a very primal, dirty, bad-boy kind of way.

While Reese stood immobilized by rapid-fire thoughts of lust, he did his talking with his hands. Camouflaged by the crowd, his right hand pulled her even closer. She could feel his sizable hard-on as he slyly rubbed her ass. His brazen display only fueled her lustful thoughts. Her head was light; she had to remind herself to breathe. She felt both wet and hot, sensations that she'd not known for years, certainly not since being married to Chris. With his left hand he slipped a note in hers, put his thick, perfectly shaped lips to her ear, and whispered, "Call me, and don't make me wait too long." He gave her a sexy leer that passed for a smile, and then he was gone.

By the time she returned to the VVVIP room with Paulette, some of the groupies had managed to cajole, beg, or barter blow jobs to gain access to the inner sanctum, and had gathered near the bar, scoping their targets. Reese watched as their eyes took in every inch of Chris's body. Many didn't refrain from licking their lips. Reese despised groupies. They hunted her man and the other players like prey in the jungle, trying any- and everything to bag one—if not for keeps, many would be just as happy with a souvenir, in the form of a baby, that could be taken all the way to the bank. She rolled her eyes at the group of them.

Just then one girl loaded up and moved in for the kill. She was formidable, with a long, silky weave, a full rack of breasts, and a butt that made Beyoncé's look like a starter kit. She slunk over to

Chris as he approached the bar. Chris was no fool; he turned his back to her.

"Those gold diggers will stop at nothing," Samantha hissed. She had good reason to; her doggish husband was one of the biggest whores in the NBA. Rumor had it that he had three outside children, and the baby mamas to go with them, and brought cases of venereal disease home to his wife the way some men brought flowers. Many of the wives, like Samantha, were tortured but well-dressed souls, who would sooner cut off a limb than part with the social status of being a player's wife.

Reese didn't have that problem, since she was convinced that she was as much of a celebrity as her husband was. The only thing necessary about Chris was his money.

"Those hussies are the worst," Paulette hissed, rolling her eyes. She was oblivious to the sharp irony of her remarks. As a realist, Paulette was well aware of her own hunt for the power that the right Mr. Right would bring, yet she still drew a distinction between *those* women and herself.

Reese had no such conflicts; she despised the gold diggers so much because she understood them all too well. In fact, she was one of the best, and look where it had gotten her, so she had little doubt that even a man like Chris could succumb to one. After all, that was how she got him.

SIX

Like a prospector prepared for a big dig, Reese had shown up at the University of North Carolina with her future clearly mapped out. She knew that to get the type of man who could afford the things a girl like her deserved, first she had to get the hell out of Queens, and since she wasn't quite ready to conquer the Big Apple yet, she needed a pit stop. The University of North Carolina proved to be the perfect outpost.

Reese surmised that any man with bankable credentials wanted his wife to at least have a college education; that much was simple to her. While most people viewed a degree as necessary for career success, to Reese it was like a sharp chisel: a precision tool needed to get better results quicker. The decision to go to UNC specifically was even more tactical: It was an excellent place to start her NBA scouting expedition.

Before Reese knew what a technical foul was, she decided that plan A was to marry a professional athlete, preferably a basketball player, and the Tar Heels always had a great team with an impressive draft record. Besides, most of the females among the hicks of Carolina offered negligible competition, so catching one of those country bumpkins with a good jump shot would be like snaring fish in a barrel for someone as clever and cunning as she was.

The Pro Plan, as she referred to it, was a step-by-step guide, outlining the tactics necessary to marry a professional athlete. It took Reese barely one week to scout out the players in each class who were favored to go pro. An NBA recruiter couldn't have done a more thorough job at picking promising talent. Her number one draft pick, LaShawn Brown, was a senior from Raleigh, North Carolina, who was a shoo-in for a high lottery pick. He was destined for a lucrative NBA contract and years of product endorsements. The boy had flashes of brilliance like Jordan, with the personal charisma of Magic. He was a true star. The only problem was that Reese was about two years too late to bag him. LaShawn already had more women in his life than he had brain cells in his head. Like most star athletes he had a main girlfriend and a second string of three or four extras, and even his bench warmers ran three deep.

It wasn't that Reese didn't feel qualified for the job or up to the challenge, but she was nothing if not realistic. After all, this wasn't sport for her; she was on a mission. Reese figured that she had only two good shots at catching the prize. The third time a girl was linked to a player she was automatically labeled a groupie—or worse, a whore, in which case, she was no longer marriage material to anyone of significance. Therefore, Reese's operation called for extreme selectivity and a well-thought-out strategy. She was playing for keeps, not for one-night stands.

Her second-draft pick was Carl Hightower, a junior who was definitely a comer. In fact, if LaShawn weren't such a star, Carl would already be flashing in the center of everyone's radar. Fortunately LaShawn was graduating this year; then everyone would realize that Carl had the *only* three-point jump shot. As promising as he was on the stat sheet, the boy also had a diction problem that was hard on the ears, but nothing that a few extra zeros in a bank account couldn't mitigate.

Her third and fourth picks were both sophomores (freshmen were too risky—who knew if a brilliant performance in high school was simply a flash in the pan or the real thing?). One was Chris Nolan, who so far showed real promise, but he was somewhat inconsistent with his game; he was also as boring as reruns of *Gilligan's Island*. If it weren't for his eye/hand coordination the boy wouldn't be able to buy pussy at a fire sale.

The other contender was Buster Russell, a ghetto kid straight out of the projects of Newark, New Jersey. He was six feet, eight inches of street thug. The boy was good—in fact, really good—but his attitude set him back just as far as his skills got him. Of them all, he was definitely the most fuckable to Reese; she loved a bad boy, but this mission wasn't about sex—or love, for that matter. She was keeping it real. It was all about the Benjamins, baby.

While the amateur groupies were busying themselves staking out locker rooms and lurking courtside at every home game, Reese was much more subversive in her approach. Her secret fuck-buddy was Bobby Hicks, the dorky team manager who was happy to catch any of the leftover tail that the team didn't consume. Reese was given the scoop on players in exchange for rounds of sex between the sheets. Through him, she found out which classes Carl would be taking the next semester, and promptly registered for his English Literature course. The first day of class she hung around outside the auditorium until she saw him go in. After he took a seat—predictably in the back—Reese quietly sat one row in front of him and one seat over, knowing that most people kept the same seat throughout the semester. Her moves were as smooth as Michael Jordan's during the play-offs. Carl never even saw the slam dunk coming.

The first two classes she wore short (but not too short) baby doll skirts that accentuated her long, curvy legs. The low sandal was just enough to further elongate her calves, but not too much to show gross premeditation. Of course, the sweaters she wore were fitted to highlight a full C-cup, but the pièce de résistance was her long, wavy hair, which she would shake and toss periodically to make sure that he was paying full attention. Aside from all of that, she did nothing for a couple of weeks! No coy batting of the eyelashes, no babbling on about his latest on-court theatrics; hers was a slow, steady seduction.

Reese lay in the cut, patiently waiting for just the right moment to hook and reel him in. It came one day as they were leaving class. She was walking ahead of Carl as a group of boys, who were horsing around, ran out in front of her, giving Reese a good excuse to stumble and almost fall, her books and bag spilling forward. Just as she predicted, Carl reached out and grabbed her, breaking her fall in the process. As rough around the edges as he was, the boy was raised by his grandmother to be a bona fide Southern gentleman.

"I'm so sorry," she gushed. "How clumsy of me." Reese played the damsel in distress to the hilt: eyelashes batting rapidly and manicured fingers spread across her clavicle as she tried to catch her breath.

"You aaiight?" he asked in a deep Southern drawl.

"I'm fine, just embarrassed." She smiled awkwardly, and quickly begin gathering her things, which had scattered to the ground.

He bent his lanky, six-foot-five-inch frame to help her. While stacking her papers and books in a neat pile, he stopped abruptly when he saw tickets to an upcoming NASCAR race at the Bristol Motor Speedway in Tennessee. "These here yours?" he asked.

"Yeah." She shrugged as though it were perfectly normal for a beautiful young girl from New York to have tickets to a NASCAR race.

"That's gon' be some race." His eyes lit up like fireflies in June.

"It should be awesome, Earnhardt Junior and Danica are both racing," she replied, as though she gave a rat's ass about the sport, and got no greater thrill than seeing cars run around a track a million times over. *What a thrill!*

After the last of her things were gathered they both stood up. "Are you a racing fan?" she asked as though the thought had just occurred to her, when her pillow talk with Bobby had uncovered the fact that he was mad about both NASCAR and Formula One racing. Not exactly a black man's sport, and most certainly not a black woman's. She'd purchased the tickets immediately and had carried them to class for a week, waiting for the opportunity to bait her trap.

"Man, I love racing." A big cheese-eating grin spread across his face. "I can't say I eva met a woman who did. Most women can't stand it." By now he was eating out of her well-manicured hand, so she continued to feed him one morsel at a time.

"I'm not most women," she said, lowering the books that she'd been holding to give him a peak at two very enticing morsels. As with most men, the sight of mammary flesh had the desired effect, killing smart brain cells by the hundreds, while multiplying the stupid ones.

From his towering perspective, Carl had a bird's-eye view down the fold of her cleavage. "I see." His mouth had slacked open, and he wore the goofiest expression on his face.

She smiled coyly, then turned to walk away, stumbling just as her weight landed on her right ankle. Again he was Johnny-on-the-spot, ready to catch her. "You sho' you okay?"

Reese grimaced, feigning pain. "It does hurt," she whined.

"You should go to the infirmary. Here, I'll help ya." He took all of her books in one arm and supported her with the other.

She limped along gingerly, clinging to him as though her life depended on it, and to Reese it did. "No, I'm sure I just need to prop it up and put some ice on it, but maybe you can help me to my room." She gave him the doe-eyed look.

"I'd be happy to," he answered. "Anything I can do to help."

Game.

Set.

Match.

SEVEN

"Hello, may I speak to Brandon Russell?" Paulette stood just inches from Gillian like an eager puppy, hanging on to her every word. If she could have gotten away with placing her ear right alongside Gillian's next to the phone's receiver, she would have done it. Paulette was one of those sadly desperate women who jump full-throttle at any opportunity—real or imagined—and the chance to meet Brandon Russell was definitely an opportunity that she could not let pass. She hadn't built a successful public relations firm on two coasts by being passive or bashful.

A man with a stuffy British accent answered the phone. "And who may I say is calling?" He stretched the word *who* out several seconds, turning the question into an accusation. Gillian automatically envisioned an English butler with a stiff upper lip, an up-turned nose, and bad teeth.

"This is Gillian. Gillian Tillman."

"And may I ask the nature of your call?"

This man was really getting on her nerves. She was barely able to swallow her irritation at having lost her luggage after suffering such a horrible flight. All she really wanted was a hot bath, a cold glass of wine, and a long nap. Gillian had to bite her tongue to keep from saying, "No, you may not." Instead, she remembered her luggage full of pricey designer gear, so she checked her attitude and gave him an answer. "There was a mix-up at the airport. I have Mr. Russell's luggage, and I hope he has mine."

"Oh, dear," the man murmured. "Mind if I place you on hold?"

Before she could respond one way or the other, a click ensued, followed by chords of classical music. Gillian sighed impatiently and wondered, *What black music industry executive programs classical music for his home phone line?*

"Brandon Russell here." His voice was pretentiously rich and melodic, smoothing over a distant twang of country. As an actress, Gillian had a keen ear for those who were cultivating an accent. Given his huffy British manservant and clearly pretentious tone, someone less exposed might believe that Brandon Russell was to the manor born, but Gillian could sniff out a fake from miles away, even through phone lines. After all, she was her mother's child.

"I'm Gillian Tillman. I must have been on your flight from New York earlier today, and somehow I accidentally picked up your luggage. I have the same bag." Next to her, Paulette looked gleeful, as though she might actually clap her hands together, jump up, and click her heels like Dorothy.

"I just walked in the door, and hadn't even realized there'd been a mix-up," Brandon said.

"So, you do have my bag?"

"I do," he answered. Unlike Paulette, Gillian didn't care if he was Prince Charles; her bag was all that mattered. Between Paulette and Reese she wasn't sure who was the bigger opportunist.

Gillian breathed a sigh of relief, happy that her designer garbs were indeed within reach.

"Let me have your address and I'll be right over," Brandon suggested. "I'm in Beverly Hills."

"If you don't mind, let's meet somewhere public." The man could have been an ax murderer, for all she knew, but her real reason for not letting him come near Paulette's apartment had less to do with fear for her personal safety than it did with not being embarrassed by her fawning friend, who would no doubt use the opportunity to do some shameless social climbing. There was no way that Paulette would miss an opportunity to place a couple of well-placed footholds in Brandon Russell.

"Why don't we meet at the Ivy in, say, thirty minutes?" Brandon proposed.

"I'll be there."

Before Gillian put the phone down, Paulette was inches from her face. "So where are you meeting him? What did he say? Does he have your bag?"

"The Ivy. Nothing really, and yes." This was truly annoying.

"Perfect!" Paulette was effervescent as she rubbed her palms together like a devilish child plotting to hold up Santa Claus. "So, what are you wearing?" she asked, turning her nose up at Gillian's stained shirt.

"Who cares?" Gillian asked, exasperated. "I'm exchanging bags with him, not bodily fluids."

"Maybe not yet." Paulette gave Gillian a sly look, and when she didn't get a favorable response she grabbed Gillian's hand and dragged her into the bedroom. "You just never know how he could help you, so at the very least please change tops," she insisted, opening up her closet as though it were Fort Knox.

Only her sense of decorum kept Gillian from turning *her* nose up at the predictably trendy and tacky garments that hung in Paulette's closet. In New York, where style was a way of life, tacky Paulette was certainly challenged enough, but now that she was spending half her time in L.A. with no barometer, her lack of fashion sense was even worse. There was something about living in L.A. that triggered serious style maladies for those who were so prone. In Paulette's mind she was a size six, only trapped in a size-twelve body, so she was oblivious to the long list of fashion don'ts she continually violated. While Gillian flipped through the hangers as if they were contaminated with the Ebola virus, Paulette disappeared into the living room.

Minutes later Gillian found a top that was marginally suitable to wear in this pinch. The fabric looked okay from afar, but up close—particularly when worn—it was only a few grades above industrial burlap. Fortunately, Gillian's Prada mules would upgrade the overall look, so she wouldn't have to stoop to wearing the atrocious Payless quality of shoes that littered the floor of Paulette's closet.

"You find anything?" Paulette yelled from the living room.

"Yep," Gillian replied as she fluffed her hair in front of the vanity's mirror. Now she was anxious to get going, pick up her bag, and get back, so she could yank off Paulette's shirt before she suffered a severe allergic reaction to it.

"The washcloths are in the bathroom closet; why don't you go ahead and freshen up."

I'm just exchanging a bag, not going to the prom. "Sure, but I've gotta hurry."

When she emerged five minutes later, Paulette had her handbag tossed over her shoulder and was standing by Brandon's now-closed suitcase, idling by the door. She was ready to go.

This was not good. "You don't have to go with me; it's not far. Plus, I thought you'd want to get ready for the party later?" Gillian prompted.

"I have to drive you there." At this point a barreling freight train couldn't have kept her from meeting Brandon, and it quietly infuriated Paulette that Gillian, like Lauren, could be so blasé about such things. But she supposed that a life of privilege resulted in such a dismissive attitude.

"Paulette, I have my driver's license, and I probably know L.A better than you do." As an actress and model, she'd been hanging out on the West Coast for many years. Besides, Paulette's driving skills left much to be desired.

"I'd rather drive you." Paulette wasn't budging; this was her only reasonable excuse to horn in on the opportunity to meet Brandon.

Gillian knew right away that this living arrangement wasn't going to work for long. She was accustomed to her independence, coming and going as she pleased, even as a child. Imelda was usually too busy chasing the next rich husband to keep up with her. "Okay, but just drop me off. I'll call a taxi to get back."

This appeared to stump Paulette. "If you insist, but it's a waste of money," she said, as if she gave a damn about anyone else's financial situation. "I'll tell you what: I'll drop you off in front and run down the street to pick up a sundress I have on hold. You can call me on my cell whenever you're ready."

"Whatever." Gillian grabbed her bag and Brandon's luggage and headed out the door.

After more than fifteen years, the Ivy was still the premier place to see and be seen in L.A. Along with great food, it offered some of the best people-watching in the world, especially at the choice tables that sat along the white picket fence, only a sidewalk away from ritzy Robertson Boulevard.

Gillian hopped out of Paulette's car in front of the restaurant's valet stand. She walked around to the trunk to retrieve the luggage, and, of course, Paulette hadn't pulled the latch to open it. As onlookers surveyed the new arrivals, Gillian hurried around to the driver's window, motioning for Paulette to open the trunk. Instead of simply pushing the little button that sat conveniently located within arm's reach, Paulette made an orchestrated show of hopping out of the car, busts bouncing buoyantly, to open it by hand with her key. Gillian smirked, and now knew why Paulette had also changed tops to simply run an errand. She now wore a plunging, bright lime green, paper-thin cotton T-shirt that was three times too small and read, I SWALLOW. The skimpy fabric hoisted and uplifted every plump centimeter of her thirty-eight-D-size chest. It was quite a sight. To make the most of her wardrobe change, after opening the trunk she proceeded to bend over deeply to help lift the large bag out of it, bringing the twin mountains ever closer to spilling out of the tight, flimsy material. Leaving the apartment only minutes earlier, she hadn't lifted a finger to help Gillian put the bag in. Now, having pushed the envelope as far as she could, she flashed a smile to those seated on the terrace, hoping to spy Brandon, in which case she would force an introduction. When that ploy fizzled, she teetered back behind the wheel, leaving Gillian to pull the behemoth-sized suitcase up the brick stairs to the hostess stand, which also sat outside. She felt like a rank, tacky tourist every laborious step of the way. But at least the luggage was Louis Vuitton.

"I'm Gillian. I'm here to meet Brandon Russell." The über-cool, L.A.-blond hostess assessed her and her luggage with a question mark on her deeply tanned face. Somehow, despite the tacky khaki green blouse from Paulette's closet, and the fact that she was rolling up pulling a piece of luggage, Gillian still managed to pass muster.

"Mr. Russell called and should be here shortly, but if you'd like I'll seat you now," she said, eyeing the luggage distastefully, as if its tackiness were contagious. "Would you like to check that?" Without waiting for a reply, she gave Gillian a claim check and led her back sans luggage, in the direction from which Gillian had just come, to the premier tables that sat along the fence. With every step Gillian regretted meeting him here. Now that she had time to think about it, it made no sense whatsoever. Why meet at the Ivy to exchange bags? The Ivy was a destination in and of itself, not exactly the place for a quick rendezvous. Halfway through her mojito, Gillian's phone rang. She checked caller ID, and predictably it was Paulette.

"Hey, girl!"

Gillian fought to keep the annoyance from her voice. "What's up?"

"Well, is he there yet?" Paulette was breathless with anticipation.

"No, and if he's not here in two minutes I'm out." This was getting very old very quickly.

"What about your luggage?" *And more important, what about my introduction to Brandon Russell?*

"I'm sure he wants his luggage as much as I want mine, so we can always do an airport dropoff."

"Don't be so hasty. Besides, we don't have time to go to the airport and still make the party tonight in Brentwood."

Gillian began looking around for a waitress to settle the tab for the drink she'd ordered, when she noticed every head on the patio turn to the valet stand, where a taupe chauffeur-driven Rolls-Royce Silver Shadow had rolled up. From the regal look of it, she'd have expected Queen Elizabeth to disembark, waving stiffly to her subjects. Gillian's mouth dropped to the floor when the driver hopped out to open the door for Brandon Russell, whom she recognized immediately from party shots in *Vibe* and *Uptown* magazines.

He was a short, barely average-looking guy, so it took a Rolls and lots of money for him to turn heads. He reveled in it, while simultaneously pretending not to notice the undue attention.

"Gillian? Did you hear me?" Paulette squawked.

"I'll call you back."

"Gillian? Gillian? Is he there? Is he—"

Gillian hung up the phone, turned off the ringer, and slipped it into her bag before the roving fanfare known as Brandon Russell approached her table.

"You must be Gillian." She was surprised, since he hadn't been escorted by the hostess; he'd simply walked right up to the table. He extended his hand, playing the part of distinguished gentleman to the hilt. He had a medium-chocolate complexion with wide-set eyes, a round, nearly pudgy face, and a mouth that was attractive because it didn't draw any attention. To be blunt, his best feature was his money. Though he wore it unabashedly, he did attempt some restraint. His shirt was a simple cream-colored Nodus linen with fine burgundy pinstripes, but Gillian knew haberdashery; it had probably set him back at least six hundred dollars. He tried for the casually elegant look with a pair of kid-glove Italian loafers that she knew were handmade and cost no less than a grand. And the watch: Audemars Piguet, another seventy grand in accessories.

"And you must be Brandon Russell?"

"I am," he said, smiling. "It's good to see you again."

She had no recollection of ever meeting him, but before she could question his comment, Brandon was seated across from her ordering a dirty martini with Grey Goose from the solicitous hostess, who'd miraculously appeared at his side. It was clear from the gleaming smile she put on display that she was one of those white chicks who would date Mike Tyson if he kept her wrapped in Gucci.

"Do we know each other?" She finally asked.

"Not as well as I'd like us to." His average appearance and humble beginnings were polished to a high gloss; only a mild trace of the skinny, gold-tooth-wearing homeboy from Mississippi remained. Like a cat analyzing trapped prey, he studied her reaction, which was to pull back and study him as well.

In seconds flat she summoned up his game. He was one of the newly but outrageously rich and semifamous people who believed in using both assets to get from point A to point B as swiftly as possible.

To put her at ease, he said, "Let's just say that I've seen your work and recognized your name. And trust me, I never forget a beautiful face." By now he was leaned back in his chair with his hand to his chin, taking her in. His mack mode was fully operational.

However, it did not work. "It's nice to have met you, Mr. Russell," she said, gathering her bag. "Do you have my luggage?" she asked, looking in the direction of the insanely expensive car. With men like Brandon, it was best to give them a taste of rejection to cleanse the palate for any subsequent encounters, not that she had an appetite for him at all. He was simply not her type.

Now he shifted in his chair. "Of course, it's in the car. But, I was hoping that we could at least have a drink?" He leaned forward. "And I do believe in fate, so there must be some reason we ended up with each other's bags."

Only good manners kept her in her seat. There was something about him that just didn't sit well with her.

"So, what brings you to L.A.?" He hoped a quick change of subject—to her—would get them past his trite mack lines that ordinarily would have worked. In fact, by now he should have tagged first base and be rounding the corner, making his way to second, but he shifted his game plan and settled down for his next pitch, hoping that it too wasn't a strike.

"I'm looking for film or TV work. Just needing a change." She shrugged nonchalantly, betraying none of the anxiety she felt about her relocation.

"Anything promising?" he asked.

"I've just gotten here. Besides, I know that it does take time."

"I saw you in *Chicago* about six months ago. I thought you were brilliant. A real talent. The direction needed some work, but your performance was flawless." He nodded his head thoughtfully. It occurred to him how to reel her in—not that he was even sure he wanted her, but at this point she was a challenge. He had to treat her like a vocal artist, and he was well known for his mike-side manner with his female singers. He had perfected the art of flattering, cajoling, and doing *whatever* was needed to tap into the emotion needed to produce a hit record. Rumor had it that one of his superstars hit a legendary note on her double-platinum single while he gave her a sample of his own oral skills right there in the studio, proving that he was from the school of By Any Means Necessary.

"Thank you." Though Gillian managed not to reveal it, she was impressed—not only that he'd seen one of her performances, but that he also understood the nuances of its production, and was accurate with his assessment.

"Your next step should be a feature film," he sat back and proclaimed as if he were Cecil B. DeMille. The only thing missing was a smoldering cigar.

"Of course, who wouldn't rather do a feature film?" she answered, ignoring his bravado.

"My thoughts exactly." He was equally undeterred by her nonchalance.

Gillian looked up to see Paulette's boobs, then Paulette herself, hovering over them like a vulture who's spotted fresh kill.

"Aren't you going to introduce me?" she asked, never taking her eyes off Brandon.

"Brandon, this is Paulette; Paulette, Brandon." Paulette bent over unnecessarily to shake his hand, her ample bosom spilling forth.

"Hi, Paulette. It's a pleasure to meet you."

Before he got the words out of his mouth, she was pivoting to find a spare chair to pull up to the table that had previously been set just for two.

EIGHT

Abyssinian Baptist Church in Harlem, New York, held a full house of well-heeled mourners. At least, some mourned; others were simply on hand to witness the passing of Priscilla Baines-Reynolds, a prominent member of East Coast African American society. Since funerals were an irresistible opportunity to socialize, to see and be seen, this one had quickly become akin to Must-See TV. Everyone who was anyone of a certain ilk in the black community was represented, including the most auspicious doctors, esteemed lawyers, and pompous Indian chiefs, in addition to politicians, and those who were just simply rich. Paulette, who helped organize the affair, wanted to have a VIP reception before the funeral, and a VVIP dinner, complete with a velvet rope, afterward. Fortunately—but to Paulette's dismay—her aunt Mildred's good taste and staunch sense of decorum prevailed.

Sister Baines would surely be missed, many agreed. Most certainly her generous tithing to the church and her plentiful contributions to numerous charities would be. Priscilla Baines-Reynolds was as old-money as black folks got, and at ninety-four she'd still reigned over her family and community with the arrogant flip of a heavily spotted, arthritic wrist, one that was nonetheless still capable of writing checks. There were some people in the congregation who were genuinely saddened by her passing, and would miss the long-standing fixture at the church. And then there was her family, many of whom had simply been biding time, waiting impatiently for her feeble heart to thump its last beat.

Lauren and her husband sat on one side of her mother, and her father, Nathaniel, sat nonchalantly on the other. True to form, Mildred looked like she'd walked out of central casting: perfectly coiffed and suitably attired for a high-profile funeral. Her suit was an ashy black, immaculately tailored Chanel ensemble, which was purchased in Paris a while ago in anticipation of this very moment. She wore a perfect face of makeup without a trace of tears, even if you could have seen past the French lace veil that draped off of a sweeping black Eric Javits straw hat.

Her sister, June, sat beside her in a bad knockoff version of Mildred's look. Not only was the suit last season's, but it was last season's Macy's! In stark contrast, her eyes were red, swollen orbs, and her makeup was smeared by tears of grief. Though June was younger, telltale creases had been etched into her face by time and stress brought on by lack of funds.

Paulette, her daughter, had boarded a flight from L.A. before rigor mortis had set in. She sat beside her mother, decked out in the shortest, tightest, and most cleavage-baring black dress that she could find along Madison Avenue. Said dress was accompanied by four double strands of pearls, a formidably wide-brimmed black hat, and a pair of large, black Jackie O sunglasses. Gillian, who'd arrived in town days earlier to audition for a second lead in Denzel Washington's Broadway production, also sat behind them.

After the interment, those who were invited milled about Priscilla Baines-Reynolds's sprawling estate, which was an impressive early-1900s Tudor-style mansion in Westchester, New York.

"The service was beautiful," Gillian said to Lauren.

"It was." Lauren sighed. "Nana would have loved it."

They each lifted a wineglass from a server's tray and toasted, "To Nana."

"I'm so glad you're here," Lauren said as they embraced. They hadn't seen each other since April, when Gillian left for L.A. Lauren missed their weekly excursions to museums, the theater, and small galleries. She had especially missed her since things with Max hadn't been going so well. He felt distant, even though he slept next to her in the same bed. She talked to Paulette about her problem, but it was never quite the same. Optimistically she asked, "So, are you moving back?"

"My old agent called to tell me about this new play on Broadway. He thinks I might have a chance at a leading role." Gillian shrugged. "So, we'll see."

"I've got my fingers crossed. New York isn't the same without you."

Lauren's mother, Mildred, made her way in their direction, fielding countless murmurs of condolence from friends and acquaintances along the way. She soaked up the attention like an actress expertly working the camera during an important close-up.

"Mom, are you okay?" Lauren asked.

"I'm fine, dear," she replied, remembering to add a wistful tone of mourning to her voice.

"I can't believe that bitch!" Paulette hissed in her mother's ear nearby as she watched Mildred with a wary eye. The angry words managed to escape the privacy of their conversation, fueled on by her second gin-and-tonic, which she swirled in a highly agitated manner among rattling ice cubes.

It pissed Paulette off that her mother assumed her secondary role so passively, as though she deserved nothing more than her barren lot in life. But she would be damned if she'd let history play out the same way between her and Lauren. The ill will between

Mildred and June had simmered steadily and quietly over the years
like an infected boil, while Lauren—who avoided confrontation
like polyester—pretended to be ignorant of her family's ongoing
drama.

From the moment Priscilla's great grandmother, a slave from
South Carolina, saw the near-white baby girl with the silky
blondish hair that her labor had produced, she vowed from then on
to protect her family gene pool from the curse of dark pigment like
her own. Ma Lizzie, as she was called, was as black as North Carolina coals, and her hair went beyond the description of kinky. A
comb would sooner break every tooth before it ever passed through
the matted tangles that covered her scalp. She had a striking presence, with the tall, elegant carriage indigenous to Africa's Zulu
tribe, but sadly it took only one generation in America to erase an
entire continent's concept of beauty and replace it with the European version. Consequently, the lighter the slave's complexion, the
closer to the big house he got, while the darkies toiled in hard,
dusty fields under the blazing-hot sun. Farm animals were treated
better. More simply put, black meant stupid, poor, and ugly, while
white stood for goodness, purity, and beauty. Those in between held
varying degrees of virtue, so Priscilla's grandmother's birth sig-
naled redemption for Lizzie, who was in the master's house only
because she was unquestionably the best cook in the state, not because of her looks. Nor were her looks an explanation for the animalistic coupling that led to the birth of her nearly white child.
Instead, it was actually the result of too much liquor, physical prox-
imity, and an inbred sense of entitlement by her master.

Late one night Master Thomas stumbled home sloshed after
his weekly poker game, and as he shuffled past the kitchen, still
clutching his empty flask, he backtracked, deciding to have a late-
night snack. When he found Lizzie bent over, removing one of her
legendary pound cakes from the stove, he decided he'd have her instead. Her face may have been lacking, for his taste, but her body

was any man's wet dream, particularly the rear view. As casually as if deciding to have a glass of milk with his cookies, Master Thomas had his way with Lizzie, humping himself to release, then zipping up his pants and stumbling off to bed. He took her the way one might relieve himself in the woods; it was a necessary physical relief performed under less than desirable conditions.

Up until the birth of her daughter, she'd maintained relations with her "husband" whenever she could sneak off to the shacks that bordered the plantation, so when she came up pregnant, she assumed the child would be black like her other two. The baby's color was as much of a surprise to her as it was a delight. Having a child by Master Thomas brought with it perks she otherwise would never have dreamed of, namely her freedom, a piece of property, and a first-rate education for her children—even the darkies. When Lizzie's lily-white daughter, Ima, was of marrying age, her sole focus was to marry her off to an acceptable light-skinned, free, and educated Negro, who came in the form of Edward Baines, the son of one of the only educated free black men in the state. From then on, the Baines women hyphenated their illustrious surname, way before it became de rigueur to do so. All, that is, except for June, whose bad marriage banned her from her family's legacy.

The fixation on skin color and hair texture continued into the next generations, so when Priscilla had June, her second daughter, hers were not tears of joy that were shed in the maternity ward. When the nurse handed her the child, she wanted to hand it right back. Somehow June had reached *way* back down the family tree and excavated the darkest genes there. Priscilla blamed the child, never forgiving her for that genetic betrayal, while on the other hand, her sister, Mildred—God bless her!—could have passed for white. So obviously she was the favorite. Sadly, June had always known that her mother didn't like her very much, even as a child. It was always Mildred who got the prettiest dress on Easter, and who was proudly paraded around, while June seemed to be a distant afterthought. When she was a little girl, she thought her second-class treatment must have been her own fault, but at the tender age of nine she learned by accident what everyone else had known all along.

As children, June and Mildred's favorite pastime was to sneak downstairs and eavesdrop on adult conversation during the many parties held at their house, listening and watching when possible as grown-ups drank, smoked, and gossiped. The two girls would giggle softly and scamper, unseen, back up to their bedrooms to mimic what they'd seen and heard—except on one particular night, when all their childhood illusions were swiftly shattered.

"Did you see the man Brenda Holton married?" Odessa, Priscilla's best friend and confidante, said to Priscilla. They were in the parlor, sipping brandy-infused tea, just the two of them after the weekly bridge game. They were both very yellow, with long hair which they wore pressed bone-straight, hanging down their backs.

"I've seen mules that looked better than that man. My word, could he be any blacker?" Pricilla huffed. They laughed.

"Let's not forget, she couldn't be expected to do much better. She's nearly as dark as he is." Odessa took a long sip of her spiked tea, pursing her lips together in disdain and harsh judgment.

"And that sister of hers! She's light, all right, but her hair is as nappy as a coon's."

"What a waste of yellow that is!" Odessa sniffed.

They exchanged knowing looks and laughed demurely, smug in the knowledge that without a doubt they could pass anybody's brown paper-bag test, and could go swimming at Martha's Vineyard without emerging from the waters with an unsightly Afro. After a few reflective seconds, Priscilla shook her head. "You just never know with children—even with the best breeding—what you're gonna get. Look at June. She's got me for a mother, and her father is lighter than I am, and she had the nerve to be born black as a skillet."

"Nothing you can do about that," Odessa sympathized.

"Except hope and pray that she has the good sense to marry someone very high yellow to stop that black curse of hers before it afflicts another generation." She talked as if they were discussing the prognosis of a terminal cancer patient.

"Well, at least you've got Mildred. She's a real beauty."

This immediately cheered Priscilla up. "Yes, she is," she preened.

Outside the door, Mildred and June looked at each other, dumb-struck. It was as if Eve had bitten from the apple, and for the first time she and Adam realized the truth: They were stripped naked, and things would never be the same between them.

After a third cocktail, Paulette felt sufficiently fortified to confront her aunt in the wood-paneled living room where most of the guests had gathered to socialize. Mildred stood huddled with Lauren, Gillian, Maximillian, and her husband, Nathan. Paulette walked up without preamble. "We need to talk about the will," she said, folding her arms across her chest, the highball still clutched in her grip. She had gotten wind of the fact that Mildred was trying to postpone the reading until Paulette was back on the West Coast.

Mildred withdrew her attention from the group, and regarded Paulette as she might an unknown intruder. "Excuse me?"

Paulette took Mildred's condescending tone as an opportunity to release her own. "I said, Aunt Mildred, we need to talk about the reading of Granny's will." The alcohol had raised Paulette's voice many decibels above the range of a private conversation. Years of anger, hurt, and resentment boiled like hot magma beneath the surface.

Mildred could sense ears perking up all around her. She took a surreptitious glance around the room, confirming that sets of eyes were following suit. "Now is not the time," she hissed between teeth clenched behind lips that still struggled to maintain a smile. Lauren was in the process of turning three shades redder; Nathaniel's jaw was tighter than a vise, while Gillian looked on embarrassed, and Max stood stoically on the sideline.

"Well, I suggest you make the time." Emboldened, Paulette moved closer, claiming a portion of the small distance that stood between them, and also affording Mildred a whiff of the alcohol that clung to her breath.

Mildred looked as if she'd been slapped in the face. Stunned, she turned from Lauren to Nathaniel and Max before realizing that it was up to her to manage her volatile, ill-bred, uncouth niece. "Paulette, I suggest you calm down, and we will deal with this later. Maybe when you're sober." She took hold of Paulette's arm to lead her out of the room and away from the prying eyes that had joined their conversation.

Paulette snatched her arm away and threw twin daggers at her aunt. "Don't think for a moment that you can placate me with a few words and your holier-than-thou attitude. I am not my mother." June stood in a corner mortified. By now everyone in the room was openly observing the unfolding spectacle, and surely Priscilla was turning over in her freshly dug grave.

"You are absolutely right. *No one* else in this family would have such poor taste," Mildred retorted haughtily. She looked down her nose at Paulette as though she were mashed debris scraped from the underside of her designer shoe. "You should have stayed in California, instead of coming here sniffing around for money already. Your grandmother's hardly cold in her grave yet."

"How's this for poor taste?" Before she thought better of it, Paulette tossed the last of her cocktail into her aunt's face.

As the ice cubes clattered noisily to the floor, a resounding gasp flowed through the gathering of spectators, their eyes widening to catch every spare detail of the drama, so that it could later be recounted and further embellished for others unlucky enough not to have had a front-row seat.

Lauren's hands flew to her mouth in disbelief, while her father backed away as if to be sure to avoid collateral damage. Max hung his head, slowly shaking it from side to side, as gin-smeared mascara trekked down his mother-in-law's previously perfectly made-up face.

June quickly appeared, pulling Paulette aside. "What the hell is wrong with you?" she hissed. "You're making a spectacle of yourself."

"You may let that bitch treat you like pond scum, but I certainly don't have to," Paulette said as she flung drops of liquid from her hand, shot a withering gaze at her aunt, turned on her heel, and stalked off.

NINE

When the alarm clock blared, Lauren rolled over and tried thinking of at least one good reason to get out of bed. Nothing came readily to mind. There was no exciting job filled with important deadlines to propel her, or young children waiting outside her bedroom door; she didn't even have a caring husband who she felt really gave a damn. In short, she didn't have a life. On second thought, she did have one; it just happened to belong to her mother.

Lauren's relationship with Max had grown steadily worse; they barely even spoke. Regrettably, Gillian hadn't gotten the role on Broadway, so her shoulder to cry on was again back in L.A. Paulette, thanks to her thriving business, was too busy to listen. She realized just how much she'd miss her grandmother. Though Priscilla Baines-Reynolds was a legend to most, she was a doting grandmother to Lauren, full of advice on everything from men to the "real" cure for the common cold. They shared a very special bond, one that certainly didn't exist between Lauren and her own mother.

Even though Lauren had slept eight full hours, her bones still felt like solid lead, as though thick Virginia molasses rolled slowly through her veins. She pulled the down comforter up over her head, willing it to swallow her. Lauren's feelings of despair were counterintuitive to her life as others knew it. She was the golden girl, who was gorgeous, born into serious money, and married to a handsome, successful man. What more could a woman want? Ever since she was a well-heeled toddler with long, curly braids, Lauren had been promised that the world was her oyster, which wasn't such a good thing if you were allergic to shellfish.

It was eleven o'clock when Max strode into the bedroom fresh off of eighteen holes of golf with her father, exuding as much energy as she lacked. "You're still in bed?" His tone was accusational, brimming with judgment, heralding the beginning of a conversation they'd had ad nauseam. He couldn't understand why she was the picture of gloom when she didn't have a job to worry about, nor the financial problems faced by most people. Plus, she had him! In his opinion Lauren was a spoiled brat, who, so far, hadn't even accomplished the one thing that *was* expected of her: to bear him a child.

The first year of their marriage they—Max, Lauren, and Mildred had agreed not to have children. During the second year, when the plan called for Lauren to get off of birth control, her mother and Max stood by anxiously awaiting word of their impending immortality. At the beginning of year three they all met and decided that it was time to bring in the professionals. The most prominent fertility specialist in Manhattan was hired, but to no avail; there was still no pitter-patter of little feet.

Before Lauren could decide how or even whether to respond to Max, the phone at her beside rang. *Saved by the bell*, she thought.

After hearing the voice on the other end, she had second thoughts. "Hi, darling. You sound as if you're still in bed," Mildred said.

"I thought I'd sleep in," she offered weakly. Why, she wondered, did she always feel the need to explain herself to her mother?

By now Max had disrobed and was headed into the bath suite for a shower, so at least she wouldn't have to continue *that* conversation.

"I hope that's not all you're doing." Mildred was so involved in their marriage that Lauren wondered why she didn't just fuck Max for her. Knowing Mildred, if she did, she'd probably get pregnant and happily birth her own grandchild.

"Mother!"

"Don't go getting in a twitter. I just called to remind you that the reading of the will is at one-thirty today." She'd succeeded in delaying it by two weeks, hoping to be well rid of Paulette, who'd thwarted her plan by taking the red-eye back in this very morning.

"Grandmother's will?" This was the first Lauren had heard of the reading.

"To my knowledge, no one else in the family has died. Though I can think of a couple of people who would be high on my wish list." Of course, one of them would have been Paulette, and the runner-up, undoubtedly, her mother. Sadly, Mildred still held a tight grip on a grudge that was decades old.

"That's a horrible thing to say," Lauren scoffed. "Will Paulette be here?"

"Unfortunately, yes, but she'll be in for a rude awakening. I'm sure Mother was smart enough not to leave a penny to her, or to her mother."

Lauren was sick of listening to this. "I've gotta go."

"See you this afternoon." There was a brusque click on the line. Lauren hung up the phone, knowing that she would be in for a long day. She'd had no idea that Paulette was even in town. More and more lately she did not call Lauren, or even bother returning *her* calls. Lauren hadn't spoken to her cousin since the embarrassing fiasco after the funeral two weeks prior. Of course, her mother had bitched for days about how tacky, classless, and generally without basic merit Paulette was, but Lauren couldn't help but feel sorry for her.

Even as a young child she'd picked up on the blatant favoritism that was shown to Lauren and her mother by her grandmother, and at the expense of her aunt and cousin. Mildred always told Lauren that it was because Aunt June had run wild at a young age, gotten pregnant, and taken off with Paulette's father. Paulette blamed the shabby treatment she and her mother received on Lauren's mother. Amidst all the conflict, it had still been fairly easy over the years for Lauren to pretend that the long-festering problems didn't exist, or that they would simply dissolve in time.

"Who was on the phone?" Max asked as he emerged from the shower with a towel cinched at his waist. He was an incredibly attractive man, almost too pretty to be handsome, with sleek, jet-black hair, a caramel complexion, and long, thick eyelashes that shaded a pair of light brown eyes that had made many a woman swoon.

Lauren listlessly pulled herself up, sitting on the side of the bed. "It was my mother, reminding me about the reading of Grandmother's will this afternoon, which I knew nothing about." She stood up and trudged toward the bathroom. She stopped short as a thought occurred to her. "Why didn't you tell me?"

Max pulled a tangerine polo shirt over his head. The color looked amazing against his glowing June tan. "As lead attorney, my responsibility is to communicate with the executor of the estate— your mother, not my wife. Plus, I obviously knew that you would be here." Shortly after Max and Lauren were married, Max's firm—thanks to Mildred—had been named the law firm of record for all family business and personal matters, including Priscilla's estate, with Max as the lead counsel. When his explanation to Lauren didn't appease her, he added, "I have to avoid every semblance of preferential treatment where you're concerned. You do understand?" He pulled himself up to his full height, sticking his chest out. Speaking legalese, he was now on comfortable ground.

"And who coordinated with Paulette?" she asked pointedly.

He ran his hand through his hair nervously. "Why do you ask?"

"I just want to make sure that Paulette and my aunt are also being treated fairly."

He visibly relaxed. "Of course, honey. Don't you worry about that." He reached out and hugged her. If she could have seen his expression, she would have seen a wave of relief instead of spousal affection. For a moment he worried that Lauren had become suspicious of his affair with Paulette.

Facing the opposite direction, she caught her own reflection in the vanity's mirror. Her complexion was sallow—even in June—and her hair was lackluster and flat. In the middle of it all sat her eyes, which looked like two holes punched into a set of puffy pillows. The image wasn't the least bit golden.

The house on Martha's Vineyard was perfectly situated to provide awe-inspiring white-sand views of the Atlantic Ocean from each of the ten spacious rooms. It was the perfect $5 million summer home. Priscilla had presided over it for the last forty years, and in the last five, as her health declined, she'd handed the reins over to Mildred, who really was to the manor born. And dear Max took to the relaxed splendor like a baby to a warm bottle.

Lauren spaced out during lunch, as Max, her father, and her mother carried on a lively conversation about contemporary civil rights issues, as if any of them really gave a shit about the plight of everyday black folk. The fact that the Baineses were long-standing Republicans was one of the best-kept secrets in black society.

"I'm sure that Martin Luther King Junior rolls over in his grave every time one of our current crop of civil rights leaders shows up for any calamity that warrants a camera crew, but are nowhere to be found on a day-to-day basis when people are starving, homeless, and institutionally marginalized," Nathaniel preached, though he certainly didn't care himself. He sat back arrogantly and reached for the cigar in his breast pocket, as if to emphasize the profundity of his proclamation.

"You're absolutely right. There has to be new blood infused into the dying carcass of what was the greatest movement of two generations." Max's pontification wasn't only for the sake of table chatter; as usual, he was thinking of himself. One of the many reasons he'd married into the Baines family was to help his political aspirations. He had the appearance; the right education, and was steadily building the necessary contacts and wealth needed to enter politics on a grand scale. Perhaps, Max thought, Congress would be a good start.

He was born with great looks and above-average intelligence, but, sadly, no money, position, or power. People often heard his name, Maximillian Neuman III, and assumed that he was from stacks of dough, when actually his mother was a cook at the local elementary school in Maryland, and his father was a mail carrier for the post office. Max changed his name from Henry to the more prominent-sounding Maximillian the minute he graduated from high school; he added "the Third" after finishing college to lend a sense of legacy to his self-appointed moniker. Yet, after all of the thought and hard work, right after they began dating Lauren had shortened his name to simply Max, and, of course, everyone else followed suit.

"What about Barack Obama, Max?" Mildred tossed out. "Now, that's a fine young man," she said, as a warm smile spread across her face, the same one she often wore when speaking of Max. As much as she loved her son-in-law, she would have happily tossed him under a bus for a handsome senator like Barack.

"I was thinking more of Condoleezza Rice. Now, there's a woman who could effect change," Nathaniel said.

The mention of the controversial figure's name pulled Lauren back from her own listless thoughts. She rolled her eyes. "Yeah, change for herself and her Bush buddies. She certainly doesn't care about the rest of us."

"Honey, you say 'us' as though *you* have any problems." This was Mildred, reminding Lauren of her silver spoon.

"Oh, I forgot," Lauren interjected sarcastically. "I have it all."

Mildred completely missed her daughter's weak attempt at sarcasm. "Yes, you do, dear," she absently confirmed.

After lunch Max, Lauren, Nathaniel, and Mildred made their way into the family library, where Theresa, the housekeeper, had already ushered in Paulette, who looked primed for a good fight, along with her mother, who seemed embarrassed even to be present, and Jim Nance, another partner in Max's law firm. Another gentleman, with gray hair and wire-rimmed glasses, sat at Paulette's side.

"Glad you all could make it," Max said, taking charge of the soon-to-be-tense situation. He shook hands and paused when he came to the stranger.

Paulette stood up. "This is my attorney, Peter West," she said.

Mr. West shook Max's hand, nodded to everyone else, and, like a boxer before a title bout, took to his corner, reclaiming his perch next to Paulette.

Max resumed his roll as ringmaster, as Mildred sat smugly, waiting for the unnecessary formalities to conclude. Everyone knew that June had been written out the will aeons ago, and there was little reason to think that daughter of hers would fare any better.

"As you all know, we're gathered today for the reading of Priscilla Baines-Reynolds's last will and testament." Max cleared his throat and made eye contact around the room. Lauren appeared genuinely bored. Mildred and Nathaniel gave the impression that this meeting was keeping them from a very important bridge game, while Paulette appeared alert and poised for attack, as her mother sat cloaked in premature defeat. "Before I continue, let me state for the record that this document was executed by me and my staff just six months ago, and it is, to the best of anyone's knowledge, Priscilla's last will and testament."

Mildred shifted ever so slightly in her chair. Six months ago? June had been written out of the will decades ago; why would it have needed to be changed? Her mind navigated through many scenarios, winding up at one that she liked: It had to be rewritten to account for Lauren's marriage and any changes in tax laws. Yes, that was it! She smoothed the crease in her linen pants and continued to pay attention, forcing herself to focus on the legalese that Max stood spouting like a broken faucet, until she'd had enough. "Max, darling, I'm sure that what you're saying is very important, but do you mind getting down to business?" In other words, who was inheriting what, and how much was it worth?

Again Max cleared his throat; this time it wasn't as much for show. He picked up a thick, crisply folded document from the desk next to him and flipped past a few pages until he found the one that really mattered. "The main disbursements in said estate are: liquid assets in the amount of fifteen point seven million dollars, securities in the amount of seventy million, and real estate holdings, including this property, the Baines-Reynolds estate, and the apartment on Park Avenue, which total an additional thirty-five million dollars, bringing the total gross value of the estate to one hundred twenty point seven million dollars."

By now you could have heard a pin drop in the wood-paneled room. No one dared to take a breath for fear of desecrating the spirit of the sacred, that being money. June knew that her mother was really rich, but since she'd never been close enough to gauge the depth, she was truly shocked by the large figures being tossed about. She had no idea so much money was at stake. Paulette sat by her side, wearing the world's best poker face. She may have been a churning mess on the inside, but outside you would never have guessed. Nathan, a man who had plenty of money of his own, believed that you never had enough, and had already gone through the permutations, spreadsheets, and pie charts that would result from merging this fortune into his own, so he sat back, veiling a smile of total satisfaction. Mildred, who was too spoiled to really appreciate the numbers, was fixated only on the personal victory at hand. While she and June had been close when they were very young, for a vain woman it took only one incident to turn the tables.

Mildred and June were born eleven months apart, and grew up playing together, going to school together, and were generally inseparable until the summer of Mildred's senior year in high school, when she developed a crush on Dexter Post, a boy whose family had just moved into the neighborhood, and whom all the girls instantly adored.

Dexter Post was a freshman at Yale, and he was high yellow, had curly, sandy-colored hair, and the cherry on top of that cake was that his father was a bona fide federal judge. Over and above the prestige of being a Baines, high school also taught Mildred to appreciate the benefits of her creamy, light skin and long, straight hair, so there was no doubt in her mind that *she* would be the girl to snare this prime catch; after all, he was the type of boy that her type of girl should have. Her mother even approved of him and, more important, of his family, the Posts. With some coauthoring from Priscilla, Mildred scripted an epic love story that opened with scenes of Dexter squiring Mildred around to the season's cotillions; then they'd become the "it couple" while he finished up at Yale, and by act two, right after graduation, they'd be married in a lavish ceremony. Several kids and an oceanside mansion would follow in act three.

Mildred had the happy ending in the can until she caught June making out with Dexter after school behind the high school gymnasium. June and Dexter were locked in a ravishing, Hollywood-style tongue kiss: lips plastered together and eyes closed, while his hands roamed her body, pulling her closer. The sight of June and

Dexter in the throes of lust upset Mildred so much that she ran up to them and physically pulled June away, then slapped the boy's face before running home to tell her mother every single detail, along with a few choice embellishments.

By the time the story made its rounds, the horny couple were an inch away from fucking, which ruined June's reputation forever. Now, not only was she the ugly duckling of the family, but was also the black sheep; Priscilla never forgave June for publicly disgracing the family and, more unforgivably, for ruining any chance of properly breeding the boy into the family. After that, the two sisters became archenemies; the battle lines were drawn as clearly as the color lines. Being the object of such scorn, June soon ran away from home with the first guy who meandered along. He wasn't educated, rich, handsome, or of good pedigree; in fact, he was darker than June, with a headful of kinky hair. He was also Paulette's father.

O f all those present at the reading of the will, Lauren was the only one who really had no interest in the outcome. As far as she was concerned, money was the cause of most of her unhappiness. She and her cousin weren't as close as they should be because of it, and she was unhappily married and drifting through life as a result of her mother's desire to create more of it.

"As per the wishes of Priscilla Baines-Reynolds, all liquid assets shall go to . . ."

Collectively the room held its breath; the walls seemed to suck inward.

"Her granddaughter . . ."

Every head, except one, turned to Lauren.

"Paulette."

The gasp of disbelief was audible. Mildred's head snapped around 180 degrees with a quickness. Her eyes registered disbelieving shock. Lauren, June, and Nathaniel all sat with their mouths agape.

Max plowed ahead. "All securities listed in the estate shall go
to . . ."

Again, silence; everyone but Paulette sat perched on the edge of
his chair; Mildred's nails were nearly piercing through the mahogany wood.

"Her daughter . . ."

All heads now swiveled to Mildred, who tried to rein in her
relief.

"June."

This time the shock registered audibly, propelling Mildred from
her chair, followed by Nathaniel, who held her elbow as if she
might fold down and collapse. If she could have made it, she probably would have lunged for Paulette's throat. At that moment, however, it was June instead who needed first aid. She appeared to be
hyperventilating, and seemed to be in shock. It had never occurred
to her to expect anything from anyone.

Paulette sat calmly amidst the eye of the gathering storm, looking like the well-fed fat cat who'd just swallowed a canary whole.

Max spoke up over the din of disbelief. "Regarding real estate
disbursements, it is the final will and testament of Priscilla Baines-
Reynolds that the apartment on Park Avenue and the main estate
are to be given to her granddaughter Lauren, and that this house
in which we stand is to be left to her daughter Mildred. That
concludes the reading of the last will and testament of Priscilla
Baines-Reynolds."

Book
Two

TEN

Los Angeles hadn't been the great escape Gillian, had imagined it would be. She felt like she'd tripped and fallen into a strange twilight zone. Everyone from the waiter from Idaho, who worked at the all-night diner, to the strip-mall nail technician considered themselves the next big star; they were only biding their time while waiting to be discovered. *Everybody* was either in the movie business or wanted to be in it, and, sadly, that included her.

Gillian's somber mood matched her disheveled appearance as she slouched on Paulette's sofa wearing a threadbare sweat suit and holey socks, with her hair scattered haphazardly atop her head. An ashtray full of rancid cigarette butts added to her despondency. Under stress, she'd chucked the idea of quitting, at least for now. Since returning from New York, after learning that she'd been passed over for the part on Broadway, she'd descended into the depths of despair. A stubborn streak was the only thing that kept her from throwing in the towel. That and the fact that she had nowhere to go.

Flipping through the trades she found herself thankful that at least Paulette was back in New York for the reading of her grandmother's will. In Gillian's current mood, she wasn't certain she could stomach an episode of *The Paulette Show*. Just as Gillian was polishing off the last of a box of chocolate-covered turtles, the phone rang. She checked caller ID and saw that the name that appeared was that of one of the best casting agencies in the business. With some vigor she tugged at her hair, trying to give it a semblance of shape, brushed away the crumbs of chocolate from her sweatshirt, and sat up straight, as if the caller could actually see her through the telephone. She took several deep breaths, waiting for the phone to ring at least four times. Though she was *truly* desperate, she didn't want to seem anxious.

"Hello?"

"May I speak to Gillian Tillman, please?" The female voice on the other end of the line sounded crisp and very professional.

"This is Gillian." Her tone was nonchalant, but aware; supremely confident, but not arrogant. She wryly noted the absurd, twisted psychology needed simply to pick up the phone in this crazy place called Hollywood.

"Hi, Gillian, I'm Annette White's assistant, Evelyn, from Perfect Fit Casting Agency." The woman's voice rose at the end of her sentence, making her statement sound like a question. "You were referred to us for a pilot we're doing, and I called to see if you might come in this afternoon for an audition."

"Can you tell me a little bit about the project?" At this point Gillian would have taken a job advertising a vaginal lubricant, she so desperately needed money, but it was always smart not to appear as desperate as you really were.

"Of course," the woman replied, as though she had actually been planning to tell her all about the project, when in fact she was acutely aware that there were so few roles available for black actresses that she felt no need whatsoever to sell the project. It was common knowledge that things were definitely harder for black female actresses than for black male actors, partly because once a black male actor went mainstream, one of the first things he demanded, in order to increase his crossover appeal, was nonblack female leads—Hispanic, white, or Asian, anything but a sister. So most black actresses would take anything and be delighted to get it.

"It's a pilot for a situation dramedy about three African American girls who share an apartment in Harlem. One is a struggling secretary trying to make a way for her three kids, all by different fathers, who are now being raised by her mother in Alabama. The second character is a party girl—you know the type—always looking for Mr. Right. And the third is the part you'd audition for. Her name is Shaniqua; she's the voice of reason for the three girls. You know, a real ball buster, a no-nonsense girl who's grown up with hard knocks, and . . ."

By now Gillian had zoned out creatively. How many times did white studio executives have to resurrect that same played-out, trifling, head-swiveling, hand-on-hip, finger-pointing, tired-ass black female character?

". . . so, we thought you might be good for the part," she sang, clearly pleased with the story she'd outlined.

Why, because I'm black?

"Are you still there?"

"Yes, I was just thinking."

"Are you interested?" the woman asked, not nearly as confident as she'd been at the beginning of the call.

Gillian was itching to give this woman a piece of her mind, but her survival instinct kicked in. She'd been living in L.A. for over two months now and hadn't made a dime and, more urgently, she was sick of being trapped in this apartment with Paulette. Having spent a chunk of her remaining money on a piece-of-shit car, she'd left her bank account precariously low.

"The part sounds interesting, and I'd love to audition for it." The actress in her had indeed surfaced; she'd even managed to muster some degree of enthusiasm into her voice.

"Great—if you could be here by two . . ."

Gillian jotted down the address and tried hard to motivate herself to really want this awful-sounding role.

The casting agency was full of the typical assortment of L.A. black girls who were eager for fame and fortune. They generally fell into three categories: The but-everyone-tells-me-I'm-so-pretty girl, who truly believed that straight hair, good skin, a pretty face, and a bright smile made her predestined for the big screen, talent notwithstanding. Then there was the overcompensator. She was the one who fell short in a major category while growing up, and quickly learned to overcompensate for this self-perceived deficiency by excelling in another area, such as a cutting wit, biting humor, Einstein smarts, or simply being the provider of the best blow job, and any one of those skills could take you somewhere in L.A. The third and most pervasive category was the fix-it-quick girl, who simply eliminated or corrected anything that God forgot to, through skin bleaching, boob implanting, hair weaving, nose chiseling, face-lifting or the most common: creating from scratch a fake, and usually annoying, personality.

Girls like Gillian were few and far between in L.A.; she was beautiful, but not preoccupied with it, intelligent—a word not necessarily synonymous with "actress"—and serious about her craft. When she walked into the holding room, instinctively the others knew that she was not of their ilk. Eyes were cut, weaves flung, and attitudes dispensed, while Gillian sat alone in a corner reading the script that the receptionist had given her. Having survived the divas on Broadway, both male and female, Gillian was completely unfazed by the onslaught of negative energy. When her name was finally called she followed an assistant into the inner office, with several pairs of eyes boring deeply into her back.

The reading room was set up with a small stage and two rows of chairs, which at present accommodated the casting agent, the director, the producer, and their assorted assistants. Before she could mount the stage, directions were barked at her from the first row.

"Read the first line and give it lots of 'tude." This came from the director, a baby-faced white boy—or, more correctly, Jewish—who had only minutes of experience in the business, but was male, of the correct persuasion, and connected.

Gillian put her backpack at the side of the makeshift stage, walked to the center, and made herself focus on the material and her delivery. She'd read the lines, but it took an act of sheer will for her to speak them. Still, she swallowed her pride and said, "Girl, you know better than to lie down with dogs, 'cause you always gonna wake up with a buncha fleas."

The director, producer, and Annette, the casting agent, all looked at her strangely. Finally the director spoke up. "That was okay, but I need you to be more"—he gesticulated, struggling to find the word—". . . black." As he said this with a straight face, he even had the nerve to cross his hands, homeboy style.

"I'm afraid I don't know what you mean. Given who I am, I'm not sure it's possible to be more or less black. I *am* black." Gillian struggled to keep an even tone, though she could feel a fire kindling in the pit of her stomach.

"Ya know what I mean?" he said with the cadence of a rapper. "Just don't speak as clearly. You know, act black. Give a little neck action and some ghetto attitude." He and the producer exchanged a little chuckle between them.

That did it. "If you think that's what being black is, then I suggest that instead of producing a sitcom you simply put on a minstrel show. You know, get some white-faced, shuffling black people to tap-dance across the stage for you. Or better yet," she said, her voice steadily rising, "just get a plain ol' monkey and an organ grinder. That should do it!" She yanked her bag from the floor and stormed out of the room, leaving her small audience truly baffled.

She was a blur going through the reception of wannabes, all anxious, eager, and willing to snatch any crumb thrown their way.

Gillian was now sure that moving to L.A. had been a mistake; the only question was what to do now? She supposed that she could tuck her tail between her legs and slither back to New York again, hoping to pick up where she left off, or maybe she should do what most everybody else in the world did: get a real job. The thought of that was physically nauseating. She was unable to envision herself sitting behind a desk from nine to five. Besides, her catwalking and acting skills didn't necessarily transfer to corporate America, even when accompanied by an undergraduate degree from Brown University.

She cursed all the way up the 405 to Wilshire, and barely heard the phone when it rang. When she saw the caller ID it occurred to her not to answer it, but when she considered that the world wasn't beating a path to her door, she decided to pick up.

"Hello."

"Hi, Gillian." It was Brandon Russell on the line.

"Hi." She was somewhat surprised to hear from him. He'd called a couple of times since they'd met at the Ivy, and she'd promptly blown him off on each occasion. Gillian was sure that he would have given up by now; a man like Brandon must have a full stable of girls, and she wasn't interested in becoming part of his herd.

"Are you okay? You sound a little tense."

"Not exactly the best day I've had." Actually, she hadn't had any good days since moving here. She didn't like L.A.—not the people, not the energy, not the seven days a week of sunshine. There was no texture in Los Angeles; everybody was a version of the same person, and to top it off, each day even looked like the one before it!

"Well, you're talking to the right guy. I called to invite you to a cocktail party tonight. It'll be full of film people." When she didn't respond right away, he continued, "I apologize for the short notice.

I hadn't planned to go—thought I'd be out of town—but a couple of meetings were rescheduled, so here I am. How 'bout it?"

Part of her wanted to say no and go home and crawl between the sheets with another box of chocolates, but Gillian wasn't a quitter, so she accepted his invitation. Why not? She realized after that horried casting call that it would take more than a contact sheet, a so-so agent, and a good résumé to get any decent work in this town. Worst case, she'd go with him to this fancy Hollywood cocktail party, hopefully meet some interesting people, and maybe even make a few industry contacts.

Before they hung up Brandon said, "I have a quick question for you. Remember when our bags were swapped at the airport?"

How could she forget? That was how they'd met. "Of course."

"When you opened my bag, did you see a flash drive in it?"

"No, I didn't."

"Are you sure?"

"Absolutely. I opened the suitcase, saw that the clothes weren't mine, and called you right away."

"Okay, babe; I'll see you later on."

She raced home as quickly as L.A.'s inexplicable, barely creeping traffic would allow. She called Lauren immediately.

"You're not going to believe this," she said.

"What happened?" Lauren asked, then said excitedly, "Don't tell me. You were offered a role in a big-time movie?"

"Nothing quite that exciting, but I do have a date."

"You're kidding! If you told me you were starring in Steven Spielberg's next movie it'd be easier for me to believe! Who's the lucky guy?"

"Brandon Russell. Remember, our bags got switched when I first moved here?"

"Of course. This is good news. Hey, it's about time you got out. What are you going to wear?"

"I don't know. It's been so long since I actually wore anything besides sweats and jeans."

"Just because you live in L.A., Juicy Couture still doesn't count as couture fashion, so do yourself a favor and really dress up. You'll feel better."

Gillian followed Lauren's advice and wore a fitted, knee-length knit dress by Zac Posen. The print was a Pucci-esque mix of coral, brown, and mustard, great contrasts and complements to her rich, dark complexion, and the whimsy of the design worked well with her wild, free curls, which she wore scattered atop her head. And, of course, she'd wear her coral wrap sandals by Ron Donovan. She was actually getting excited about going out, and smiled genuinely for the first time in weeks.

ELEVEN

Reese emerged from the shower smelling of ripe grapefruit and fresh lavender. Her dewy skin was newly exfoliated and as smooth as whipped butter. Staring into the mirror above her vanity, she objectively took an inventory of her physical assets. The bottom line: She loved everything about herself. Her skin was smooth and poreless, thanks to a series of glycolic treatments from Mario Badescu. Her hair was long and luxurious, her figure curvaceous—full and flat in all the right places, even after giving Chris a child, something she would rather not have done. But, ever shrewd, Reese accurately calculated the true value of those nine months of hell. Like every smart gold digger, she knew that having a baby drilled the last nail into her poor victim's coffin. Married or not, a baby was a guaranteed eighteen-year financial commitment.

With a wry smile, she turned her thoughts to Carl, her first baller boyfriend, and how she'd dropped him like a piping-hot potato after he sustained a career-ending injury at the beginning of his senior year, shattering his NBA dream before it could become a reality. Carl was showboating his renowned slam-dunk skills during a pickup game when he took a violent elbow to the chest, lost his balance, and came crashing down hard on the pavement, shattering his right knee. While he lay crumbled on the floor, writhing in excruciating pain, clutching his crushed knee, Reese was already doing a situation analysis, quickly deducing that his injury was career-ending, and subsequently started plotting then and there exactly how to dump him and score with Chris, her second-round draft pick, all at the same time. In mere nanoseconds, Reese made the agile leap from Carl's bed right into Chris's.

Up until then she'd had Carl on lock, so much so that the campus groupies had even thrown in the towel on bedding him. The two some were the premier "it couple" on campus. Bets were that he'd be the number one NBA draft pick, and they'd be married before the ink dried on his rich new contract. In fact, Reese, unbeknownst to Carl, had already picked out her wedding gown and gone for several fittings before his junior year even began.

When Carl realized that the dream he'd dedicated his whole life to achieving was over, he was quite obviously seriously depressed. Reese spent a couple of weeks playing the supportive, stand-by-her-man girlfriend, while publicly insinuating (especially to his teammates) that Carl was so depressed that he wanted to be alone, and was pushing her away. But Reese truly deserved the Bette Davis award the night she showed up at Chris's room, again playing the role of damsel in distress. She cried on his shoulder, recounting how Carl had asked her for space and didn't want to see her anymore, and how devastated she was, and how badly she wanted to be there for him during his time of need. A shoulder to cry on quickly became a mix of arms, lips, and legs.

For the coup de grâce, before Reese left his room the next morning she sneaked into the bathroom and pulled out a new cell phone, using it to anonymously text-message Chris's soon-to-be-ex-girlfriend, asking her to meet Chris in his room right away. At the appointed time, Reese emerged from the shadows wearing one of

Chris's extra-large T-shirts, with her hair freshly disheveled. She looked every bit like a woman who'd recently been fucked.

From that moment on, Reese seduced, cajoled, and badgered Chris until she was finally able to lead him down the aisle, but not before his mother insisted that she sign a prenup. This was a hitch that she had been unable to graciously avoid, making childbirth more financially beneficial than the marriage license. After fifteen hours of hard labor she promptly handed the screaming child over to a flight of nurses and nannies. She was just thankful to have weathered the ordeal without the physical catastrophes of stretch marks or extra pounds of fat that plagued so many women she knew, instantly diminishing a girl's physical value.

Polishing off her beauty routine with a touch of glitter lotion smoothed across her cleavage and clavicle, she felt good knowing that the rough part was over. Now was the time for her to cash out and trade up while her personal stock remained at an all-time high, a fact that was confirmed for her every time she looked into the mirror. Chris had served his purpose; now she wanted someone more exciting, handsomer, and definitely sexier. She only needed to bail out with as tight a grip on as much of Chris's money as possible.

Reese propped herself up on the silk damask chaise longue that graced a corner of their massive bedroom, with a glass of French cabernet sauvignon in one hand and a seldom-used ultraprivate cell phone in the other. Chris didn't even know it existed. Reese paid the monthly bill from a checking account she'd wisely held on to from her poor days.

She took a sip of wine, then dialed Kira, who, besides Paulette, was her closest confidante. They were two of a kind, so Reese felt that she could trust Kira with her more dastardly secrets. "Hi, girl."

"Hi, yourself," a groggy voice on the line replied.

"Sounds like someone had a long night."

"When don't I?" Though it was two o'clock p.m. on the West

Coast, for Kira this was a wake-up call. She normally rolled out of bed about three o'clock, was in the gym by four, and back at home at seven-thirty to dress for her evening activities.

"Was part of it spent with my husband?" Reese asked.

"No, but it wasn't because I didn't try. The man is a hard sell." Reese had come up with the brilliant idea of having Kira seduce Chris, have it secretly taped, and then use it as leverage to break the prenup, which had a fidelity clause buried in it. Reese figured that, unless he was an alien, like most NBA players he was having affairs on the road anyway, so why shouldn't she just surreptitiously arrange a little tryst and then benefit from it?

Reese sat up from her reclining position, her relaxed mood suddenly replaced with angst. "What happened?" This was not good news; her little covert mission was supposed to be a fait accompli. The Knicks were in L.A. playing the Lakers, and there was a big after-party that everyone was going to. Chris had even confirmed to Reese that he'd be there. For someone with Kira's seduction skills, snagging Chris should have been like shooting big crabs in a small barrel, especially since he had no idea just how close the two women were. Plus, at the end of the day men were men, and usually thought with the smaller of their two heads.

Kira was up now, ready to defend her scandalous reputation. "He was at the party, and we *did* have a couple of drinks together, but when I invited him upstairs to my suite for a nightcap, he declined!" Kira herself sounded just as surprised that her target had escaped her clutches, something that rarely happened to her.

"Shit!" Reese slammed the glass of wine down onto the side table. "Now what are we gonna do?" She collapsed on the chaise, deflated.

"You know you're my girl, but that's your problem now. Not mine."

"You've obviously forgotten about the money." Reese had offered her ten grand to sleep with him and produce video or photographic proof of the deed.

"Girl, you know me; ten grand is chump change. I go through that on a light sprint down Rodeo Drive."

Reese knew she was telling the truth. Kira rocked the fashions as hard as Reese did. Reese's problem was that, while she had liberal access to lots of credit lines for charging goods and services, which meant that Chris or his accountant had detailed access to every penny she spent, unfortunately her cash access was more limited, so ten thousand was the most that she could get away with without attracting suspicion. Suddenly an idea came to her. "What if I gave you ten grand now, and another fifty once the divorce is final and I get a settlement?"

The phone line was quiet as Kira pondered the new proposal. Ten thousand was one thing to sleep with a friend's husband, but fifty thousand was something else. The most she'd ever been paid for a one-night stand was twenty grand. There were risks involved. What if word got out? The last thing she needed was a reputation as someone who set up her lovers, many of whom were married. That could be bad for business. But she and Reese had agreed earlier that she would say someone installed the video camera in her hotel room without her knowledge, and she could feign as much outrage as Chris would feel. "Now, that's a different story."

"We've got to move quickly." The relief was loud and clear in Reese's voice.

"Shaun must be taking care of his business," Kira teased. She and Paulette were the only people whom Reese had told about Shaun, her new boyfriend, or more aptly put: Her new fuck buddy. He was the man she'd met when he introduced himself by grabbing her ass instead of shaking her hand at the Knicks party that Kira had also attended in New York. The brazen move had worked: Reese had phoned him the very next day, and they'd been fucking like horny bunnies ever since. He wasn't the marrying kind—didn't make enough money—but if orgasms were publicly traded, homeboy would be Warren Buffett.

"He is amazing," Reese reflected. Just thinking about him had diverted her attention, at least momentarily.

"But back to Chris," she said, snapping out of her lustful reverie. "The Knicks will be in town for another two play-off games. Last night he was probably just tired, and may have been worried that you two had been seen together at the party. You should just show up at the Mandrian Hotel two hours after tonight's game. His room number is sixteen-twenty-five. I'll call him before the game and make sure he'll be around. Maybe I'll say that Rowe wants to speak to his daddy before bedtime." The churning wheels in her swiftly calculating mind were a blur as her new plan came blazing together. "Show up in a coat and nothing underneath. That drives him crazy." By now her chemically whitened smile spanned from ear to ear.

"Cool." Reese could hear Kira's cell phone ringing in the background. "Listen, gotta go. I'll stop by his room tonight, and we'll talk tomorrow. Ciao."

Pleased with the new plan, Reese got up from the chaise, dressed, and prepared for a rendezvous of her own.

Using the same secret cell phone, she called Shaun and purred, "I'm on my way."

Thirty minutes later Reese was nervously knocking on another hotel room door, praying that no one she knew—or who knew her—would see her. She wore a baseball cap pulled down low over her face, with her hair stuffed underneath, and a pair of large Christian Dior sunglasses that covered much of her face. Though her jeans and stack-heeled boots were pricey designer pieces, they weren't nearly as flashy as most of the clothes in her wardrobe. By her standards she was dressed down.

Before the third knock landed on the hotel room door, it swung open to a dark room with music playing softly in the background. Reese took two steps in and was grabbed by her collar, then roughly yanked into the room and into a deep, passionate kiss. Pushing the door closed with one hand, her shirtless lover unbuttoned her jacket with the other, all while moving her steadily against the wall and kissing her with an urgency that took her breath away. His passion was raw; in fact, she could feel him already straining mightily against the baggy jeans he wore. It was with grateful surrender that she allowed herself to be pressed against the wall. Her lips left his and her head rolled back. She inhaled deeply and let a long, low, throaty moan escape. Her mind was completely detached from her demanding three-year-old son, from her boring, unromantic husband, and from the self-imposed pressure to always look as if she'd stepped off of a runway. Her only thoughts were those that would lead to a long and satisfying night of being satisfied by a man who knew how to do it right.

"You ready for me?" His lips caressed her ear, and the sexy voice was followed by his wet, hot, and proven-to-be-talented tongue. His husky breathing sent shivers down her spine.

"Always, baby," she managed to say. By now he was grinding into her, making them both wish that the layers of clothes between them would simply melt away.

He nibbled down the side of her neck, lingering along that sensitive path of nerves that ran from her ear down to her clavicle, leaving intense shudders of anticipation in his wake. "Let's see how bad you want me." With one hand he ripped her shirt wide open, scattering her buttons to the floor and revealing a skimpy red lace bra that barely constrained her augmented thirty-six-Cs. With his teeth he pulled the flimsy material aside and began licking, biting, sucking, and just short of mauling her breasts. Without wasting a movement he deftly unfastened her belt and plunged his hand into her G-string, not bothering to unbutton her low-riding hip-hugger jeans. His middle finger came to rest between her slippery lips, which he parted, causing her to take a deep breath and begin moving urgently against his probing finger. But he denied her the building friction by removing it, bringing the coated digit to his mouth for a taste. "I think you're *very* ready," he said, offering her a taste of the creamy evidence, which she accepted.

Shaun was a master of sexual manipulation, and he had Reese exactly where he wanted her. She was the picture of sexual abandon. Her baseball cap had fallen off by now; her hair was a mess of tangles. Her cheeks were flushed a shade that Revlon could never replicate, while her breasts swelled well beyond the flimsy bra and torn blouse. Happy with his handiwork, he unbuttoned her jeans and pulled them off. While looking deep into her eyes, which were fixed on him as though he were the Dalai Lama, he slowly unzipped his own pants, removing ten inches of power. Reese's gaze was drawn to him as he stroked himself for her viewing pleasure. When she reached for him, he lifted her up and penetrated her sex, pinning her to the wall. With a strong, steady rhythm he gave her every inch. Reese was on another planet by now, and a three-alarm fire couldn't have driven her away from this spot. Through hooded eyes she took in the sight of Shaun's upper body as his muscles flexed and bulged in time to his powerful, relentless thrusting. She wanted the feeling to last forever, but he took her to the edge of pleasure, angling himself just right to push her over. When it happened and she could no longer fend off the inevitable, she hugged him tightly, burying her face in his neck as the intense sensations racked her body.

When she caught her breath again, she also felt the earth move, and soon realized that Shaun was walking them toward the bed, not missing a stroke or a step. When they got there he lowered her, never breaking contact, and took her with animalistic force. She felt him expand inside of her, heard his moans escalate, and saw his muscles tense as his orgasm built, crashing to the surface. He carried her along with him to the precipice of pleasure and they both went crashing over the edge. Her body shuddered from head to toe as a ringing chorus filled her head.

All of a sudden he froze. She opened her eyes and saw that he hadn't been overcome by a body-seizing orgasm, but that his head was cocked to one side, listening. That was when she also realized that the ringing wasn't the result of her own resounding, mind-blowing orgasm, but filled the room. The hotel's fire alarm was blaring loudly, and a blinking red light pierced the darkness. "Oh, shit." Shaun hopped up, followed by Reese, who was naked from the waist down, with her torn shirt on top.

"There's a fire in the building, and you must evacuate the hotel right now," a detached, mechanical voice implored.

While Shaun scrambled into his pants and shirt, Reese searched frantically for her panties and jeans. She could do nothing about the torn top, so she tied it at her waist and threw her cap back on. When they ran out of the room to gather with everyone outside the hotel, she looked exactly like what she was: a woman who'd just been fucked very well. Her makeup was a smeary mess, and clearly visible since she hadn't had time to search for her sunglasses; her hair was a tangled nest under the baseball cap; her ripped top looked as disheveled as she felt; and, to top it all off, she could feel traces of him flowing down the insides of her legs, staining her jeans.

To make matters worse, the whole thing turned out to be a false alarm.

TWELVE

Reese started ringing Kira's phone at noon West Coast time the next morning, dying to know whether her girlfriend had succeeded in bedding her husband. And, more important, whether she had evidence of the dirty deed; even a stained blue dress would suffice, though she was certain that in Kira's case it would not be from the Gap. Imagine having an affair with the most powerful man on the planet, and you're wearing a forty-five-dollar dress from a chain store! Monica should have been indicted for that alone.

Careful not to smudge her freshly painted nails, Reese dialed the phone number for the fifth time, and again she got Kira's voice mail, imploring the caller in a sexy, throaty voice to leave a message. Where the hell was she? Reese wondered as she blew on her nails to speed the drying process.

She picked up the phone again and called Paulette on her cell, since it was a crapshoot these days to determine which coast Paulette was on.

"How are you, and where the hell are you?" she asked.

"On cloud nine," Paulette enthused.

"Now, which area code is that?" Reese asked, chuckling. She assumed that Paulette must have just gotten laid by her mysterious new boyfriend.

"It's the one with lots of zeros!" Paulette answered with a sly smirk.

"Do you mean Os, as in orgasms?"

"No, honey, I mean the zeros behind the comma."

"What the hell are you talking about?" Reese asked.

"My grandmother's will was read last week, and let's just say that I'm in the money!" she sang. "Yesssss!" Paulette was having a party with herself to celebrate her tremendous windfall. In the days since the reading of her grandmother's will, she had gotten a head start on being rich by running up all her available credit, and generally spending money as though she were Donald Trump.

"That's great," Reese said, though she was thinking that it would be even greater if it were happening to her. Anyone in her family could keel over, and she'd be lucky if they left enough money to be buried.

"Yeah, girl, I finally got mine."

"So, Paulette," Reese joked in a TV-game-show-host voice, "you just won millions; where are you going?"

"I can tell you it ain't Disneyland!" Paulette laughed. "I'm headed up Madison Avenue."

"Let's hope after I divorce Chris that I'll be right alongside you."

After their brief chat, Reese hung up feeling anxious. Her thoughts were racing. What if she did end up poor? *Don't panic*, she told herself. Maybe Kira had spent the night in Chris's hotel room, and that was why she wasn't answering her phone. She decided to call Chris and see what the hell was going on.

"Hi, babe." She smiled at the thought of Chris answering the phone all nervous because he had another woman in his bed. Reese hoped, for her friend's sake, that her husband performed better with her than he did at home. Having sex with Chris was like rid-ing a treadmill: It took you nowhere.

"Oh, hey." He sounded strange, not his usual relaxed self.

Gotcha, she thought. "Are you okay?" she asked. Now she felt sure that Kira was lying next to him buck naked.

"Yeah."

"You sound like something's wrong. What's up?" She leaned back on the bed, settling in for the final act.

He took a deep breath and said, "We need to talk."

Interesting, she thought. Maybe he was feeling so guilty that he had to confess. "I'm listening."

"Not now. I'll be home in the morning. We'll talk then."

"Okay, I'll see you later." She hung up the phone, wanting to jump for joy; her freshly painted toenails were all that prevented her from doing so. He'd never sounded this serious before, so her plan must have worked like a charm—and not a minute too soon.

After last night with Shaun—false fire alarm notwithstand-ing—she was more anxious than ever to kick Chris aside and keep it moving. Shaun was magical, possessing skills that ordinary men could barely imagine, doing the most amazing things to her body. She was getting warm, wet, and flushed just thinking about how thoroughly he sexed her; Chris had never come close to giving her that kind of satisfaction, and now that she had a taste of it she was nowhere near ready to stop. She needed to be free to savor it com-pletely without the annoyance of sneaking around hotels and tak-ing the risk of getting caught. So now was the perfect time to dump Chris, something she had no compunction whatsoever about doing.

The next morning when Chris came home, Reese still had not been able to speak to Kira to confirm that the dirty deed had in fact been done, but given his tone she was pretty confident that her friend had pulled it off. And knowing Kira, she probably left town on a jaunt with one of her many male friends.

She heard his key in the door of their three-floor town house, and hurried down to meet him. "Hi, babe. How was your trip?" When she stood on her tiptoes to kiss him she immediately felt a chill. The team had been beaten badly on the road, ending their chance at the finals, so he was probably just in a sour mood, on top of being remorseful at having cheated on her.

"Very interesting, actually." He sat his bag down at the foot of the palatial winding staircase, and kept going until he reached the den.

Reese followed him, perplexed. "Are you okay?" she asked feigning worry and concern for him.

"Not really." He sat on the leather club chair and crossed his long legs, one over the other.

Reese wanted to jump for joy. She was sure that he was feeling guilty about his rendezvous and wanted to come clean, but he needn't bother, since she was leaving him no matter what.

"What's wrong, baby?" She was prepared to play the hurt, betrayed spouse to the hilt. She already had her tears on tap.

"I should be asking you that question." He crossed his arms.

She observed him more closely, taking note of the coolness that she had mistaken for guilt. "I don't understand."

He reached into his pocket and pulled out his BlackBerry and pressed a couple of buttons. "A picture is worth a thousand words, so why don't I save us both a few?" He handed her the device, smirked, and watched her expression change from confusion to shock to anger.

Reese had been perplexed when she took the phone from Chris, still wondering what it had to do with him and Kira. Why would he show her a picture of himself caught in the act? It made no sense—until she took a good look at the image on the LCD. It wasn't the picture she expected; instead it was a picture of her and Shaun standing outside of the Four Seasons Hotel after the fire alarm sounded, with his arm wrapped protectively around her. Her torn blouse was sloppily tied at the waist, her makeup was badly smeared—on her face and his—and her hair was a disheveled wreck. She was mortified, and there was no denying what had happened between them last night, when she'd told Chris that she was turning in early with a headache. But she had to try to defend herself. She was not going down without a fight.

"Baby, it's not what it looks like," she pleaded. By now the color had drained from her face, but Chris's was flushed with anger.

"It looks pretty clear to me," he said, standing up angrily. "You've been fucking around with some nigger!" he yelled. "I should have listened to my mother. She knew right away that you were nothing but a gold-diggin' slut!" He shook his head. "I gave you everything, and you still couldn't keep your fuckin' legs closed."

"It's not like that." Tears from fear, not remorse, streamed down her face, taking traces of her mascara and eyeliner along the trail.

"You're just a cheap, lying bitch." He walked up to her, using his full height to add to the intimidation.

Desperately she reached for him, instinctively wanting to use her body to assuage the dicey situation, trying to physically hold on to him. If she could just hug him, arouse him, and get him into bed, maybe they could get beyond this. Maybe she could explain that she was lonely because he was always on the road. *That's it, blame it on him!* "No, baby, listen. I didn't do it. I promise. It's all a big mistake." Her denial sounded weak, even to her.

He grabbed her hands from his shoulders and dropped them coldly. Chris looked at Reese as though she were the lowest form of life on the planet. "Reese, don't insult me with more of your lies. Trust me; I know exactly what's up. It's time for you to get the hell outta here." When she stood frozen in place, he bent down into her face. "Now!"

"Chris, please—"

"Don't waste your breath or my time. I want you out of here tonight. So go upstairs, pack your shit, and get the fuck out."

Her head was spinning. Reese was not at all prepared for this. "But where will we go?"

"What do you mean, 'we'? You're not taking my son anywhere. Not tonight or ever."

This scenario was her worst nightmare come true—to be kicked out of the comforts of her $11-million home without her only real asset: her child. She retorted, "What are you gonna do, take him on the road? As much as you travel, you can't possibly take care of him!"

He laughed in her face. "And you can? You're a sorry excuse for a mother, Reese. The only thing you do for Rowe is arrange for other people to take care of him. But don't worry—not that you ever do. My mother's on the way over, and she'll take care of her grandson."

"You can't do this to me. You can't take my child," she begged. She had to hold on to something.

Chris grabbed her forearm and led her to the stairs. "Go get your shit and get out. Now!"

At this point Reese was crying uncontrollably as her world came crashing down at her feet. All of her plans had gone terribly wrong, and she was so terrified that she never considered what had really happened with Kira last night. "B-b-but where will I go?" she pleaded again.

Chis looked at her and snorted his disdain. "To quote Rhett Butler, 'Frankly, my dear, I don't give a damn.' "

THIRTEEN

Paulette rolled off of Max. She'd just finished riding him cowgirl style, her favorite position: on top. She'd been waiting patiently to celebrate her newfound wealth with him before heading back to L.A., and what better way than a frisky romp between the sheets?

"You were wonderful," she lied. The truth of the matter was that Max was a subpar lover, at best. The problem with Max was his looks. He'd always been told how handsome he was, and therefore was convinced that his mere presence did the trick. He had no idea how to please a woman, so a girl had to work hard to achieve an orgasm with him, which wasn't a problem at all for Paulette; she loved his dirty drawers. At least, it was Paulette's version of love; Max represented everything that she had been denied, and the fact that Lauren had him made him even more desirable.

She reached over to the nightstand for their two glasses of champagne. "Here's to a brilliant mission, masterfully executed!" They raised their flutes to toast, careful not to spill any champagne on the just purchased Pratesi sheets in Paulette's brand-new trendy loft apartment in SoHo. It was one of the many spoils from their victory. Already Paulette had maxed out every credit card she had and rapidly applied for new ones, while also leveraging her company assets to access even more credit for her loft, a place in Beverly Hills, and a shiny late model Mercedes.

Six months earlier, when it was obvious that Nana was going downhill fast, she and Max had hatched the plan to change her grandmother's will, fake the signature, and split the money. It had come off without a hitch. Since Max was the attorney for the estate, thanks to Mildred, his doting mother-in-law, it was a seamless operation. "The look on Aunt Mildred's face was priceless." Paulette threw her head back and laughed heartily, clearly a very happy woman.

"I'm just glad it's over." Max reached for a cigarette, something he never did in public or at home, lit it, puffed a few times, then lay back on the pillow to enjoy the nicotine rush.

"I'm glad it's over, too," Paulette said, snuggling closer to him. " 'Cause now you can finally leave her." First she'd gotten Lauren's money, and now she'd get her man.

Max glanced at her out of the corner of his eye, but decided not to comment.

When seconds ticked by and he still hadn't responded, Paulette did what Paulette did best: She took the direct route. "You are leaving her, right?"

Max took the cigarette from between his lips and turned to face her. "Now, Paulette, I never said that I was leaving Lauren. What we have is great, but leaving my home is another matter altogether." He had no idea why Paulette would think he'd leave his trophy wife for a loudmouthed publicist, even if she was a rich one now. He simply went along with the plan to sock away some money of his own. He hated knowing that *all* of his wealth was tied to Lauren. Now he had his own nest egg. But this didn't mean that he was done with Lauren; her family had another purpose to serve: launching his political career.

She slammed the champagne flute down and sat upright in bed. "You may not have said it, but you damn well insinuated it."

He sat up, too. "What are you talking about?"

"You said that you were only in the marriage for the money, which I now have," she said smugly. "And let's not forget I gave you half. So why would you stay with her? That bitch can't even give you a baby!" Paulette was not above hitting below the belt.

Max got up from the bed and began gathering his things. "I'm not having this conversation." Carrying on an affair and concocting some financial shenanigans for profit were one thing, but having a real relationship with Paulette was quite another. He did have an image to uphold, and someone like Paulette, money or not, just didn't fit it.

"Don't you walk out on me." She jumped up out of the bed naked, with her melon-sized boobs bouncing like buoys. "I just gave you millions of dollars, not to mention the best sex I'm sure you ever get, especially if it's coming from Lauren, and you're just gonna walk out?" She planted her hands on her wide hips.

The stress leading up to their heist had led Paulette down the familiar road of binge eating, and making off with the money and thus being able to afford fancy restaurants only added more pounds to her burgeoning weight problem.

"Listen, Paulette, there is no reason we have to have this conversation now. I didn't say that I'd *never* leave Lauren, just not now. It wouldn't look good; in fact, it would look pretty suspicious if all of a sudden we ended up together after the reading of the will." When he saw that his desperate logic was working, he pressed ahead. "We have to wait. It's for the best."

She visibly calmed down, unable to deny the truth in what he said. "Okay." She pouted. "We'll wait a few months, and then I want you all to myself." She walked up and hugged him tight.

"Let's just play this thing by ear, okay? You got what you want, so enjoy it." He gestured around at the grand loft.

Not exactly, she thought. Her grandmother's money was only the beginning of her ambitions; now she needed the man to go with the status, and Max was the perfect specimen. It didn't hurt that he also belonged to her cousin.

Max dressed in a hurry. "I do have to go; I'll call you tomorrow," he said, kissing her forehead. He had to give some serious thought to how best to extricate himself from this gold digger's clutches. Or, more accurately, from between her legs.

Like many guys, he'd heard rumors about the elusive snapping pussy, and the rare woman who held that mythical power between her legs. Paulette was the best sex he'd ever had; she had the power to put a death grip on a man's dick, and since he wasn't the best-endowed man, it was rare that he ever achieved a truly snug fit. It was hard to walk away from such great sex, but blazing orgasms or not, it was definitely time that he did.

She closed the door behind him and leaned against it, wondering if he really thought that he could just walk away after all they'd been through. There wasn't a chance in hell. In fact, if he tried to, she could threaten to reveal how he'd altered the will, which would ruin his reputation and his career. Besides, he could never prove that she had anything to do with it. She sighed. Men could be so naive; who did he think he was fucking with, anyway?

She was about to walk back up the stairs to pack for the red-eye to L.A. when there was a knock at the door. He must have come to his senses, she thought. Smiling, she tugged the bedsheet a little tighter around her chest and opened the door. "Oh, Max, I knew . . ." The words caught in her throat. It wasn't Max at the door; instead it was Reese, looking uncharacteristically thrown together, but more important, she was wearing a shocked look that soon transformed into a cat-that-ate-the-canary expression.

It didn't take Reese long to deduce the implications of what she'd just seen, nor the fact that she'd certainly be able to use it to her own advantage.

"Max, huh?" She walked past Paulette into the loft, leaving three suitcases outside the door. "I thought I saw him coming out of the building. You sneaky little girl, you." Though she was still reeling from her own drama, she couldn't help but be intrigued by the one playing out in Paulette's apartment.

"Reese, what are you doing here?" Paulette demanded. This was the last thing she needed.

Reese looked her up and down, shrewdly taking in the fact that she was covered in only a sheet and her hair was a frightful mess. "I might ask you the exact same thing."

FOURTEEN

After arriving in L.A. the next day, Paulette wasted no time hitting Rodeo Drive with a vengeance. After her spree she walked back to the new bungalow that she and Gillian had moved into, both arms loaded down with shopping bags. When she saw that Gillian wasn't wearing her usual long face she asked, "What's up? Did you just win the lottery?"

"No."

"Why the sexy outfit?"

"Nothing special, just going out." After her first "official" date with Brandon a few weeks before, and many phone conversations since, she'd realized that he wasn't such a bad guy. He was courteous, charming, and generally a nice man. And best of all, he didn't try to hit on her. So, tonight they were going to an exclusive cocktail party given by one of the biggest producers in the business.

"Oh?" Paulette said. "And may I ask with whom?"

Gillian started to lie, but thought better of it. L.A., regardless of its sprawling size, was really a very small town. "Brandon Russell," she finally said.

Paulette's expression froze on her pudgy face. "When did you start dating him?"

"We're not dating," Gillian retorted. "He's simply invited me to a cocktail reception."

"Where is it?"

There was no way that Gillian was going to mention that the cocktail party would be at the home of William Rutherford, the famous film director; she'd have to bind and gag Paulette to keep her from tagging along. "He didn't say," Gillian lied. Before Paulette could respond Gillian walked out of the room, heading for the privacy of the bathroom.

Before she reached it the phone rang. She checked the LCD and saw an unfamiliar number and no name.

"Hello?"

"Daaaarling, it's your mother." Imelda spoke as if she were a 1920s movie star, a rhythmic blend of long vowels and sharp consonants, a preposterous combination of Zsa Zsa Gabor and Eartha Kitt.

Gillian was accustomed to her mother popping in and out of her life without warning, so a call out of the blue wasn't a surprise. "I didn't recognize the number. Where are you?"

"I'm in Rome, daaarling, with Stephan. We'll be here for a few months and plan to be in the States in October."

This *was* a surprise. "Stephan? Who is Stephan?"

"Don't you worry, sweetie; you'll meet him soon enough. I just wanted to check in with you to see how things are going with your movie career."

"I don't have a movie career, Mother."

"Well, you will soon, darling. No one is as beautiful and talented as you are; besides, you're my daughter. You'll be bigger than Halle Berry."

Before Gillian could say another work, Imelda had plowed

ahead. "All right, darling, see you in a few months. Ciao." And she was gone.

Gillian stood staring at the phone. The last she knew her mother was married to a baron and was living happily ever after in Barcelona, so what the hell was she doing with a guy named Stephan traipsing around Italy? And why were they coming to the States?

She hung up and finished her makeup. *I've got my own problems*, she thought.

Thirty minutes later the buzzer to the apartment rang. "Miss Tillman, this is Mr. Russell's driver; we're parked downstairs."

"I'll be right down." Gillian took one more look in the mirror, blew herself a kiss, and headed for the door.

When she walked out of the building Charles stood like a wooden statue next to the back door of a black Maybach, waiting to open it for her. She slid inside, where Brandon and a chilled flute of Champagne Paul Goerg awaited.

"Hi, babe." Brandon wore a tailored Armani suit with a bright Nodus shirt open at the neck, and a pair of Italian handmade loafers. Everything about him was crisp and expensive, the very essence of new money. He leaned in for a kiss.

She gave him her cheek. "How are you?" she asked.

The inside of the quarter-of-a-million-dollar car was the epitome of decadent opulence. Tan handcrafted grand napa leather and rich Italian mahogany transformed the backseat into a posh living room on wheels, complete with a well-stocked bar, a humidor, reclining seats, and a state-of-the-art computer and entertainment center.

"I couldn't be better, but more important, how are you?" He was taking in her appearance, her exotic beauty and quiet confidence. He didn't drool, but it was clear that what he saw was very appetizing.

"I suppose I could complain, but that's never very productive," she deadpanned.

"It depends on who you complain to." His lips curled into a confident smile. "So, tell me, how are things going with your career?"

"Not exactly according to plan," she admitted.

"I can't say that I'm surprised."

She turned sharply toward him. "What's that supposed to mean?"

He held up his hands in mock surrender. "Not what you think." He gave a low chuckle at her reaction. "I really meant that as a compliment."

"If that's a compliment, I'd hate to be on the receiving end of one of your insults." She folded her arms and shot him an icy glare.

"No, Gillian, what I'm trying to say is that you're different. You don't fit the mold of the Hollywood starlet, so it doesn't surprise me that they don't get it, but I do." He reached into his humidor and pulled out a Cuban Cohiba, an eighteen-karat-gold cigar cutter, and a diamond-encrusted cigar lighter.

Before she could respond, a phone rang from inside a wooden panel between them. He held up a hand to let her know that it'd be just a moment, then picked up a sleek Bluetooth headphone. "Brandon here." He listened for a while, and puffed on his cigar, agitated. "Listen, you're worrying for nothing. Don't go getting nervous on me. I told you I'd find it." He pinched the bridge of his nose, resting his elbow on the coffee table between them. After another fifteen seconds of listening, he decided he'd had enough. "Listen, Sam, you're worrying for nothing, okay? Have a drink, and we'll talk later." Without another word he removed the earpiece and disconnected the line.

"Problems in paradise?"

Without humor he said. "There's no such thing as paradise, only temporary respites from purgatory."

Fifteen minutes later they drove through a ten-foot-hedge-surrounded gate that proceeded ceremoniously up a winding curved driveway to a mansion nestled in Beverly Hills. An unrivaled collection of Rollses, Bentleys, Porches, and Mercedeses snaked along the incline, and a staff of white-jacketed valets stood at the ready. When Charles pulled up, two butlers dressed in black tuxedos opened each side of the car for Gillian and Brandon to disembark.

When they met along the walkway, Gillian whispered, "A small cocktail party, huh?" She suddenly felt a craving for a cigarette, and she did have a pack in her bag. She thought about sneaking away somewhere, perhaps the ladies' room, for a quick fix, but knew that it could ruin her image in Tofu Land if she were caught. So she sucked it up and kept moving.

"As you'll see, with me, Gillian, everything is relative."

Upon entering the palatial home, Gillian crossed the threshold into a habitat populated by one percent of society; the women wore diamonds the size of small fruit, and were nipped and tucked so tightly that smiling risked a rupture. The home was owned by William Rutherford, one of the most commercially successful, if not critically acclaimed, film producers in Hollywood. He strolled through the crowd, looking quite dashing in an Asprey silk ascot, sipping a dirty martini. He was of the old-Hollywood school of style, believing in glamour above all else.

When Brandon and Gillian entered the room, since they were the only black people in attendance, their DNA seemed to alter the very chemical balance of the elite gathering. Scapel-perfect noses immediately picked up the whiff of a foreign scent.

Gillian looked stunning and wore her dark beauty with casual grace, and Brandon reeked of money. Though his face was not one readily known by the readers of *People* magazine, or the *National Enquirer*, people in the know, knew. The sight of the two of them at this exclusive enclave brought about all sorts of conjecture as to who they were. Of course, the easy money would have bet that he was an athlete (football, not tall enough for basketball) and that she was his trophy girlfriend, though some might have guessed an entertainer, perhaps some new breed of rapper, and his model girl-friend.

"Brandon, glad you could make it," Rutherford bellowed, swirling his martini. The only accoutrement missing was a smoking jacket, though he probably owned a few.

"Thanks for the invite, William. I'd like you to meet Gillian Tillman, the actress I mentioned to you."

Gillian took note of his statement, but registered nothing. When would he have mentioned her to William? And why?

William peered at her thoughtfully, "You're right; she is absolutely stunning."

Gillian extended her hand and pretended that he'd not spoken as though she were an object instead of a person. "It's a pleasure to meet you." She even managed a smile.

He shook her hand, his pinkie ring glittering like the North Star. "The pleasure is all mine." Slipping his arm about her waist, he guided her through the grand room out to a bar at the poolside terrace where more of L.A.'s power players were gathered like a thirsty herd of cattle. "What would you like to drink, my dear?" He turned to Brandon, who trailed behind them. "I'm afraid you'll have to fend for yourself," he teased.

Brandon laughed lightly and turned to Gillian. "I have to warn you, he's quite the ladies' man."

"She's a big girl, and I'm sure that she can take care of herself." William smiled. "So," he said, turning away from Brandon to focus his complete attention on Gillian, "what can I get you to drink?"

"I'll have a French martini," Gillian said, keeping her ice-princess cool.

After returning with her cocktail, he asked, "How long have you been in L.A.?"

"A few months now."

"Are you working on any projects?"

This was the part she hated, when she had to admit failure. "I can't say that I am," she reluctantly admitted. Happy for the distraction, she took a sip, enjoying the champagne's rich effervescence.

"Brandon and I are planning to do a film together," he said, watching carefully for her reaction.

"I thought he was in the music business," she replied nonchalantly. She didn't want this guy or anyone else thinking that she was so familiar with Brandon that she would audition on his casting couch.

"True, he is, but he and a group of investors are interested in putting some money into a film project."

She took a sip of champagne and glanced around the room, as if the conversation were of only marginal interest to her. "Uhmmm."

"It's really an exciting project. It's an urban drama, but with a breezy mainstream story line. I think it could be big, just the sort of project to completely legitimize urban films."

Gillian wasn't exactly sure what that last phrase meant. "Sounds interesting," she said.

"What are you two talking about?" Brandon walked up carrying a small plate of Petrossian caviar and toast points, which he offered to Gillian.

Gillian took one and popped it into her mouth, which put the onus of answering the question squarely on William. "Our project and Ms. Tillman's acting career, two perfectly compatible subjects, the way I see it." Again William was looking at her as though she were an object rather than a living person. Clearly, at this juncture Gillian didn't care about his lack of manners.

Though she managed to remain cool on the outside, on the inside she throbbed with a renewed energy and purpose. She could hardly wait to get home and call Lauren. Finally, something positive had happened.

FIFTEEN

While things were finally looking up for Gillian, Lauren felt trapped inside a gilded cage. Her life, which was supposed to be a charmed cakewalk, was turning into a slow stroll across smoldering hot coals. Since the explosive reading of her grandmother's will, things had gone steadily downhill. Her mother had all but physically attacked Paulette, so sure was she that her niece had had a hand in stealing her inheritance. Then Mildred suddenly and dramatically turned on Max with a vengeance. He fought back, stoically wielding client confidentiality, insisting that Priscilla was of sound mind, and had freely chosen to atone for the favoritism that she'd always shown Lauren and Mildred. During all of the fireworks, Paulette had gloated like an arsonist at the scene of a five-alarm fire. Not only did she now have wealth and social redemption, but the best part was witnessing her aunt Mildred's humiliation. Through it all, Lauren sat strapped amid a rock, a hard place, and hell.

Dressing by rote, she slipped into the easiest garment possible, a simple sundress, brushed and styled her hair, added makeup to give life to her sallow, lifeless complexion, and reluctantly headed out the door to Stephanie Green's bridal shower. The last place on earth she wanted to be was in a room full of black Barbie dolls, but she'd known Stephanie since third grade, and Stephanie had been a bridesmaid in Lauren's own wedding.

As she was driving out to Rochester, New York, her cell phone rang. She saw the caller ID and answered the call. "Hey."

"How are you?" Gillian asked with an upbeat tone that Lauren hadn't heard in quite a long time.

"Obviously not as good as you are. You sound great," Lauren enthused, glad that someone was in a good mood. "Your date must have gone well."

"It did. He's a very nice guy, and even better than that is the fact that he is financing a film project with William Rutherford, and they want me to be in it!"

"That's great!" Lauren was genuinely happy that Gillian was catching a break.

"I don't want to get too excited, but it does sound promising."

"I'll keep my fingers crossed."

"And I'll keep my *legs* crossed. I just hope that he doesn't have plans to audition me on his casting couch." Although Gillian was enjoying Brandon's company, she feared that he wanted only one thing, and it wasn't a screen test.

"I doubt that a legitimate producer like William Rutherford would do that, especially with someone as talented as you are."

"It's not William I'm worried about; it's Brandon."

"Has he mentioned anything suggestive?"

"No So far he's been a perfect gentleman. I just hope that he doesn't, because he is definitely not my type."

"Who is?" Lauren said. All the years she'd known Gillian she'd never once seen her with a boyfriend. "My exit's coming up. Gotta go. I'll call you later."

Minutes later Kathy Hill greeted her at the door, chipper as a sorority girl before homecoming. "Hey, girl!" Though the women were all in their thirties, the glee surrounding one of their own bagging one of the men they called the Eligibles was palpable, like being at a party for a bunch of three-year-olds, all high on glucose. An Eligible was the quintessential Jack from Jack and Jill; he was well-bred, well educated, successful, and not too dark.

"Congratulations," Lauren said as she made her way over to Stephanie. She even managed a degree of conviction. "I'm so happy for you."

"Thank you." Stephanie blushed in a way that a thirty-four-year-old shouldn't be capable of, but there was no greater joy than that of a BAP on the brink of fulfilling her life's destiny by marrying an Eligible.

To balance her sour mood, Lauren grabbed a glass of white wine and took a seat in the corner of the room, bracing herself for the next two hours of bridal-shower hell.

After muddling through the first forty-five minutes of giddy but inane conversation, Lauren propped herself up with a second glass of wine, preparing to bear witness to the obligatory but painfully stupid bridal-shower games.

"Now, I have a special surprise for you ladies," Kathy stood up and announced. She was even clapping her hands together and grinning like the Mad Hatter. "We have some very exciting entertainment scheduled, and I think you'll all enjoy it." On cue, Nelly's sex romp song "Hot in Here" filled the room, and in walked a dark, sexy, well-built man with chiseled arms, wearing a tailored UPS uniform and carrying a brown box. He had the raw sexual energy that elicited a chemical reaction from the women just by his walking into the room. Every woman, except for Lauren, who was still waiting for an appropriate moment to leave, leaned forward in her chair, eyeing him like a rack of half-price Manolo Blahniks.

He began his seduction by slowly unbuttoning his shirt, teasing his audience as he revealed a smooth, muscular chest. His eyes were locked on Lauren. She was the the least engaged of the group and the biggest challenge for him, but when she saw those soulful, slanted brown eyes, she couldn't help being drawn in. As a warm-up to the bride he approached Lauren, dropped his shirt, stood in front her, and begin moving his hips seductively to the music as he unzipped his pants. Her breath caught in her throat; she was sure that a blush must have spread across her face like wild kudzu. She was both uncomfortable and, at the same time, more stimulated than she'd been in years. She couldn't remember the last time the sight of a man's body had aroused her. Sex with her husband had become perfunctory, and then nearly nonexistent once it became clear to Max that they wouldn't be making a baby.

These thoughts were pushed aside as his pants slid past his hips, revealing the impressive imprint of his manhood caught under-neath black silk boxers. The women roared their approval. He sud-denly turned away, leaving Lauren relieved that he was gone, yet desperate for him to return, which he did after opening the brown box and removing a long, bright red silk scarf, which he slowly trailed around her neck, letting one end slither down her front and between her legs. But he didn't stop there; he took the scarf and tied her hands behind her back, then began massaging and caress-ing her neck and shoulders. His touch was so erotic that her breath caught in her throat.

After scant seconds that seemed to last an eternity, he gently un-tied her hands, giving her a look that summed up her own thoughts, and withdrew his attention, moving toward the bride for the coup de grâce of his performance, which included a little dirty dancing in the middle of the room as her guests cheered them on. She blushed like a bride would, but was clearly enjoying the attention. When the music stopped, he kissed Stephanie on her cheek, gathered his things, and walked out, looking back over his shoulder at Lauren, who turned away, embarrassed by her own thoughts.

Minutes later Lauren left the bridal shower, but wasn't quite ready to return home, so she stopped off at a Starbucks a couple of blocks away for a caramel macchiato, and a chance to be alone with her scandalous thoughts. If she focused hard, Lauren could relive the tingling excitement that she'd felt at the stranger's touch, and with her eyes closed tightly she could vividly imagine the enticing feel of the silk scarf moving seductively against her skin. She sighed, marveling at just how turned on she had been, pleased that it was even possible.

"Do you mind if I join you?" The unfamiliar voice snatched her mind away from her thoughts.

Looking up, she saw Mr. UPS, sans the uniform and the box. She was speechless. Sitting there with her eyes closed and her imagination running wild, she'd felt as if he were an unreal memory, or a piece of a fragmented dream, yet there he stood, in the flesh.

"I hope that means okay." He flashed the smile that he'd undoubtedly used on many occasions to render women speechless. "I'm not a stalker, but I couldn't resist the chance to properly introduce myself." He'd been parked talking on the phone when Lauren pulled out of the driveway, and on impulse followed her to Starbucks.

For a minute she couldn't find her voice. "Sure, I almost didn't recognize you," she managed to say, which was a lie. She could have picked him out of a cast of thousands, even wearing the jeans and T-shirt he now wore, instead of stripped down to his boxers.

"I suppose I do look different with my pants and shirt on." He chuckled. "But if it helps, I can take them off." He pretended to pull his T-shirt over his head.

"No, no, that's okay." She laughed, putting her coffee down and holding both her hands up in mock surrender. His wisecrack broke the ice, and she suddenly felt a bit more comfortable. Flirting had never been her strong suit—she was always so attractive that she never had to cultivate that skill—and after being married for the last five years, she was essentially clueless. She marveled at how some women, particularly Reese, did it so naturally. Reese, she imagined, probably came out of the womb winking at the doctor.

"My name is Gideon." He reached over to shake her hand.

She took his, still remembering how good it had felt on her neck and shoulders, and imagining how his hands might feel on her breasts and . . . "I'm Lauren," she finally said, snapping out of her fantasy.

He leaned back, appraising her. "An elegant name for an elegant lady."

"Thank you." She blushed in spite of herself. Then she felt incredibly silly for behaving like a schoolgirl over a male stripper.

Before she could gather her things to leave, Gideon asked, "So, Lauren, what do you do, besides drive men crazy?"

"You must be thinking of another Lauren, but to answer your question, I'm a housewife."

"Oh, so you're already taken?" He snapped his fingers. "I should have known; all of the good ones usually are."

"Yes, I'm married," she said, trying to put a little enthusiasm into her voice.

"Do you have kids?"

"No." She braced herself. Why did she always feel the need to apologize for not having kids—even to strangers?

"So, tell me about yourself."

She shifted uncomfortably. "Let's talk about you instead. How long have you been . . . stripping?" She didn't know what else to call it.

He laughed at her discomfort. "Today was my first and last day. My cousin just started a party entertainment company, and one of his dancers called in at the last minute. We drew straws and I lost. But now I'm glad I did." He gave her that smile again.

"So, what do you normally do?"

"I'm a documentary photographer."

She was surprised and intrigued by his answer. "What do you shoot?"

"I travel to obscure places around the world and document the cultures. Lately I've been spending a lot of time in Africa."

Lauren was taken aback. She really had had no idea what to expect from him, but Gideon seemed deep and very real. "I love art and photography. I'd like to see some of your work sometime," she said, without thinking. For her, it was a pretty forward suggestion, so maybe her flirting skills weren't nonexistent after all.

"Lauren, you can see me—or my work—anytime you want to." Though his eyes smiled, the rest of his expression was very serious.

Lauren sat back in her chair and for the first time in months she really smiled.

SIXTEEN

Reese gripped the newspaper and savagely tore it to shreds, throwing the small pieces to the floor as if she were a bratty two-year-old. The only thing stopping her from having an all-out meltdown was a blistering headache, which was also the by-product of too much cheap red wine consumed the night before. Any sobbing and heaving would only add insidious pressure at her temples, thus more pain, and since last month she'd had enough.

Reese figured that Chris had sat on the scandalous story and photo to strategically leak it as a negotiating ploy, sending a message to her and her attorney that they needed to settle on *his* terms. Given the prenuptial agreement, the fact that Reese was caught in flagrante, and her less-than-stellar track record as a mother, Chris definitely held all the cards and was now playing his trump.

In a few short weeks she'd slid from her lofty perch atop the world, down a slippery slope right into the depths of hell, and she'd never even seen the precipice that loomed before her. In this deep abyss, she was without money or credit cards; Chris had cut them all off. She had no fancy house, and even her lover, Shaun, was gone with the wind; he hadn't returned any of her urgent phone calls since that fateful night.

She'd had to beg Paulette to let her stay at her New York loft apartment. When begging didn't initially work, she'd resorted to a subtle form of blackmail; after all, she had caught Max, Paulette's cousin's husband, tipping out of their love nest. She didn't come right out and blackmail her, but the insinuation was so clear that Stevie Wonder could have seen it clearly.

"What the hell are you doing?" Paulette walked in from the airport to find Reese ruminating amid her ruins, a smorgasbord of empty doughnut boxes, discarded tissues, and partially eaten plates of food. "I agreed to let you stay here, but I didn't say you could trash the place. Hell, I just bought this apartment." She tossed her brand-new Louis Vuitton carry-on onto the leather sofa.

"I'm finished," Reese cried, grabbing fistfuls of hair. "Did you see today's *Post*?" She was half hoping that Paulette would say no; then she could hold out some hope that she wasn't the butt of jokes for *all* of New York.

"Yeah, I saw it," Paulette said, shaking her head in disbelief. "That shit's pretty fucked-up." Her summation was proclaimed without any emotion or empathy for her suffering friend.

Reese rolled her eyes and barked, "Like I don't know it?" The scintillating story, detailing how superstar Knicks player Chris Nolan's wife was busted at a Midtown hotel with another man, had leaked to the press, along with a most unflattering picture of Reese looking like a drowned raccoon washed up outside of the Four Seasons Hotel. The headline read, "Baller's Wife Caught Way Out of Bounds."

Reese wasn't sure which was more upsetting to her; the sordid story, or the horrid picture. She looked a dreadful mess. Certainly it was one thing to be caught up in a seedy scandal, but quite another to look bad while doing it. It was morbidly unfair, since Reese was never seen in public looking less than fabulous, and the one time she'd been forced to, because of a faulty hotel alarm, it had ruined her life.

"You've gotta stop sitting around here feeling sorry for yourself and come up with a plan." Paulette plopped down on the sofa. Truth be told, things were going so well for her that it was hard to feel sincere sympathy for Reese. Plus, she was sick and tired of picking up the pieces for these spoiled-rotten divas. Both Reese and Gillian had always strutted around as if they were holier-than-thou, yet both were now living under *her* new roofs.

Paulette wasn't telling Reese anything she didn't already know, but it was a tad difficult to come up with a solid plan when the world was crumbling down around you. "I know; I've gotta get a new lawyer."

The *Post* article had the desired effect. She'd just gotten word from her old one that without payment, which she didn't have, he wouldn't be doing any more work. Undoubtedly he had little faith that she'd end up with anything worthy of his time. "And I need you to work on my publicity again. My image has to be scrubbed clean before I can ever dream of a decent settlement," she said.

"How can you afford my monthly retainer when you have no money?" Paulette cruelly reminded her.

Reese wanted to slap her, but remembered that she could attract more bees with honey than with vinegar, and right now she needed a whole colony. "I know that I can't pay you right now, but after the settlement I'll pay your fee, *plus* a bonus," she said sweetly.

Just the thought of her divorce settlement ramped up Reese's headache. The no-cheat clause in the prenup applied to both of them, so her little rendezvous with Shaun could cost her the millions that she had been sure to get if she'd simply divorced Chris. Of course, now she wished she'd done just that, rather than bothering to try setting him up to get more. This shifted her thoughts to Kira; she was still missing in action. She hadn't heard from her friend since the night before all hell broke loose.

"So, will you do my PR?" Reese implored.

Paulette leaned back, kicked off her Chanel pumps, and carefully considered the situation. Though they were friends, this *was* business. What exactly did she have to gain from helping Reese? The answer wasn't money, at least, not at the moment. The woman didn't have any, and frankly her prospects weren't looking so hot for the future either, especially now that Paulette was independently wealthy herself. Besides, there was no prestige in representing the whore wife of a superstar ball player. On the other hand, she needed to get Reese on her feet so that she could march her right out of the door, but she couldn't push her, or, knowing Reese, she might slip and tell Laura about Max, and it was too soon for that. In a matter of seconds, all of these permutations sifted effortlessly through Paulette's calculating brain, and she came to a rapid conclusion. "I'll tell you what. I'll do it, but let's leave it off the record." What PR person needed a famous ball player as an enemy, especially when she wasn't getting paid for the trouble?

This gave Reese a glimmer of hope, so she allowed herself to take another leap. "What about Max—you think he'll help with my legal work?" When she saw the word *no* about to form on Paulette's lips, she pressed ahead. "Think about it; The sooner I get a cash settlement, the sooner I'll be out of your—and his—way." This was a slick way of extending her extortion to Max's side of the ledger.

Paulette did not miss the thinly veiled threat. "I'll talk to him about it, but for either of us to be able to help you, I need to know *exactly* what happened." Paulette's well-honed PR instincts told her that there was much more to the story than she'd heard or read, and to help Reese, she'd have to know all of the skeletons that rattled around in her closet, not to mention that she was just plain old nosy.

"Chris and I had been having some problems, and I met someone else—"

Paulette quickly interrupted her; she didn't need to hear a canned speech. "Tell me what *really* happened."

Reese weighed her options, just as Paulette had minutes earlier. She could hide the sordid details, which would probably not gain her anything, or she could confide in Paulette and Max and, with their help, figure out some way to get out of the mess she'd gotten into.

"I can't help you, nor can Max, unless we know everything," Paulette lectured. "And you have to realize that some things that you may not think are important could be crucial. So tell me everything."

After careful consideration, Reese made a decision. She took a deep breath and jumped in, telling Paulette the whole sordid tale.

SEVENTEEN

Gideon lived and worked in a *real* loft in Williamsburg, New York, not one of those yuppie lofts, like so many that were scattered throughout Manhattan, with their superslick marble finishes, perfect, state-of-the-art stainless-steel appliances, and the requisite doorman downstairs. His building was authentically rustic, even a bit grimy, but it was also steeped in character that only the passage of time could design.

In the late 1800s the building had been an iron-welding factory, and still bore a lot of gritty reminders of that bygone era. The structure's conversion to lofts had been a pioneering adventure for a few renegade artists, rather than a developer's urban project, so there wasn't a Starbucks around the corner, nor a Gap midblock. Gideon considered the area to be the last frontier in New York for the true artist.

To Lauren, who was the poster child for creature comforts, seeing his world was like getting a glimpse into a third-world country. It was a far cry from her domain of elite private schools, expensive designer clothes, sprawling homes, and four-hundred-thread-count

Pratesi bedsheets. When the taxi dropped her off on the barren industrial-looking block, her first reaction was to yell for the driver to come back. She felt there must be some mistake; no one she knew lived in a place like this. When the Yellow Cab turned the corner, she took a deep breath, gripped her Hermès Birkin bag a little tighter, and slowly walked toward the building that bore the number she'd written down as his address. There was a rusty old intercom with names and buzzers to the left of the door. She nervously scanned the list until she found Gideon's name, then pressed twice, anxious to get in off of the street. Hopefully the contraption worked.

"Hello." With relief, she recognized his voice.

"Gideon, it's Lauren." A timbre of fear resonated in her words.

"Come on up. I'm on the third floor." His voice was as light and airy as hers was tight and nervous.

She heard a clicking noise, and then pulled open the large stainless-steel door. As skeptical as she had been all along, her trepidation hit another level as she entered the antique, cage-enclosed freight elevator. She almost turned around and headed for posher pastures.

Not for the first time that day, she asked herself, *What the hell are you doing? You must be crazy!* She didn't know Gideon, or anyone like him. Though he'd been hired for Stephanie's shower, she was sure that the arrangement was purely transactional. He was simply the hired help. Besides, she couldn't very well call Stephanie up and say, "Hi, how are you? By the way, tell me about that fine stripper you hired." In her close-knit world, all inhabitants were a mere two degrees of separation away, certainly not the customary six, and clearly, this man was far outside of her social orbit. For all she knew he could be an ax murderer. By the time the elevator opened into his living space, she was nearly paralyzed with fear.

"Push the lever there to open it," Gideon said with a smile. He stood just on the other side of an intricately designed wrought-iron gate, wearing a pair of holey blue jeans, a short, well-worn gypsy shirt, and bare feet.

This was her last chance; she could push the button for the first floor, hop off the elevator when it opened, walk out the front door, and then run for her life. But run back to what? Her distant husband, her controlling mother, or her nonexistent career? Realizing there was little or nothing to run back to, she pushed the lever and entered Gideon's world.

"Come on in." His smile revealed a sexy mouth and a set of white teeth that were attractively imperfect. The star of his face was a pair of coal-brown eyes, which were surrounded by a full set of Maybelline lashes. He looked at her as if he could see right though her well-groomed facade, but wouldn't make an issue of the truths he saw hidden there.

"Hi, Gideon." She stepped off the elevator into a large space whose west wall was all paned windows. The ceiling was twelve feet high, and the floor was covered in well-worn, dark brown wooden planks. They appeared to be original to the structure. The rest of the large room was a creatively assembled mix of interesting rugs, furniture, and artifacts from all over the world. The other three walls were covered in the most compelling photographs, both black-and-white and color, including a collection of electrifying images of Africa's nomadic sheep-herding tribes, a selection of soul-searching photographs of the Ashanti tribe in Ghana, and a series of regal shots of beautiful Senegalese, Somalian, and Ethiopian women in their traditional garb. The images pulled Lauren into the room, moving her steadily from one to the next. "Wow," she breathed, without even realizing that she'd spoken.

"I'm glad you like them." While she was completely absorbed in the gallery, Gideon observed her the way he might a subject through his camera lens, registering every nuance reflected in her body language, her posture, and her aura.

"They're really quite amazing." What was also amazing to her was that this guy, whom she'd initially written off as little more than an erotic dancer, seemed to be as deep as his work revealed. She turned to face him, feeling as if she were seeing him for the very first time.

"Would you like something to drink?"

"What do you have?"

"I'm afraid I'm out of French champagne," he teased. "But I do have an excellent South African Pinotage."

She wondered for a split second how to take that comment about French champagne, knowing that it said something about who she was, or at least whom he perceived her to be. "That sounds good," she answered.

"Make yourself comfortable," he said, gesturing to a cluster of large Czech-designed multicolored pillows nestled in a corner. A low coffee table, which was actually the base of an enormous tree, sat nearby covered in art and history books.

When he turned to walk away, a smile toyed with the corners of her mouth. She shrugged, tossed her bag onto the table, and plopped down onto the pillows. They were surprisingly comfortable; in fact, so was she.

When he returned with their wine, she was flipping though a book about the history of art in Africa. He handed her a glass, then joined her on one of the oversize pillows.

She closed the book and turned to face him. "I love your place. It's very . . . interesting." She was sure there was a more fitting adjective, but at the moment it escaped her.

"Thank you. Though I'm sure it's a far cry from all that you're accustomed to."

"Which is what makes it so interesting," she countered.

"Oh, I get it. You're down here slumming for the day. To see how the other ninety-nine percent live, huh?" he teased.

"I wouldn't say that."

"Of course you wouldn't; you're much too polite."

"Why do I have the feeling that you're making fun of me?"

"It's not that. Really, I think you're cute. You're an interesting . . ." He paused and held up his finger. "There's that word again. An interesting study in contrasts, and you realize that photography is really a visual representation of contrasts. You know, light versus dark, soft versus gritty. It's almost impossible to show one element without contrasting it with another." He looked at her as though his deepest desire were to penetrate a layer of her skin, to see her more clearly.

She took a sip from her glass, fully enjoying the wine, the environment, the conversation, and the man. It was intriguing to her that he was so intellectual, yet not the least bit stuffy. "So what contrasts do you see in me?" She propped another pillow behind her, and reclined to hear his explanation.

He leaned in and lowered his voice. "In you, I see a range of personal conflicts."

She shifted slightly, suddenly feeling exposed, as though he really could see through her. Oddly enough, she subconsciously hoped that he could, and then maybe he could tell *her* what was there.

"You have it all, but you aren't sure you deserve or want it; you're gorgeous, but you'd rather people didn't see it; you are strong and independent, but you like to keep that to yourself as well." His gaze never wavered as he read her like an open book.

She took another sip of her wine, unnerved by his insight into her personality. She doubted that her own husband or mother, understood her as well. "So, what are you, some kind of psychiatric photographer?" she asked, hoping to lighten the conversation.

"Take a look at that photograph." He gestured to a black-and-white shot of an elderly West African man. "The etches carved into his face, the very subtle dilation of his pupils, and the set of his jaw all tell a story that no screenplay writer could come close to creating. It's impossible to capture the raw essence of a person in a photograph without gazing into his soul."

Again, contradictions prevailed; Lauren was as comfortable as she'd been in years, but at the same time she felt precariously on edge, as though she too were at a precipice, but not quite sure if the slide would take her down or help her to escape. "What if you don't like what you see there?"

He tilted his head, shrugged his shoulders, sighed, and said, "People are who they are. None of us is perfect. I mean, look at that lame excuse for a striptease I pulled off." He laughed at himself, and then became serious again. "But, perfect or not, it doesn't matter. We are all the sum of our imperfections, and we are who we are as a result of them, for better or worse. What matters most is how we grow as people, and what we do individually to make the world better."

Lauren took a thoughtful sip of the wine, absorbing his simple but profound words, along with the grapes from a country she'd yet to visit. She didn't reply; no words were necessary. She just nestled more deeply in the pillows that surrounded her, feeling better than she had in years—more centered, more understood, and more interested in what the next moment might bring.

"Are you okay?"

"I am."

"Can I get anything for you?"

"No, I'm just fine." She felt oddly at peace, as if she could stay in this moment for hours.

Without comment he wrapped his arm around her, and she fit perfectly against his chest. The gesture was an easy one, with no pressure or expectations attached to it; nor was it an overtly sexual move; however, it did reveal an intimacy that her husband would never have been capable of. Suddenly, Martha's Vineyard, Westchester, and the Upper East Side all felt worlds away.

EIGHTEEN

melda descended on L.A. like a blustery nor'easter. Gillian could easily imagine her mother's grand entrance, blowing into the Four Seasons lobby, dripping in sable—even in sunny California— with a barrage of Louis Vuitton steamer trunks following in her wake, and a trail of bellmen nipping at her heels. Though you could pick your friends, you weren't as fortunate where family was concerned, so she dutifully placed the call to the hotel to speak with her mother.

"Hello, daaahling," Imelda's affected effervescence reverberated through the phone line, making her sound bigger than life. She was the quintessential drama queen. Gillian often thought that her mother should have been the actress in the family.

"How was your trip?"

"First-class travel just isn't what it used to be, unless you're on Virgin Atlantic. But, boy, do I miss the Concorde! These days any old yokel with enough frequent-flier miles can get a first-class seat." She blew an appalled gust of air aimed at the ill-fated airline industry. "I remember a time when they served French estate wines with dinner; now you're lucky if you get a regional Californian." It was telling how drastically different her sentimental reverie was from those of most women her age, who might just as fondly remember the low price of bread.

"How long are you planning to stay?" The answer Gillian really wanted was to the question, When exactly are you leaving?

"Oh, we aren't really sure, maybe a week or two, or perhaps a month." Since Imelda had never had a job, she also didn't appreciate the context of time that most people conformed to.

"Speaking of 'we,' who is this guy you're traveling with, and what happened to your latest husband?"

"We'll get into all of that later. Right now I'm a bit jet-lagged, but I've made a reservation for the three of us at Spago at eight o'clock. Okay, darling?"

Gillian hung up the telephone with an unsettling feeling of foreboding. She was the only person she knew who had more cause to worry about her mother's judgment than the other way around. Long before Gillian had ever even heard the term *gold digger*, she'd recognized the color of her mother's stripes. All of her life she'd seen the way Imelda had masterfully manipulated, cajoled, and used any means necessary to get what she wanted from men, and once she got it—or something better came along—they became instantly disposable, like last year's news. Gillian had hoped that Imelda's last marriage would have been enough for her, and that she would finally settle down like a normal person, instead of flitting around the world selling her wares—which, by the way, were getting a bit worn. Though her mother seemed oblivious to it, quite a few of the petals had fallen from Imelda's bloom, so she was not the beauty she was when she began trading up husbands the way some people did their automobiles.

Gillian shook her head as her thoughts centered on the father she never knew, the first of many men to be sucked into the tsunami known as her mother. For years, Gillian had tried to persuade Imelda to tell her who her father was, and how she might find him. She secretly hoped that he would ride in on a white horse, scoop her up in his arms and rescue her from never-never land. Even though she knew exactly who Gillian's father was, Imelda ignored her pleas, telling her daughter one story after another, denying Gillian the right to know him, simply because she had no desire ever to face her past, once she'd left it behind. What Gillian got instead was one "uncle" after another, and a history of issues dealing with men that prevented her from forming lasting relationships.

"What's your mom doing in town?" Paulette asked as she breezed into the room. She'd just returned to L.A. for two weeks—just long enough to have liposuction and a breast-lift. Though Gillian had been living with Paulette for six months now, dealing with her cloying personality had not gotten any easier. Actually, it had gotten worse since Paulette had come into her inheritance. Modesty and humility were two words that had never been introduced to the woman, so she bragged incessantly about her pricey New York loft, her big, buldging bank account, and lately about her hot new man, who she swore was God's gift wrapped in organza and silk bows. She never revealed his name, explaining that she wanted to keep the relationship private for now, which was a first for Paulette. Whenever she'd managed to trap a man in the past, she promptly put the poor man on display like a caged white Bengal tiger. Whatever, Gillian thought, she couldn't care less which schmuck would be stupid enough to hook up with Paulette. She had her own—and her mother's—problems to deal with.

"How long is she staying?"

"Who knows? The woman is—"

"—my hero," Paulette interrupted. "Any black woman who can travel around the world marrying one rich man after another is the shit, as far as I am concerned."

"That's debatable."

"So, what's going on with you and Brandon?" Paulette asked. "I saw from the phone's ID that he's been calling."

It was just like Paulette to come home and immediately go trawling through the caller ID log. She was insufferably nosy. "Nothing, really." In truth, she and Brandon had been spending a lot more time together, but there was no way she'd divulge that to Paulette.

"A friend told me he saw you two at Jerry's Deli having lunch." Paulette raised her brows and fixed her eyes on Gillian, hoping to pry away something gossipworthy.

Gillian was not about to be baited. "And . . . ?"

"Nothing, just curious, that's all, though I did hear some interesting industry gossip about Sunset Records." Paulette waited for Gillian to now pry the gossip from *her* loose lips, but Gillian wasn't interested in continuing the conversation.

"I'm gonna take a nap. I'll need my energy for dinner tonight with my mom."

When Imelda made her grand entrance into the famed Spago, Gillian was already seated at the prime center table that her mother had reserved, sipping a dirty martini with Grey Goose. She was just about to check voice mail on her cell phone when she felt her mother's presence before she even turned to see her enter the restaurant. Imelda didn't just walk into a room, ever. She conquered all four walls, making sure that every head turned and that all eyes tracked her like heat-seeking missiles. At the age of fifty-five, she was five feet, ten inches tall, and in excellent shape. Her complexion was honey brown, and she wore a sassy short haircut that was dyed a warm platinum blond. Package that with the tight, bright red Versace dress, and she was impossible to miss. Trailing behind her was a dark-haired, handsome young Italian with a rich olive complexion. He appeared to be at least half her age, if a day.

"Daaahling, you look fabulous." She made a show of kissing both of Gillian's cheeks, then holding her at arm's length to get a good look.

"And, of course, so do you," Gillian said. And she did; even with the hint of crow's-feet that were creeping from the corners of her eyes, and a few other telltale signs of age, she was a handsome, elegant woman who knew all too well how to work her assets.

"Oh, thank you, sweetie." She turned to introduce the Italian stud into their conversation. "Gillian, this is my fiancé, Stephan. Stephan, this is my beautiful daughter, the actress, Gillian." This exchange started another set of air kisses from him, but didn't stop there. Gallantly Stephan bent at the waist and kissed the back of Gillian's hand, while his eyes remained locked with hers.

"Pleased to meet you," Gillian said.

"The pleasure is *all* mine." And he looked like a man who really meant that. Stephan had that oozing sexuality that many Italian men possessed, which could turn a mere gaze into an intense sexual encounter.

Gillian was nearly speechless. Fiancé? Just when she didn't think it was possible, her mother managed to shock her again.

After the fawn-fest concluded, with a rapt audience, they sat down for dinner with Imelda, of course, in the power seat, perfectly positioned so that as many people in the restaurant as possible could see her. In fact, she took the seat that Gillian previously had, gingerly moving her daughter's cocktail aside.

"So, how are things going for you here, dear?" What she really meant was, Have you gotten any acting jobs yet? She was totally enamored of the idea of her daughter being a Hollywood actress. The way Imelda spoke of Gillian's career to friends in Europe, her daughter was bigger than Julia Roberts.

Gillian felt a strong desire to down the other half of her martini, but took a tame sip instead. "Let's just say that I'm learning patience."

"As beautiful as you are, you shouldn't have any trouble at all getting work. You must be doing something wrong. Are you getting out, meeting people? Maybe I should meet with that agent of yours. He obviously isn't doing his job."

The last thing Gillian wanted was to discuss her teetering career on an empty stomach with her mother and her boy toy. Fortunately, before she had to respond, the waiter came to take drink orders from Imelda and Stephan. Imelda ordered an eight-hundred-dollar bottle of vintage Dom Pérignon, so obviously the new husband-to-be must be doing well.

When the waiter left the table, Imelda turned back to Gillian. "You were saying?"

"Mom, I do have some things in the works, but it does take time," Gillian patiently explained.

"Some things like what?"

Gillian was hoping that she could just keep the conversation moving in another direction, but leave it to her mother to be relentless. "Brandon Russell and William Rutherford are producing a film called *Gold Diggers*, and they're talking to me about a starring role." She really hadn't planned to divulge this to her mother, but hoped that this little tidbit might temporarily satiate her ravenous appetite.

"That's wonderful!" Imelda beamed, turning to look at Stephan as if to make sure the he too understood how important this was, namely for Imelda. The wine steward walked over with the champagne and went through the uncorking, and pouring ritual, after which Imelda went through the swirling, smelling, tasting, and approving ritual. After all glasses were filled, she raised hers for the others to join. "Here's to my gorgeous daughter and her sensational film career."

After taking a sip, Gillian said, "Mom, remember nothing's final."

"But it will be." Now Imelda picked up the menu and changed

the subject. "Everything looks divine, especially after those pitiful meals they serve on airplanes these days."

"Excuse me." Gillian got up to go to the ladies' room, not ready for another discourse on the horrid state of first-class travel.

Once in the ladies' room she powdered her nose, fluffed her hair, and thought of anything else she could do to kill time. That was when she remembered her cell phone, which she'd left at the table. Brandon's record label was having a fancy album release party for Sweet Cakes, one of the biggest female rap artists in the world. Her last album had gone triple platinum, and she had endorsements with everybody from Chanel to Lancôme. He'd insisted that Gillian come for the exposure, to beef up her profile before her film debut. He'd promised to make sure that she walked the red carpet and was photographed for print media, but Gillian had forgotten to find out where the party was being held. She'd just call after dinner. She took one last look in the mirror and left to rejoin her mother and Stephan.

When she got back to the table, her mother handed her the cell phone. "Dear, a call came through while you were in the ladies' room."

Gillian took the phone, but didn't see a missed call or a new-message indicator.

"I went ahead and answered it for you, knowing that it might be important."

"Mother!"

"Well, it's a good thing I did, because it was Brandon Russell, calling about tonight's party."

"You spoke to him?" This was the last thing that Gillian wanted—for Brandon, whom she wasn't sure about to begin with, to meet her mother.

"Of course, darling, and he's such a nice man. He invited Stephan and me to be his guests this evening. Isn't that lovely?"

"Mother, this is business!"

"I know, sweetie. We won't be in the way, and in fact I may even be able to help you."

"Did he say where the party was?"

"Believe it or not, it's at the Four Seasons, which is perfect. We'll finish up here, I'll go back to the hotel, change clothes, and we'll go to the party."

As usual, it was all about Imelda.

NINETEEN

Sweet Cakes's album release party was held in the spacious but cozy roof garden atop the Four Seasons. It was a must-attend for hip celebrities. Brandon spared no expense entertaining his high-profile guests, including the top executives in the entertainment business. He hired the renowned event planner extraordinaire, Colin Cowie, to transform the rooftop into the Garden of Eden, with apple trees and waiters dressed only in fig leaves as they served Champagne Paul Goerg, and a host of other delicacies, starting with caviar on apple crisps. At the moment Sweet Cakes was the glittering jewel in Sunset Records' shining crown, and Brandon was pulling out every stop to milk her for all she was worth.

Legend had it that Brandon started Sunset Records in Mississippi fifteen years earlier with less than two thousand dollars cash and one marginally talented wannabe rapper. Sheer determination and a really good ear for hit records enabled him to parlay his meager, struggling basement operation into a thriving $100-million business. Over time he carefully groomed himself by meticulously emulating those executives and moguls he admired. He copied their way of dress, the cars they drove, their mannerisms, and the way they spoke. He'd all but lost his Mississippi twang, and hadn't been back to his hometown since he left for New York after his first big hit—not even to see his eighty-year-old mother, even though he made sure that she was well taken care of.

Finally he would set himself apart from the cadre of other black music-industry titans by making his long-awaited move into film. It was the deal that Brandon had been praying for every day as he struggled to build his empire. Just as he'd fled the Delta and never looked back, he now wanted to rid himself of the grit and grime of hip-hop. When he was younger, dealing with the madness was one thing, but now that he was in his mid-forties it was not good for his health or his sanity. Decades ago, when he envisioned making millions, he did not foresee working with drug dealers, gangsters, and thugs forever, and recently things had gotten even worse. These days a rap artist without a couple of felonies or bullet wounds to his credit wasn't even marketable. He craved a more dig-nified life producing films, traveling between the States and a hill-side villa in the South of France that he planned to buy, and simply enjoying the finer things in life. He'd say good-bye to all of the lame chicken heads with bad grammar and worse weaves, and the stupid, ignorant gangbangers, and spend his time with a real lady, like Gillian, someone with class. He loved the regal way she carried herself, and how she never seemed affected or impressed by wealth. In other words, his Bentley didn't cause her tongue to hang from her mouth and saliva to drool from its corners. Unlike most women he met, she wasn't a gold digger. She was perfect for him; she looked good on his arm, she was well educated—Brown University, no less—and he could apply his star-building skills to make her the next award-winning superstar actress. They'd be the perfect power couple.

Meanwhile, back in her hotel suite Imelda slipped half an Am-bien into Stephan's tonic water and slipped herself into a Swarovski crystal–covered cocktail dress and matching sling-backs, before scur-rying to the hotel's loading dock. She'd bribed one of the managers to allow her driver to pick her up in the back of the hotel, so that she could then be chauffeured around to the front, where she'd make her grand entrance stepping out of the limo in front of the star-studded gathering. Her brilliant plan could be ruined if anyone happened to see her hovering around the loading dock before taking a limo to the other side of the hotel. What a desperate loser she'd look like!

While her mother was concocting her scheme, Gillian was strongly considering not going to the party at all. She could tell from the look of glee in Imelda's eyes when she said that Brandon had invited her that there was sure to be drama involved. After the phone call Imelda rushed through dinner, anxious to get back to the hotel to dress for the party. At first Gillian couldn't figure out why her mother would be so excited about going to a record-industry hip-hop party, but it didn't take long for her to come to the conclusion that it was related to Imelda's favorite accessory: green cash money. Knowing Imelda, she realized that there would be en-tertainment executives there, both black and white, who were flush with cash. But what about her fiancé? And whatever had happened to her husband?

Gillian's cell phone rang. "Hello?"

"Hey, babe, it's me."

"Hi, Brandon."

"Just wanted to make sure you got my message earlier."

"Yes, I did."

"Also, I'm sending Charles for you. He'll be downstairs in an hour."

Gillian didn't reply; she was still considering whether she wanted to go or not.

"Also, William's coming, and he wants to spend some time get-ting to know you better, now that we've gotten the film fully funded." He let the last few words sink in.

When they did, Gillian jumped up from the couch. "Did you say that you got the film funded?" Miss Calm, Cool, and Unaffected was now affected. It was one thing to have a film in development, where most died a slow death, but quite another to have it funded for production.

"Absolutely, and you're gonna be the star. So get here within the hour and we'll open a bottle of champagne."

She plopped back down onto the couch, dumbstruck. "I can't believe it."

"Don't forget to really work the red carpet. You are about to be a big star. I'll instruct our publicist to make sure that you get plenty of coverage from *Access Hollywood*, *Extra*, and the print media."

"No problem with that."

"Cool. Oh, by the way, your mom sounds great."

"She's a piece of work."

"I can't wait to meet her. Gotta run."

Gillian hung up the phone in a daze. She had become so accustomed to disappointment that even after meeting the famed producer and hearing Brandon talk about the film nonstop, she never really expected that it would happen. The good news vanquished all thoughts of her mother.

Thankful that Paulette wasn't there to give her the third degree, Gillian slipped into a tangerine-colored Roberto Cavalli cocktail dress, bronze mules, a stunning Ethos Art Collection necklace, and long chandelier earrings that brushed her perfectly sculptured shoulders seductively, preparing for her own grand entrance. She practically skipped down to the lobby, where Charles stood ready to open the door for her to climb into the black Bentley. Maybach, Bentley, it didn't matter—he could have sent a horse and carriage and she would have been just as happy. Finally, she was on the verge of starting her film career.

The red carpet in front of the Four Seasons was a swarm of press, handlers, partygoers, and onlookers waiting to catch a glimpse of the next celebrity to make an appearance. So far they'd feasted their eyes on Jay-Z, Beyoncé, Denzel, Kanye West, 50 Cent, and Terrence Howard, and were salivating for the next boldface name. When the black Bentley pulled up, every head turned to see who would step out of it. Dutifully Charles hopped out, dressed in his formal uniform, replete with black cap, and opened the door as though Gillian were the Queen Mum. Ever elegant and in control, Gillian set one smooth, long leg on the pavement, followed by the other, until all five feet and ten inches of her stood up in total splendor. Aside from being gorgeous, her look was so un-L.A., so non-fake-boob-wearing and light-skin obsessed, that she was literally a breath of fresh air, causing a pause from those gathered.

Brandon's publicist, CoAnne Wilshire, rushed to her side bearing a clipboard and a fake smile. After a brief introduction she ushered Gillian to the red carpet, where camera flashes immediately burst in the night like fireflies. Gillian could hear a chorus of:

"Who is that?"

"She's gorgeous, but who is she?"

"She looks familiar; was she in the last Rainforest film?"

Everyone played the Gillian guessing game, which was just what Brandon wanted to accomplish. As cameras continued to flash, Gillian handled the red carpet like a seasoned pro, gliding along without stopping to pose for every available cameraman, as many an aspiring actress would be tasteless enough to do. The trick was always to appear unaffected. Toward the end, CoAnne guided her to Shaun Robinson from *Access Hollywood* for an on-camera interview.

"Gillian, you look amazing. I guess L.A. agrees with you." Shaun flashed a bright Hollywood smile and put the microphone to Gillian's face.

"I've always loved L.A.," she lied fluidly.

"I caught you on Broadway a couple of years ago and you were great. What are you working on now?" This was also a well-executed lie; Shaun had simply read the notes provide by CoAnne, realizing it was best to appear to know the beautiful creature in front of her, even though she'd never laid eyes on her before in her life. She had been in the business long enough to know a comer when she saw one.

"Thank you . . ." But before Gillian could answer the question posed, she caught a blur of crystal and platinum moving toward her at a swift clip. She turned to see what the moving galaxy was, and there stood Imelda, already hovering over Shaun's microphone and wearing a smile as bright as her garb.

"My daughter is in L.A. to star in a new film by William Rutherford and Brandon Russell. Oh, by the way, I'm Gillian's mother, Imelda von Glich." She gave Shaun an unexpected kiss on each cheek, as though they were long-lost friends, while Gillian silently fumed.

"Mother, why don't we get inside," Gillian said, managing a tight smile. When she felt her mother hesitate, she latched on to Imelda's elbow and firmly guided her away, stopping only for a moment to say to Shaun, "Let's catch up soon."

After they were off the red carpet, Gillian demanded in a harsh whisper, "Mom, what the hell are you doing?" Imelda *would* wait to appear until it was time for Gillian's close-up. She was truly insufferable.

Imelda stuck her nose in the air arrogantly. "I was only trying to help."

The rest of the night proceeded downhill fast. After they joined Brandon, who was holding court in the VIP area, Imelda flirted with him shamelessly before latching on to Samuel Becks, the chairman of UTI Entertainment, a multimedia conglomerate. He was an old, gray, but distinguished-looking and filthy-rich man. He was also a legend and titan of the entertainment business, and was there along with many other prominent and wealthy men to show support for Brandon, who was the current golden black boy in the industry. Men and money were everywhere, and Imelda was like a hungry pig in a field full of black truffles; she smelled money all around her, and wasn't quite sure where to dig first.

By the time Gillian caught up to her, the woman was three sheets to the wind and flying high. After much prodding, Gillian managed to coerce her into the ladies' room. Once inside she grabbed Imelda by her forearm and turned her around. "What the hell is wrong with you?"

Indignant, Imelda pulled her arm away and smoothed her dress down over her hips. "I am just fine."

"Mom, you are *drunk*!" Gillian nearly screamed. "And you're hanging all over one man, while some guy you say you're planning to marry is upstairs, and another guy who was supposed to be your husband—the last I heard—is in Europe!" she fumed. "What the hell is going on with you?"

Imelda was a master at ignoring reality, but to hear her life so harshly articulated by her daughter stunned her. Tears began to burn her eyes, and her lips quivered as she fought back emotions that she never bothered to face. "My husband has no money, and neither do I. I have nothing!" she sobbed.

This made no sense to Gillian at all. "But I thought he was a baron or something."

Imelda sucked her teeth and rolled her eyes, pouting. "Yeah, but a very broke one. It would be my luck. All the man has is a title, a big, cold castle, and a bunch of land. You can't exactly go shopping on the Champs-Elysées with that, now, can you?" she snipped.

"So, you're divorcing him for that?" Gillian couldn't believe her ears. It was one thing to be a gold digger, but to be so callous was another.

"What better reason?" Her tears had dried up, and Imelda became as serious as a heart attack.

"But I thought you loved him," Gillian naively said.

Imelda fixed her with steady, cold eyes and said, "What's love got to do with it?"

TWENTY

"Mommy, why don't you live here with me and Daddy anymore?" Rowe looked at Reese with big, round, quizzical eyes and a pout on his upturned face. He was a cute but precocious little boy. Reese sighed, tired of having to answer this same question during each visit. Her attorney, Justin Brookes, a colleague of Max's, had insisted that she maintain a regular visitation schedule whether she wanted to or not. It was important that she begin establishing a track record as a good mother.

"I told you, Mommy and Daddy are not together anymore," Reese said in a barely patient tone. "But I'm still your mommy, and we'll see each other all the time." Rowe's three-year-old's attention span had already latched on to something of greater interest. He was happily pulling things out of Reese's bag while Reese sat nearby, distracted by thoughts of her recent bank statement. Rowe struck pay dirt upon finding a tube of MAC lipstick, and prepared to make a magenta mess on the cream-colored carpet.

"Rowe, you're not to play with Mommy's things. Where is your paint set? You can paint in your playroom, but not in here."

"But I like *this* paint," the child whined, putting a death grip on the tube of lipstick. When she took it away from him he folded his arms firmly across his little chest and stamped angrily on the floor.

"This is for adults, not kids." On some level Reese did love her son; however, she'd just never managed to truly bond with him, mainly because his birth began as a means to financial end.

"But I waaaannnnttt iiiit," Rowe whined, as he began stamping his feet adamantly in place. The child was becoming increasingly spoiled, due to the fact that his mother ignored him, his father was never home, and his nanny thought her job was to comfort and entertain him, rather than instill discipline. Having his grandmother around hadn't helped the situation; her solution to everything was another home-baked cookie.

"What did I say?" Reese asked sternly. *The little tyrant*, Reese thought. When she was a kid a fit like this would have been brought to a swift resolution with the help of a well-worn belt, but these days you could barely raise your voice at your own child without the risk of being reported to the authorities.

"I don't care what you said! You're mean! And you're not my mommy anymore anyway." Rowe stuck his tongue out at her defiantly. "I have a new mommy now."

Reese was about to snatch the little brat up by his collar and call out for his nanny, until she realized what the child had said. "You have a new mommy?" she repeated, her unwaxed brow furrowed in question.

By now, Rowe had sidetracked his hissy fit, and was sitting on the floor calmly playing with a jigsaw puzzle. "Yes, and she's *very* pretty," Rowe said without looking up.

Reese calmed herself down and clasped her hands together, stemming the nearly irresistible urge to wrap them around the boy's neck. "What's your new mommy's name?" She'd known it was only a matter of time before Chris would have some hoochie up in there, but so soon? She wouldn't admit it—even to herself—

but some part of her was still in denial, and was sure that Chris would come back to his senses, and realize that he still loved her madly and couldn't possibly live without her. It was irrelevant that she didn't want him; this was a matter only of ego and her own selfish principles. *She* should be the one to end it, not him.

Rowe looked up, leveling a steady gaze, wanting to witness his mother's reaction. "Auntie Kira." Even at his tender age, Rowe instinctively knew that what he said would punish his mother, but he had no idea the impact of the bombshell he'd lobbed her way.

Reese's face froze in shock, and her mind reeled back to her sordid deal with the devil, and how the horn-wearing bitch had disappeared like Casper the Friendly Ghost after the shit hit the fan. Heat rose through her body like vinegar separating from oil. Her anger started from the very core of her being, and steamed upward and out. *The nerve of that fucking slut-bitch!* No wonder the whore hadn't bothered returning her calls; she'd been too busy getting in position to stick the knife farther into her back.

Calm down, she told herself. She had to get more information. "Does your new mommy live here?" she nonchalantly inquired. By now Rowe was over the fleeting excitement of delivering bad news and was back to his puzzle, trying to fit a square-shaped piece into a round hole.

"She just visits, like you," Rowe said, smiling sweetly, but devilishly.

She left him in the living room and charged into the library, making a beeline for Chris's cabinet, where he kept his bills. Reese began rummaging through the files with an obsessive vengeance. She cursed and flipped folders until she came across the one she wanted, a file containing his cell phone records. Starting with the most recent one, she scanned the log with a chipped nail until she came across the familiar numbers she'd called to contact Kira herself. "That bitch!" she screamed. She cursed herself for not continuing to try reaching Kira, but after her life hit the skids, she'd become most preoccupied with figuring out how to survive, and easily assumed that their plan hadn't worked and Kira had just gotten busy. She was right on that account: The backstabbing hussy had gotten busy, all right—busy stealing her husband. She may have hired Kira to fuck him, but that certainly didn't give her leeway to be his damned girlfriend!

She stuffed the bill into her back pocket and snatched up the phone, frantically pounding out Kira's phone number.

"Hello?" Kira answered on the fifth ring, sounding like she'd just woken from a dead sleep, or, more likely in her case, she'd just rolled over from a good romp in the sack.

"Wake the fuck up, bitch," Reese spit.

"Who the hell is this?"

"The woman whose husband you stole. Though I'm sure that where a whore like you is concerned, that's not much of a distinction; it only makes me one of many." She'd always heard that Kira was a guiltless barracuda, but she never imagined that the woman would bare her fangs at her.

"Oh, it's you."

"You damned right it's me, and I want you to stay away from my husband."

"The last time we spoke you wanted to pay me to fuck him, so why don't you make up your mind? Which is it?"

Reese's nostrils flared in anger. "You don't know who you're fucking with, Kira. I'll kick your sorry yellow ass." The south Bronx surfaced, smothering years of social exfoliation.

"Listen, Reese, you need to chill. If you hadn't been so damned greedy this never would have happened. You asked for it; now you deal with it."

"You fuckin' bitch—" Before she could finish the sentence, the phone was snatched from her hand.

Reese spun around to find Chris standing behind her, pissed off and ready to spit hollow-points.

"I should have known you were fucking around with that slut!"

Chris put the phone back on the receiver. "It takes one to know one." He turned to leave.

She silently prayed that Kira hadn't told Chris all about their scheme to trap him in bed with her. That would only make her settlement discussions with him that much harder. Maybe she had only told him about her affair with Shaun. Reese ran around him, blocking his exit. "What did she tell you?" she demanded.

"Everything." He folded his arms across his chest, ready to stand his ground and fight if she wanted to go there. "Now, if you'll excuse me, I need to get back to my son."

"She's lying."

"How would you know what she was lying about if you weren't involved in anything?" he asked.

Frustrated and caught, she passed him, blew into the family room, snatched up her purse, and was out the door, not even bothering to say good-bye to Rowe, who looked after her questioningly.

The minute she got into Paulette's new Mercedes, which she'd borrowed, she pulled her cell phone from her purse and dialed her friend's number. "That bitch is sleeping with my husband," she said without a greeting or preamble.

"Which bitch?"

Reese slammed her fist down hard on the steering wheel. "Kira! She and Chris are fucking."

"I don't know why you're surprised. You set it up, remember?" Paulette let out a long yawn.

Reese stared at the phone, then screamed into it, "I asked her to fuck him, not be his girlfriend, damn it!"

"What did you really expect? The girl's a gold digger." Even Paulette grasped the irony of calling someone else that term, but she also knew that, like bitches—as in dogs—gold diggers came in all shapes, sizes, and pedigrees, and she considered herself head and shoulders above the rest.

Reese sighed heavily. The whole world seemed to have turned against her. "It's just fucked-up."

A click sounded on the phone. "Hold on, Reese; that's my other line."

While Paulette took the call, Reese sat dejectedly, going over the log of calls on Chris's bill, torturing herself as she noted how often Chris and Kira had spoken on the phone during the days before and after D-day. As she sat lamenting the situation her eyes fell upon another familiar set of numbers. She blinked, sure that she was seeing things. When she opened them, sure enough another other ten digits on Chris's cell phone log were familiar. They belonged to Shaun, her lover!

Her heart lurched in her chest. Not only did they talk regularly, but there was a call made from Shaun to Chris on that fateful night they were together at the Four Seasons. Her face flushed with anger. Not only had Chris played her where Kira was concerned, but the sneaky bastard had set her up with Shaun. In her anger another possibility bubbled to the surface: Maybe Chris *and* Kira set her up. After all, Kira was in town and at the party when Shaun mysteriously appeared. She felt like such a fool! Their plan had worked brilliantly, while hers had fallen apart at the seams.

"Sorry about that." Paulette was back on the phone. "Reese, are you there?"

In a monotone she said, "You're not going to believe this." Reese sat there slowly shaking her head.

"What now?"

"It's Shaun."

"What, is Kira fucking him, too?"

Reese rolled her eyes. "Maybe."

"What are you talking about?" Paulette was sounding impatient.

"Chris and Shaun."

"What? Is Chris fucking Shaun?"

"No, but they both fucked me."

"I know that; now, what's the big deal?"

Reese exhaled, exasperated. "Chris, and probably Kira, set me up with Shaun. Chris and Shaun are boys! I'm looking at the phone records!" she yelled.

"You're kidding! Wow!"

"That dirty, low-down muthafucker!"

"Which one?"

"Both of them. No, all of them! That's fucked-up."

"Yeah, it's exactly what you were planning; he just beat you to it."

"Hey, whose side are you on?"

"Don't even go there. Remember, I'm the one who's letting you sleep at her place, has hired an attorney for you, and has your back in the press."

"Speaking of attorneys, we need to call Justin. Since Chris is fucking around with Kira, maybe it could help my case." Her attorney had been in contact with Chris's lawyers, and so far they were still playing hardball, protesting any financial settlement at all since Reese had broken the marital vows, and Chris was seeking full custody of Rowe. Under the original tenets of the prenup she would have been entitled to $2 million, plus child support. That sum had seemed piddling a couple of months ago, but at this point she would have welcomed every penny of it.

"That may not be a good thing," Paulette cautioned. "Chris filed a legal separation, so it won't matter who he's sleeping with now, unless you can prove he did it before you split up. Besides, if you drag Kira into court and she testifies that you plotted with her to set him up, it could hurt you more than it hurts him."

"You're right, but we've gotta do something. What about press?" Reese was biting her chipped fingernails, something she would never have done months ago.

"You have to trust me, Reese. The one thing that I know from being in this business for the last six years is that everybody's got a skeleton or two buried somewhere, so I've got a private investigator digging around. Once we find something, then I'll start the press campaign. We will need public opinion moving toward your side in order to get Chris to settle out of court. He can't afford to have skeletons walking around, not with all of those lucrative sponsorship contracts he has on the table. All we have to do is a little digging, strike gold, and then you'll get paid."

And then you can get the hell out of my house, Paulette thought to herself.

TWENTY-ONE

"Oh, baby. That's sooooo goooood," Paulette panted and hissed. Forget Halle; Paulette's performances were truly Oscar-worthy. "Omigod, omigoooood. That hurts soooooo good. You've got the best dick eveeeer," she lied.

Max had no sexual technique whatsoever, and couldn't find a clitoris with the help of a global positioning satellite system. The saving grace was that usually the whole bumbling act was over within a few minutes, at which time he'd roll over heavily, as if he'd slain a fire-breathing dragon. But Paulette was so in love that he could have come at her waving a limp noodle, and she'd have happily spread her legs and faked a climax. To Paulette, Max represented social redemption for her and her mother. He was the one who got away—from June, and from Paulette.

He pushed and poked around on top of her, with his head buried deeply in her cavernous cleavage, emitting grunts of effort here and there. For all of the intimacy on his part, Paulette could have been a mail-order blowup doll. After another few minutes of thrashing about, he stiffened like a seizure victim, cocked his head way back, and came. Paulette didn't remember the last time *she'd* had an orgasm, and Max never bothered to inquire whether she did or not.

He rolled off her onto his back, his arms splayed at his sides.

"That was wonderful, baby." Paulette continued lying like a Persian rug.

He patted her thigh in response, the way one might an eager and obedient puppy. The thing he liked best about Paulette was how little effort it took to make her purr like a kitten.

With Lauren he never felt as if she were ever satisfied, in or out of bed. Aside from her looks, his wife's money and social position were what attracted him to her to begin with, yet they were also the things he resented day to day. Though he and Paulette man-aged to heist a good deal of the Baines fortune by forging the will, that *je ne sais quoi* that rich people wore like a cloak couldn't be confiscated; borrowed, or imitated.

"What are you thinking about?" Paulette asked, snuggling closer to him, clearly craving postcoital intimacy.

He hated when women asked that question of him, especially after sex. It was obvious that they wanted to hear that he was thinking about them, which was rarely the case. In fact, with Paulette, it was *never* the case.

He sometimes wondered why he had ever even started the affair with her to begin with, though he knew the answer. The psycholog-ical explanation involved typical passive-aggressive behavior. By fucking Lauren's cousin, he could get back at his wife without having to confront her or his own deeply rooted issues with her. He could bring her down a peg or two and make himself feel better— mentally and physically—in the process. So, as much as Paulette de-spised being Lauren's cousin, it was really the only thing that she had going for her, as far as he was concerned. And of course, the purely physical reason was that magical thing that she did with her vagina.

She nudged him to get his attention. He was daydreaming,

about her, she hoped. "A penny for your thoughts." She snuggled even closer.

She was so needy, he thought. Max had a barely contained urge to push her away from him, dress in a hurry, and bolt out the door. And it was probably time that he did just that. They'd gotten the money, had a little fun, and now it was time to call it a day. "You wanna know what I'm really thinking?" he asked, summoning up his courage. Enough was enough. It was time to end this before someone got hurt.

She smiled, but it looked more like a pained grimace. "Of course I do."

He rolled onto his side to face her. "I was thinking about the future." He was running his it's-not-you-it's-me speech through his head.

The prospect that he was thinking about *their* future increased the show of Paulette's teeth as her lips spread across her mouth; then she turned to face him, too. "That's exactly what I've been thinking about," she interrupted. "We've been seeing each other for a while now, and we're great together." She rolled over onto her back and gazed toward the ceiling. "And I've been thinking: What could possibly make our relationship even better?"

"That's what I want to talk about, our relationship." There was no easy way to do this; he just had to say it. "It's not going anywhere."

"You're right, and I want to change that. In fact, I have something to tell you that will." She sat up in bed, excitement hanging over her like a halo.

The conversation wasn't going exactly the way Max had hoped. She seemed to cling to some far-fetched fantasy that they'd live happily ever after. It was definitely time to bail out. "Listen, Paulette—"

She couldn't hold it anymore. "Max, I'm pregnant!"

The muscles in his face went slack, and his mouth hung open like a Venus flytrap.

She badly misread his shocked expression. "I know; I was surprised, too! But isn't this great?" she shrieked.

Max felt trapped in an underwater bubble. He could see Paulette's mouth moving, but couldn't hear the words that were coming out of it. A stream of drool reminded him to close his own mouth. "This can't be," he finally managed to say. He wore a rubber religiously; in fact, he kept a stash in her nightstand.

Paulette must have been locked her own bubble, because she seemed to hear nothing he was really saying, only what her fantasy required of him. "I don't know how it happened," she lied. "You know we always use protection." She gestured over to the nightstand, which contained the box of condoms. The problem wasn't a lack of condoms, but the little pinprick she'd used to "prep" them before he even arrived. Since Paulette always slid the contraceptive on for him after reaching into the nightstand and pretending to tear open a new package, he was never the wiser. After sex she'd gently remove the condom and head into the bathroom to clean up, but not until she locked the door and lay in the tub on her back with her legs up against the wall, where she'd then squeeze the remaining contents into her sex.

The bubble finally burst, propelling Max up. "Paulette, you don't understand. This can't happen."

Paulette shook her head, still ignoring the words that came from his mouth. "Oh, yes, it *can*. I'm three months pregnant."

He grabbed her shoulders. "There can be no baby."

Paulette looked at him as though she'd been physically slapped. "What do you mean, there can be no baby? We *are* having a baby."

"First of all, there is no 'we,' " he said sternly. He could see that kid gloves weren't going to work here.

Now her face really cracked. Her daydream was shattering into pieces right before her eyes. "What are you talking about? We're getting married."

He'd heard enough. Max got up and pulled on his underwear,

pants, shirt, and shoes as rapidly as possible. "You're crazy! I never said that we were getting married, and I certainly never wanted to have a baby."

"But you did." Having a baby was all he ever talked about.

"Yeah, but with Lauren!"

"That selfish bitch! Why her? Why does everyone love her?" Paulette sobbed.

She was up, chasing him across the room, clutching at his shirt. He pushed her aside, rushing out of the bedroom. Paulette ran after him. Before he reached the door she slipped to the ground, but continued grabbing at the hem of his pants. On her knees, she begged. "Why Lauren? Why not me?" Tears ran down her face, chin, and neck, and streamed into the crevice between her huge breasts.

When the door slammed shut, Paulette remained crumpled in a sobbing heap on the floor. This was not how she had envisioned the happy scene that would play out when she told Max the blessed news. In her version he held her and praised her for giving him what he wanted most—a child. They were supposed to grow closer, more and more in love every day, but something had gone horribly wrong; he obviously hadn't read the same script.

Time passed, and she had no idea how long she lay there, wallowing in her sorrow, but sometime later the door opened and she rose to her knees, her arms outstretched. "Max, you're back. I knew you'd come back."

But it was Reese, who was supposed to be with Rowe all day, who walked through the door. "What happened to you?" She stared at Paulette as though she'd grown two heads since that morning. "You look like shit!"

Paulette crumbled back to the floor, deflated and emotionally wasted. "He's gone," she cried.

Reese knelt beside her. "It's okay; he's just a man." Hell, she had problems too, but you wouldn't see her bawling just because a man left her—only when he took his money with him.

"It's easy for you to say. Look at you. You can always get another man. It's not so easy for someone like me." She began sobbing uncontrollably. Paulette had never articulated those feelings out loud, so it was devastating to confront the demons that normally lurked quietly within her subconscious. Though Paulette had assumed that money and the power that usually came with it would make her happy, she was beginning to realize that her issues ran much deeper.

That was the saddest thing Reese had ever heard. How must it feel not to be beautiful? she wondered. "Paulette, we'll get you all fixed up, and you'll have men lined up at your door," she lied.

"That's not all." Paulette took a deep breath. "I'm pregnant. I'm having Max's baby."

Reese raised her brows and stood up. "Now, that's just plain stupid." She walked out of the room, leaving Paulette alone.

Book
Three

TWENTY-TWO

Max surreptitiously watched Lauren apply a coat of lipstick at the vanity in her boudoir, while he stood across the room, dressing for a dinner meeting with a new client. While Lauren slept soundly beside him, he'd barely closed his eyes the previous night, tormented as he was by Paulette's deranged plan to have a baby—his baby! He'd tossed and turned like a trout caught on a line, cursing the day he'd let himself be hooked by Paulette. For him, their relationship began as a tantalizing flirtation—fodder for the sexual imagination, not a consciously planned affair.

One weekend Paulette "happened" to stop by while Lauren was on Martha's Vineyard. She wasted no time baiting him, and before he could say "slut" she had him spread-eagled, flat on his back, with his penis at full mast. She took him in with a vacuumlike suction, wrapping him in her tight, warm, wet cocoon. Then the most amazing thing happened: On the upstroke her sex literally snapped his penis, causing the most amazing sensation experienced by man! The pleasure was so intense he nearly passed out as she worked her magic over and over again, driving him nearly insane. At the moment of climax he felt a jolt of electricity surge through him like a cattle prod.

Until then, as far as he was concerned, the snapper was pure legend, like the Loch Ness Monster: No one he knew had ever actually encountered one. At first he thought there was witchcraft involved, or black magic in them thar' lips, but he later learned that there was a perfectly reasonable and purely anatomical explanation for the snapping action. A small, infinitesimal percentage of women had cervices positioned at such an angle that the penis moved over its ledge and back during sex, resulting in an intense snapping sensation; therefore, the snapping pussy was not some special paranormal hat trick, but actually a physical deformity. In any regard, now he perfectly understood the concept of being pussy-whipped; even though he hated Paulette at the moment, and had never really liked her to begin with, he still felt an unwelcome craving for her magical snapping cervix. He wished to God that he'd never had the pleasure. That Venus flytrap was like a dangerous drug—crack cocaine, one hit and you were an addict. After taking the plunge, he found himself unable to extricate himself, no matter how much he disliked her brash personality or her tacky ways.

He shook his head, a vaguely defeatist gesture, wanting to erase from his mind—and loins—the muscle memory associated with Paulette's snapping pussy. Of all people, why did Paulette, Lauren's cousin, have to be one of the few women on earth who actually possessed one?

Weekly rounds of sex with Lauren had continued after the affair initially began, though it became more of a chore for them both, not much different from doing laundry. They'd never had explosive chemistry to begin with, but sadly his affair with Paulette—or more accurately put, her pussy—extinguished any flicker that might have ever existed.

As Lauren blotted her lips, evening the coat of color, he suddenly noticed that something was very different about his wife. A sparkle glimmered seductively in her eyes as she leaned toward the mirror to stroke a touch of mascara through her lashes. He was sure that she'd be humming a happy tune if it were not for his presence. Lauren was literally glowing. Knowing that it wasn't the result of anything *he'd* done, he felt a desperate need to get to the bottom of it.

With his chin held high, Max straightened his tie, attempting to appear nonchalant. "Where are you off to?" he asked.

"A gallery opening downtown," she answered. Her focus never wavered from her own image in the mirror.

She was meeting Gideon at a SoHo gallery that was premiering his latest collection of black-and-whites. Since her visit to his loft, they'd met for lunch twice and talked on the phone nearly every day. She thought of him often, sometimes lying awake fantasizing that he lay next to her, instead of the insensitive log who did. After their last lunch he'd kissed her on the cheek, and she had still felt the touch of his lips hours later.

Max watched her, riveted, waiting for her to inquire about his plans for the night. When she didn't, he frowned and offered, "I'm meeting a new client for dinner at Cipriani."

"That's nice." She took one last appraising look at herself in the mirror, condoned what she saw, and headed for the door. "See you later." She didn't even look back!

There was a time—not so long ago—when she would have tried to engage him, all but begging to know where, with whom, and at what precise time he was doing what, but now she didn't really seem to give a damn.

Puzzled, he watched her stroll out of the bedroom door. There was something intrinsically different about her recently that had dissolved the impenetrable cloak of sadness that had become her fixture. Lauren's newfound happiness troubled him deeply. At least when she was unhappy he could rest assured that it *was* because of him, which affirmed his sense of power and control.

Due to a pathetic combination of ignorance and arrogance, his narrow mind refused to accept the most obvious explanation for the pep in her step. He simply could not imagine his pure, beautiful, blue-blood wife engaging in a torrid love affair with another man, not when she had him. After all, affairs were messy endeavors, and this unfortunate business with Paulette was certainly proof of that.

His thoughts bounced like a bungee cord back to his most pressing female concern: Paulette was pregnant with his child! He felt like one of those dense, brainless athletes who carelessly spread their sperm around, oblivious to the fact that his seed was the equivalent of liquid gold, a substance readily mined by swarms of well-trained gold diggers. He'd always shaken his head knowingly when hearing the woeful tale of yet another baby mama using her spawn to extort money from an unsuspecting man who'd been driven to despair by the smaller of his two heads. Now he was the idiot with no control of his own dick.

As savvy as he perceived himself to be, he couldn't fathom how this could have happened; after all, he'd *always* worn a condom. The more pressing matter at the moment was figuring out how to get out of this mess unscathed. Though he and Lauren's relationship was barely functioning, he had no intention of letting her go just yet, even if she couldn't bear his child. Her family's clout was invaluable, opening important doors in both finance and politics. He had to make this situation go away, but he also knew that Paulette would never go for the solution that suited him best. She had waved the news of her pregnancy at him like a homeless drunk with a winning lottery ticket, so there was no chance in hell that she'd ever have an abortion. More drastic measures were definitely in order.

Before Lauren made it out the front door, the phone rang; she stopped and picked up the receiver in the foyer. "Hello?"

"Hey, girl." It was Paulette, whom she hadn't heard from in months.

Max tiptoed out the bedroom, down the hall to the top of the stairs, listening carefully, hoping to get a clue to the new Lauren. He felt silly—girlish, really—eavesdropping on his wife. It was a strange role reversal; she was usually the one trying to figure out what he was up to.

"Hi, Paulette, stranger! I haven't heard from you in forever," Lauren chirped. "What's going on?"

Max's ears really perked up when he heard Lauren say Paulette's name; then his blood cooled quickly as fear flowed through his veins, freezing him on the spot. Was Paulette crazy and cruel enough to tell Lauren about their affair, and her pregnancy? Oddly, he'd never feared being caught before, knowing that he'd vehemently deny an affair even if his penis were caught trapped in the pussy, but a child was living, breathing proof, a form of physical DNA evidence that was irrefutable.

"I won't hold you, but I've got good news." Paulette sounded elated about whatever it was.

"Well, don't keep me in suspense; tell me your news." Lauren set her purse on the table, waiting.

Max felt the muscles around his heart seize as he held his breath.

"I'm having a baby!" Paulette blurted out. Her tone was understandably exuberant, but with a tinge of malice. Beneath her joyous words she taunted, *I'm having a baby, and you're not,* and buried more deeply between them was the evil satisfaction she felt for having Lauren's husband's child, the one thing Lauren had been unable to do.

"A baby!?" Lauren was shocked, since Paulette hadn't even mentioned a boyfriend to her in well over a year.

Assuming that Paulette had told Lauren everything, Max felt his heart pound ferociously in his chest. His first instinct was to rush down the stairs to defend himself.

"Yes, a baby."

Paulette was obviously thrilled, so, regardless of the circumstances, Lauren was too. "I'm happy for you, if that's what you want."

Max was on the first stair step when he suddenly froze in place, puzzled. This certainly wasn't the response to be expected from a woman being told that her husband was having a baby—especially by her cousin.

"So, who's the lucky guy?"

"He's an old friend," was all Paulette said. "I'll tell you more about him later."

"Well, we have to get together to celebrate! I've got a great idea! I'll have a baby shower and invite the girls. How many months are you?"

Paulette frowned at the phone. This wasn't nearly as much fun as she'd thought it would be. She'd imagined her cousin being choked up with jealousy because she was having a baby when apparently Lauren couldn't, rather than gleefully planning a party to celebrate. She was tempted to really get her attention by dropping the other shoe and telling her who the father was, but that would be premature. First she had to help Max come to his senses, and then they'd tell her—and the rest of the world—together, as a couple. "Just short of four months," she said.

"We should do it next month in L.A. and make a girls' weekend of it!" Lauren said. This was sounding like a really good idea. "We haven't gotten together since Gillian left for L.A." Plus she needed a good reason to get away from Max, to rethink her own life.

"S-s-sure, that sounds good."

"Great! I'll start planning it and be in touch with the details."

"Thanks, Lauren. I really appreciate that." The wind seemed to have escaped Paulette's sails. Why was Lauren so happy, anyway? Paulette liked talking to her much more when she was sad and depressed.

"Gotta, go. Congratulations!" Lauren hung up the phone even

happier than she was before picking it up. Though her mother was still livid at Paulette, and convinced that she had somehow hijacked the will, Lauren couldn't care less about any of it. She had enough money from her trust funds to last her a lifetime, so what was another few million? She grabbed her bag and dashed out the door.

Only after he heard her exit did Max finally move a muscle. He felt as if he'd stumbled into the twilight zone; nothing made sense to him. He had an illegitimate baby on the way, thanks to his wife's cousin's snapping pussy, and his normally docile and melancholic wife was suddenly happy and infused with life, and he had no idea why. He had to do something, so he decided to deal with Lauren first, and he'd take care of Paulette later.

Feeling a little more empowered, he marched purposefully into Lauren's boudoir and carefully went through every drawer there. He was obsessed with finding out why she was suddenly so happy. After fifteen minutes of searching through sweaters, underwear, toiletries, and scarves, he was about ready to give up, when he opened a jewelry case that was stuffed in the back of a drawer that was filled with socks. Inside there was a pouch, and inside the pouch was a package that contained quite a few little white and green pills. A prescription label was on the package, and he noted that the date was current.

He may have been stumbling around blindly in the dark up until now, but one thing was blatantly clear to him: These weren't barbiturates, uppers, downers, sleeping pills, or Ecstasy. No, they were something much more alarming. All this time, while he and Mildred waited with bated breath for his wife to produce an heir, Lauren had still been taking fucking birth control pills!

He crumpled to the floor, feeling like the biggest loser in the world. His own wife didn't want to have his baby, and yet he had a delusional, near-psycho bitch ready to give birth, whether he wanted it or not. Something had to be done about all of this.

He only had to figure out what.

TWENTY-THREE

When Brandon began preproduction on *Gold Diggers* he offered Gillian the choice of an apartment or a wing in his palatial estate.

"We can get you a place tomorrow, but you don't need the stress of finding, furnishing, and settling into an apartment, or buying a car. You've got to prepare for this role in record time. Here you can have your own suite of rooms, complete with servants and a driver," he'd argued. Feeling her apprehension, he added, "I'm suggesting this to protect my investment; I can't have the lead actress in my film stressed out, and not at her best."

"As long as you realize this is a business move, not a personal one," she insisted.

"You know I respect you too much to assume that."

The timing couldn't have been better. Even though Paulette spent a lot of time in New York, their living arrangement had run its course.

Lately Paulette had become as unpredictable as an unmedicated schizophrenic. And, of course, the surge of hormones from her pregnancy didn't help matters. One week she was totally supportive, and the next she was bitching about how long it was taking for Gillian to get out of her apartment. After her inheritance, Gillian thought she'd calm down, that the money would take the pressure off. Instead, it had made Paulette even more volatile. A part of her believed that she no longer needed other people—especially her friends—now that she had money.

It had always riled Paulette that Reese, Lauren, and Gillian all had more going for them than she did, whether it was money, looks, or class. Now that she had been redeemed by the great equalizer—cold, hard cash—she felt that putting them in their place was her just due. The way Paulette saw it, they were now all losers.

Even with her highfalutin, glob-trotting mother, Gillian—Miss Untouchable—had been trawling around L.A. just like a gazillion wannabes, with no money or connections. She didn't even have a place to live! And Reese, who had been the queen diva, with her rich, famous husband, long, pretty hair, and unlimited funds, really fell hard. Paulette had Reese's future in her hands, from the next meal she ate to the very roof over her head.

And then there was Lauren. Every time Miss High and Mighty's husband came, it was Lauren's face that Paulette saw behind her closed eyelids. The secret pleasure she got from hurting Lauren was much more intense than any orgasm Max could ever give her. Seeing the mighty fall was a healing salve that superficially soothed Paulette's open wounds.

So, when Gillian told her that she was moving in with Brandon, Paulette's anger was visceral. Gillian was about to be taken care of by a wealthy, eligible celebrity who seemed to worship her. Paulette had *enjoyed* seeing Gillian close to being broken, both financially and spiritually. Whenever she would insist that Gillian find her own place, knowing that she couldn't afford to, it wasn't because she wanted her to move, only that she wanted to inflict upon her friend a dose of the insecurity and hopelessness that Paulette had felt and nursed for as long as she could remember.

To Paulette's dismay, Gillian's move was proving to be a perfect arrangement. Those long days eating chocolate in sweatpants sprawled out on Paulette's sofa were light-years away as she lay prone and perfectly motionless on a rattan chaise longue near Brandon's Olympic-sized pool soaking up the sun's rays. The California sun warmed the undertones of her smooth, dark skin, and painted golden brown highlights throughout her hair. She was taking a break from studying the *Gold Diggers* screenplay, which she found to be brilliantly witty. The characters were devilishly passionate, and the dialogue crisp and catty. Her role, in particular, was an actress's dream, with excellent character development, well-written lines, and great interaction with the other characters. It was a part that she could really sink her teeth into.

While preparing for her role, Gillian was perfectly at home amid the beauty of Brandon's sprawling Tuscan-style estate. Since Brandon was at the office much more than he was home, she was able to enjoy the beauty and solitude of the elegant house in total privacy while learning her lines and preparing for her debut film role. Calling it a "management account," Brandon also provided Gillian a bank card with a balance that never dropped below four zeros, in addition to leasing her a champagne-colored Porsche Carrera, insisting that his star drive around town only in the very best, when she cared to; otherwise she had carte blanche access to Charles. In other words, Gillian was chillin' in the lap of luxury.

Of course, her mother, who would have happily taken up with Brandon herself, strongly advised Gillian to close the deal with him from the outset, both professionally and personally. In many ways, she schooled, he was the mother lode. The man had money, position, and power, *and* he could help set up Gillian's film career.

"Child, are you crazy? Of course you should move in! I know

women who would kill for that chance." This was not a figurative statement on her part, since this population most likely included her.

After spending two weeks getting on Gillian's nerves, Imelda left L.A., but without her Italian stallion. When they went to check out of the Four Seasons hotel, he deferred payment to her, causing quite a big ruckus, with Imelda doing most of the screaming. Apparently he was under the impression that she was a very rich older woman who needed a companion, or gigolo (the male version of a gold digger), and of course, she thought that he was very rich and wanted her. Imelda was so pissed and insulted that she stormed out of the hotel into their waiting car, where her things—*and his*, including his airline ticket—were already loaded, and took off. She wasn't sure how, or if, he ever got back to Europe.

"Yeah, and there's a name for them." While Gillian had taken to luxury like a baby to a warm bath, something about her new arrangement still gnawed at her. She'd always prided herself on being independent, and turned up her nose at women—like her mother—who would sell their bodies and souls for a set of designer clothes and a sizable bank account. Nonetheless, here she was reclining by the pool of a $20 million estate compete with every known creature comfort, owned by a man who, under any other circumstances, she wouldn't have given the time of day. Sure, Brandon was a nice guy, but certainly not someone who would be the catalyst of a wet dream. Though she hadn't slept with him, they both knew—talent notwithstanding—that this was what it was all about. In other words, she'd traded up from a casting couch to a casting chaise, only surrounded by a mansion.

To emphasis her point, Imelda continued. "You'd better get real; men like that don't come along every day. And remember, its just as easy to love a rich man as it is to love a poor one—and a lot more rewarding!"

"So, I'm supposed to just lie down and open my legs?" Gillian asked rhetorically. The question was really one that she posed to herself. Gillian shuddered to realize how closely she might ultimately resemble the mother she'd always disdained.

"Women lie down and open them for a whole lot less. A lot of these young fools run around giving pussy away like they're passing out flyers." She *hhmmppff*ed. "If I'm giving it away, you'd better believe I'm getting something for it." Imelda was the original black gold digger; she had been mining since way back in the day, when most black women were still figuring out how to perm their hair.

"Which is why you're broke?" Gillian said, the sarcasm dripping heavily. She didn't enjoy twisting the sword that was already planted in her mother's back, but someone had to make the woman take note of reality. In her most recent marriage she'd spent all of her own money prospecting fool's gold. Her grand plans had ended disastrously, and now that she was older, with fewer wares to peddle, she was desperate, perhaps hoping to barter her daughter's assets for the next great dig.

"Miss Tillman, there's a phone call for you. It's Mr. Russell."

Gillian shielded the sun from her eyes, squinting as she reached for the portable phone, turning her thoughts away from her troubled mother. "Hello?"

"How's my girl?" Though he was trying for casual, he sounded tense.

"I'm good. What's up?" He never called her during the day.

Out of the blue he said, "I have a question for you, and its very important. Was anyone else with you when you discovered that you had my suitcase?" His tone was measured and very precise.

This was the second time he'd brought this up. "Just Paulette," she replied.

"Was she ever alone with it?" he asked.

"What's this all about?"

"Gillian, please, just answer the question." He never spoke so firmly with her.

She was about to say no, when she remembered leaving the bag in the living room and going into Paulette's bedroom closet, at her insistence, to find a blouse to wear. "Yeah, but not for long." She also recalled Paulette going through his things, pulling out his designer wear and commenting on each label. For all Gillian knew, after she left the room, maybe Paulette had continued rifling through Brandon's personal effects.

"Damn!" he muttered.

"Brandon . . . Brandon?" He'd already hung up the phone.

TWENTY-FOUR

The moment Gideon made his appearance at the chic downtown art gallery, which was full of New York's coolest aficionados and wannabes, Lauren could feel the heat of his presence; or perhaps she smelled him in that primal, instinctive way that has driven animals to mate throughout eternity. Though her reputation was for being prim and proper, since their lips had first touched weeks ago, Lauren had thought of little other than making love to this man. To hell with Max, who had personally killed any spirit that her mother left unspoiled. As far as she was concerned, whatever happened between her and Gideon was long overdue.

When Gideon looked at Lauren from across the room, her spine tingled deliciously, and when his eyes caressed her from head to toe, turning his lips into a conspiratorial smile, the warm sensation traveled southward. Enjoying the building anticipation, she lifted a glass of chardonnay from a passing waiter and sipped it slowly, savoring the sight of him as he wooed both art critics and collectors alike. His humble confidence was very intoxicating.

"Lauren, darling! It's great to see you!" Lauren snapped back to reality, only to find one of her mother's snotty sorority friends wearing a plastic surgery–altered smile plastered cruelly across her face. It was hard to tell whether the woman was really smiling, or grimacing in extreme pain. Her skin was so tight it looked like a handheld Halloween mask, holding hostage a pair of eyes that darted nervously about, looking for an escape.

It took Lauren a moment to transition from the rapture of lust, past the gruesome sight of this poor woman's desecrated face, to some semblance of proper social etiquette. "Oh, hi, Mrs. Lansing."

"Darling, you look wonderful, but then you always have." The woman tried for a broad, endearing smile, but it was truly a scary sight. She was sipping a cocktail in a tumbler, and it was clearly not her first—or second. She barely managed to stand straight, so her reed-thin frame teetered precariously on a pair of four-inch stilettos.

"Thank you," Lauren managed.

Beth Lansing was an it girl from way back in her day. Though she was long past her prime, the memories were still very fresh in *her* mind. She didn't see the atrocity that haunted her mirror, only the much-desired debutante she once was. More and more of Lauren's mother's friends were having plastic surgery and turning themselves into the walking dread; even Lauren's mother had scheduled her first "touch-up" for next month. This sad by-product of self-obsession affirmed that the direction Lauren's life was traveling in would be littered with shallow corpses hanging on to self-imposed social limbs, a virtual spiritual cemetery.

"What brings you to a downtown art gallery? The Upper East Side is more your speed," Beth said through collagen-impregnated lips. "Do you know Mr. Miller?" She was a bad cross between Lil' Kim and Joan Rivers.

Lauren was not sure how to respond. "Y-yes, I do know his work." She couldn't help but feel guilty, like she'd been caught with her hand in the cookie jar.

"Handsome man, huh?" She struggled to wink one of those frightening eyes, and nudged Lauren's elbow, glancing in Gideon's direction. "A tad dark for my usual taste, but boy, is he sexy."

Lauren brushed off the deeply bred ignorance and concentrated on not getting busted. "I hadn't noticed," she said nonchalantly. She had the unnerving feeling that everyone present could see that she was a married woman who was out to cheat on her husband.

"You'd have to be visually impaired not to, my dear. The man reeks of sex appeal. If only I were a few years younger. I can't say that I'd marry him, but we could have a little fun." She chuckled, taking a sip of her drink, but never letting her eyes roam far from Gideon.

Lauren was appalled at Mrs. Lansing's conversation; it wasn't as if they were contemporaries having a little girl talk. She was her mother's friend for God's sake, however drunk! "How is Judith?" Lauren asked, attempting to change the subject. Judith was Beth's daughter and, sans surgery, an exact replica of her mother.

"She's fine. She married a doctor, one of the Phillips boys, you know, Judge and Mrs. Phillips from Boston." Before Lauren could answer she plowed ahead, turning over a subject that was well tended. "They bought a home, a really big one, up in Westchester, and they have my granddaughter, Ella. She is gorgeous, of course. Pretty hair, light skin. She's perfect."

Lauren grew up subtly aware of the premium her ilk placed on light skin and "pretty hair," but to hear it here and now by this woman was absolutely appalling! It was even more obscene voiced among the beautiful images of Africans Gideon had captured, and that now surrounded them. The strong dignity and grace captured in these photos wasn't a function of Ivy League schools or the right neighborhoods, and certainly not of features that resembled those of the oppressor. She felt embarrassed to be associated, in any way, with the hideous woman who stood before her, especially knowing that she represented everything that Lauren's life had also represented, at least up to now. How sad, she thought, that she'd followed the dictates of an uninformed society like a mindless lemming.

"How is that handsome husband of yours?" Mrs. Lansing asked, taking another long sip of her joy juice.

"H-he's fine."

"Where is he?" She looked around as though Max might pop out of the woodwork.

"He had a client dinner tonight."

"Oh." She gave a knowing look. "So while the cat's away . . ."

"Hey, gorgeous." Gideon was suddenly at her side. He wore a fitted black knit V-neck T-shirt and cream drawstring pants that draped nicely over a pair of black loafers.

"Oh, hi." For a second she forgot about Tight Face and all the vileness that she represented.

"Mr. Miller, I love your work," Mrs. Lansing interjected, batting her eyes the way a teenage girl might. "I'm a friend of Lauren's family." She extended her hand to shake his, holding on a beat too long.

"Oh, I'm sorry. Gideon, this is Mrs. Lansing; Mrs. Lansing, Gideon Miller."

Sensing Lauren's unease, Gideon nodded and said, "Thanks for coming. Lauren, it's good to see you." He eased away, greeting the next cluster of eager fans.

When he was gone, Mrs. Lansing turned to Lauren with a raised, questioning brow. "You two seem awfully . . . how shall I say . . . familiar."

Fifteen minutes later, when Lauren managed to disentangle herself from Tight Face's grip, Gideon slipped her a note. It read:

Meet me at the loft in an hour. Can't wait to see you!

Many kisses,
GM

She smiled and tucked the note into her jacket pocket, unconcerned with the gossip that was surely percolating at the root of the black social elite's grapevine. In the time it took for Mrs. Lansing to leave the gallery and extract her cell phone, Lauren's unsubstantiated affair would become a bona fide fact that would be wildly embellished before sunup.

Exactly an hour later she pulled up to Gideon's loft, even more nervous than before. This time she wasn't uneasy about the neighborhood, but about the personal boundary that she was prepared to cross. She pressed the buzzer, heard the beep, and vowed to leave the old Lauren behind on the sidewalk. Stepping out of the elevator she walked into the large loft, which was dimly lit with candles.

"Gideon?" A second later she felt his arms wrap around her from behind, and she melted into his embrace. He swept her hair to one side and kissed the nape of her neck, sending wild shivers racing through her body. She wanted him to stop, because the feeling was too intense to be tolerable, but at the same time she would have pleaded without shame for him to continue. Though they'd yet to shed clothes, their closeness was deeply intimate, their connection very real, erasing all thoughts of her family, her mother, and most especially her husband. Bravely, humbly, stoically, she turned to face him, keenly aware of all that doing so implied.

"God, you're beautiful," he murmured. Their lips met like two wispy clouds blending together in a clear, blue sky. Time stood still for her, trapped, as it were, by the pressure of his lips as they joined hers, the first taste warm, wet, and sweet, his tongue probing, teasing, and deeply sensual.

Lauren's heart raced toward an unknown destination. She was barely conscious of her body's rhythmic effort to keep up with him, or the steady flow of adrenaline that coursed through her veins.

Instinctively her pelvis moved against his as she searched for fulfillment and oneness with him. His hands roamed her body, pulling her closer, caressing her at the right times, in all the right places, fearlessly exploring the unknown landscape of her body. They moved against each other, drawn together like magnets seeking the exact moment of complete contact. Through the layers of clothes and undergarments, she felt his mass massaging her at just the right place. Nothing could have kept her from chasing the ever-ascending levels of pleasure that every movement he made provided.

With her arms wrapped tightly around his neck, she clung to him, bracing herself for the moment when there would be no control, when she would surrender to her own desires. Gideon seemed to know her body better than she did, so he held her tightly, refusing to let the building sensations subside. He made her go there. Lifting one of her legs for positioning, he never missed a beat. When she did let go it felt like a free fall, traveling to a magical, ethereal place that existed somewhere between earth and the heavens, a place she'd never been before. She stood in the middle of his loft, clinging to him for dear life as she had her first orgasm ever.

When both feet finally touched the ground, she found herself still holding on to him in the middle of the room. Until that moment she'd never been able to figure out what was so damned good about sex, what all of the fuss was about. But now she knew. She also knew that she had a lot of making up to do.

Without wasting another precious moment, she led him to his bed, where she worked all night to make up for lost time.

TWENTY-FIVE

Being a star NBA player was as close to nirvana as the average young black boy reared in South Carolina was ever likely to come, so with good reason Chris loved having all eyes follow his every sure step, as he dribbled upcourt with a cocky confidence and a sure swagger. He was cheered, revered, adored, and catered to by legions of fans, especially those of the female persuasion. Babes drooled over him—and, of course, his money—like overexcited puppies tossed their first bone. They came to his games in packs and droves, each hoping to catch his eye, have his baby, and spend his money happily ever after.

As a result, the majority of his fellow ball players needed custom racks to hold the belts upon which they notched their sexual conquests, but Chris, who was not the average ball player, had always managed to duck and dodge, effectively evading the fleshy temptations offered by the scores of beautiful women who stalked him as if he were prey. One explanation for his superhuman resistance was certainty that his "devoted wife" would like nothing better than to catch him with his pants down, so she could take *him* to the cleaners.

If he were honest with himself, Chris would admit knowing that Reese had never loved him, and furthermore, that if not for his fame and fortune, she wouldn't have given him a moment's notice. But, in college he had deluded himself, falling for her dreamy looks of love like a fish into freshwater. After they were married, the only time he saw stars in her big brown eyes was when she was spending his money, and then her face lit up like the Rockefeller Center Christmas tree.

All things considered, he wasn't surprised when Kira told him about Reese's plot to break their prenup. Kira sold her girl down the river without batting a false eyelash. Ever shrewd, she arranged for Shaun's "introduction," and happily cashed the check that Chris had given her for her trouble.

He laughed at the irony of it; while Reese was busy spinning her flimsy web, she was already hopelessly entangled in one that had already been well set. Together he and Kira planned the infamous rendezvous at the Four Seasons hotel, the fake fire drill, and, of course, the hideous picture that was later plastered all over the tabloids and the Internet. Being underestimated and classified as a dumb jock proved to be a blessing for Chris, because Reese never saw the approach of her own demise. All was fair in love and war, and make no mistake about it—with Reese, love was war.

Now she was nearly out of his life, and he had an eight-figure Nike deal days from final execution; in other words, Chris had the world at his talented fingertips. To make things even better, finally, Reese had agreed to give up custody of Rowe and had verbally accepted his settlement offer of a measly two hundred thousand dollars, even though the sum would dwindle like sand through a strainer once her attorney and Uncle Sam got their unfair share. The way Reese spent money, she'd be lucky if the balance lasted three months. Clearly she was desperate and couldn't afford the time or financial commitment to hold out, in hopes of a bigger settlement. Besides, she had no chips to play, while he had a full stack.

Chris felt as if he were cruising at the top of the world as he expertly maneuvered the rented black Escalade along the hairpin curves of Mulholland Drive, with Kanye's title track, "Gold Digger," thumping from the speakers, and his boy Damon riding alongside him. It sure was good to be king!

"Man, that shit's tight!" Damon said, bumping his head to the killer beat. They had been best friends since high school. Damon was one person whose motives Chris never had reason to question. He was down-home and regular; both were qualities that Reese had despised.

"Yeah, man, Kanye and Jamie put it down on that track," Chris agreed. "And you know, I could write a book on the subject." They were chillin', rolling through L.A. in a tight ride, sporting Sean John sweat suits, brand-new gym shoes, and enough bling to be taken seriously. They were headed to a private party given by a mutual friend.

"I'll bet you could." Damon laughed. "That bitch Reese was crazy. I never understood why you had to go and marry her in the first place. Just 'cause she got pregnant? Man, that's the oldest trick in the book."

"Yeah, but I fixed her. She'll have to find another sucker to leech off of. I am free at last!" They high-fived each other and continued rocking to Kanye's funky beat, soon pulling up to the Peninsula Hotel, where Chris hopped out of the car, tossed the keys to a valet, and bounced inside. They took the elevator to the penthouse suite.

Five hours later, at four in the morning, exhausted from some serious partying, they came out of the swanky hotel. It had been a long night, and Chris had a big game with the Lakers the next day, so he felt no compunction about stepping ahead of a couple and two other guys who were also waiting on their cars. Chris broke in line, as was his right—after all, he was a star NBA player—and handed his ticket to a valet, not caring about the angry looks that were thrown his way. The Escalade was quickly driven around and he jumped in and took off, oblivious to the commotion erupting behind him.

As they cruised up Wilshire Boulevard, jamming to KKBT the Beat, the music was so loud that neither he nor Damon heard the siren blaring or noticed the blue lights twirling madly in the night sky behind them. It wasn't until the LAPD cruiser pulled alongside the Escalade, the driver motioning him over, that Chris realized that he was being stopped by the cops. Being a black male in L.A., he felt unbridled fear as his natural reaction, until he reminded himself that he wasn't just an average young black boy from South Carolina; he was a renowned superstar NBA player. Besides, he was also clean. Sure, he'd had a few drinks, but he was six-five and 220 pounds. Over the course of five hours, there was no way he was anywhere near drunk. After reassuring himself, he pulled the Escalade over to the side of the road, killed the engine, and rolled down his window. A tall, lanky white cop approached him, shining a bright flashlight through his window.

"License and registration, please," the cop said as he peered into the car, sizing up the situation.

Chris squinted into the bright light, but with confidence said, "No problem, Officer." He spoke clearly—no slurring of his words. He was respectful, was not drunk, and therefore had nothing to worry about, he told himself. Damon, on the other hand, was visibly nervous. A sheen of perspiration had appeared across his brow and upper lip, and his eyes had the look of those of a deer caught in bright headlights. Chris leaned toward the door to reach into his back pocket, tossing Damon a look that said, *Chill; I got this.*

"Slowly . . ." the officer cautioned. His hand was near the revolver, his fingers already drawn toward the trigger. Two shifty-eyed young black boys, an expensive sports car, and four o'clock in the morning—it all added up to trouble in his book. To him, all black men fell into the same category: lowlifes. Some were just more polished than others. Besides, he wasn't a basketball fan, so Chris didn't look at all familiar.

Taking note, Chris showed his palms and slowly reached into his back pocket, pulling out his wallet, and from it his driver's license. He handed the ID through the window to the cop, and then reached over to the glove compartment to get his rental agreement. Right away he knew something was wrong; instead of the folded piece of paper that he'd left within easy reach, there was a small leather bag that he'd never even seen before.

The officer's radio crackled. "Got a five-oh-three on the license plate."

Suddenly the cop got antsy, shifting his weight from one foot to the other, his semicordial demeanor gone with the wind. "Get out of the car with your hands on your head," he demanded. His gun was drawn now, and the barrels were pointed squarely between Chris's eyes. A second cop, who'd remained in the patrol car up till now, was suddenly prowling on Damon's side of the car, looking very nervous and menacing, while Damon looked like a runaway slave facing a tight noose.

"Wait a minute. What's going on here?" Chris was baffled. Something was terribly wrong.

"Our records show that this car is stolen, so I need you both to get out of the vehicle slowly, with your hands in the air," the first cop said, never lowering his weapon.

"Listen, Officer, there's gotta be some mistake here. I'm Chris Nolan, with the New York Knicks." This was the card he always played when things needed to go his way, but this time it was trumped.

"I don't care if you are Don King; I need you to step out of the vehicle right now!" Tension was visible in the cop's face; the veins along the side of his neck throbbed, and his complexion had gone from pale to pink—red was next. Chris suddenly understood the term *trigger-happy*, because the cop's fingers were actually twitching involuntarily, as if only the release of a bullet could possibly scratch the itch.

Damon was looking at Chris for an explanation and reassurance. Chris slowly opened the door and got out, then was promptly manhandled by the second cop, who frisked him, then slammed his body against the car, yanking his hands roughly behind his back, where they were joined in a pair of tight handcuffs. It wasn't until his face was jammed onto the top of the car that Chris noticed a very important detail: The car was midnight blue, not black. Somehow in his haste he'd left the hotel in the wrong Escalade!

Finally realizing what had happened, he immediately felt a sense of relief, a shining glimmer of hope that he could wake himself up from this awful nightmare. All he had to do was explain how he'd inadvertently taken off in the wrong new Escalade; then they could all laugh about it, and he could get on his way, head to the hotel, climb into bed, and forget this madness ever happened. "Officer, Officer, listen, please. I just valet-parked my rental car at the Peninsula, and somehow I left in the wrong one."

"Oh, yeah, so you just happened to take a brand-new Escalade by accident. Save it, buddy; you're going down." He yanked the cuffs, dragging Chris to the patrol car. Out of nowhere a photographer had shown up, offering Chris the second flash of light in his face in the last five minutes.

"I want to call my attorney," he demanded angrily. The reply was his head being shoved down as he was unceremoniously tossed into the backseat of the patrol car.

In a surrealistic state he watched as Damon went through the same humiliating process. He was clearly terrified; his eyes were the size of dollar coins. When the officer frisked him he called out to his partner, and both men converged behind Damon, examining something that had been taken from his pocket; then a flurry of activity ensued. Though Chris couldn't hear what was said, the fear in Damon's eyes was loud and clear. Damon had something on him that he shouldn't have. Chris dropped his head, shaking it from side to side, praying that this was all a bad dream. Another patrol car pulled up, and the officers hopped out and quickly begin a methodical search of the car, stopping every now and then to place pieces of evidence into plastic bags. Chris shivered as he absorbed the full calamity of the situation that was unfolding before him.

After torturous hours of interrogation, booking, and processing, Chris's attorney finally had them released at nine o'clock that morning. He walked out of the precinct looking like death warmed over, and was greeted by a swarming mass of reporters and photographers, all snapping a frenzy of pictures and popping off rounds of questions:

"Chris, Chris, why did you steal the Escalade?"

"Were you high on the meth they found in the car?"

"What'll happen to your Nike deal?"

"Who is your friend?"

"Where had you been all night?"

Courtesy of a reporter looking for his reaction, a newspaper was shoved in his face. The erroneous headline read, "Knicks Star Chris Nolan Steals Escalade During Drug-fueled Rampage."

And, of course, there was the requisite grainy photo of him doing the perp walk—head down, hands shackled behind his back—into the police station. There was no way *not* to look guilty under those circumstances. This was his worst nightmare come true.

Though his lawyer assured him that the auto-theft charge would be dismissed, based upon proof that he had just valet-parked a similar car at the same place, the drug charges could be a problem. Not only did Damon, unbeknownst to Chris, have Ecstasy on him, but there was meth and cocaine found in the car as well. Proving that they weren't his would be tricky, since the car's owner was unlikely to step up and claim the drugs himself. Regardless of what happened in court, his reputation was already tainted by the scandal-hungry media.

He thought of his son, Rowe, his mother, his coach and team, and how disappointed they would all be when they got wind of this. It brought tears to his eyes. But most of all he thought about Nike, and the multimillion-dollar contract that had just sat in the palm of his hand merely hours ago. Given the character clause, it was fair to assume that defeat would be snatched from the jaws of victory. Forget a misting of tears; the enormity of *that* loss rendered him unable to hold back a tidal wave.

With his head in his hands, the six-foot-five-inch superstar athlete cried like a lost child. At that moment being a star NBA player was worthless to him; in fact, he'd rather have been just an average black boy from South Carolina.

TWENTY-SIX

Normally Brandon was the portrait of calm, cool, and collected, his feathers rarely ruffled. But lately Gillian had noticed that he seemed just a tad anxious, a little jittery, and ever so slightly on edge. Of course, he was charming to her, but there was a barely perceptible frisson beneath the smooth surface of his impenetrable facade. She chalked it up to the stress of producing his first feature film.

On the contrary, starring in *Gold Diggers* was exhilarating for Gillian, like jumping from a soaring jet with a weightless chute that opens just in the nick of time, but without any effort or energy. To William's delight, she proved to be a perfectionist where her craft was concerned. She pushed herself harder than any director would dare, happily enduring countless hours of shooting—and reshooting—scene after scene, perfecting a simple glance that would speak volumes, or delivering a powerful line with just the right balance of emphasis and restraint. Each night she fell into bed drained, but never had she been happier. Her director, Christopher Bythewood, was a genius, the screenplay was brilliantly written, and her role was tailor-made just for her—as was Brandon, she was also discovering.

Her feelings had begun to change a couple of weeks before. She'd fallen asleep exhausted in the media room while looking over outtakes that Chris had given her to study. Sometime in the night Brandon came in, lifted her from the chaise, and took her to her room and tucked her into bed. She had a sleepy, partial recollection of this, but a very clear remembrance of the sense of security that the gesture gave her. In every way he was unfailingly generous, providing her with everything a woman could ask for; he was kind and loving, and ensured that *all* of her needs were met. And the bonus was, he was also a perfect gentleman! Surprisingly, he had not once come close to crossing the line she'd drawn in their relationship, even though his desire for her was obvious. Oddly enough, his maintaining a distance seemed to draw her closer. More than anything else, the sense of security that she'd never experienced from a father was deeply comforting and very enticing.

A lazy smile crossed her face, and she slipped farther down into the milky bath she'd drawn, letting the warm water lap over her hair, untangling the coils, caressing her body, and quieting the stream of static in her mind. A chilled glass of sauvignon blanc sat on the marble ledge that surrounded the Jacuzzi tub, waiting to further erase any stubbornly tangled nerves. In these minutes of pure relaxation, Gillian experienced an unshakable satiation with her life; in fact, she hadn't thought about a cigarette in weeks now.

She had always felt just a little out of place in the world until now: a little too tall for her grade-school classmates, a little too dark for Jack and Jill, hair just a little too kinky to be considered good, and a little too rich for the kids in the hood, but still a little too poor for the jet-setters—she was never *just right* for anything. These ambiguities made her a truly unique and special person, but taken out of context the result was unsettling. Brandon, however, provided an environment created just for her, so the fit was like a kid-leather glove pulled taut. He accepted Gillian for exactly what she was, and blindly worshiped all of her: the good, the bad, and the rest.

Deeply content, she turned her hazy thoughts to her friends. She wondered whether they were anywhere near as happy as she was at this moment. Though Paulette was expecting and seemed pleased as spiked punch about it, Gillian personally thought the pregnancy was a nine-month disaster in the making. And Lauren had been mysteriously missing in action lately. Aside from a quick call to set up Paulette's baby shower, she hadn't been heard from, a development that was way out of character for her. And then there was Reese, who'd gotten beat at her own game. Even so, it was hard to *really* worry about her. The girl was a survivor, the type who would be left standing when all others fell. It would be good to see them at next week's shower.

Gillian stepped out of the tub, wrapped herself in a plush white towel, and took another lingering sip of wine. She padded out of the bathroom into her enormous suite, which had its own land-scaped balcony, an entertainment/sitting room, and a personal boudoir. After smoothing a rich Biotherm lotion into her soft, buttery skin, she slid into a creamy lace nightie and tossed a matching robe over it. Gillian was about to go to bed when she decided to do something that she'd been considering for the last week, as her attraction to Brandon grew. Even though she realized that it was probably a father-figure fixation, the idea still tugged at her, teased her, coaxed her to join Brandon in his sitting room, where he would undoubtedly be smoking a stogie and nursing a single-malt.

And there he was, wearing a cranberry velvet Armani bathrobe with matching slippers and black drawstrings house pants. The cigar had long since burned out, and the snifter was low on fuel. He looked melancholy, but perked up the moment she walked into the room.

"You're a sight for sore eyes." He gave her a weak smile, but his eyes still danced at the sight of her.

She marveled at her ability to elicit such an unguarded response from such a powerful man, realizing that he truly worshiped her. She slowly walked over to him and perched on the armrest of his chair, wearing her sexy negligee and a nice warm smile. He looked so vulnerable, causing her to feel a deep affection for him, a desire to make it all better, whatever it was that troubled him.

"Can I get anything for you? Another cognac?" she asked. Her words were simply put, but the real question was as complex as the faceted shades of brown and gold that flickered in her eyes. There was nothing literal about their conversation, but then again, Brandon was not a literal man. She was beginning to see the many layers of his personality, those that weren't obvious to most people.

He reached up and gently slid his hand behind her head. "How about this instead?" he asked, pulling her toward him for a kiss.

She caressed his lips with the soothing touch of her own. Opening her mouth ever so slightly, she invited him in, tasting, teasing, and testing him, skimming the surface of his desire. He literally shivered under her touch. An epiphany revealed itself to Gillian: If she'd brandished a whip and snapped it overhead, Brandon would have happily succumbed to any demand she made. But her desire was only to soothe him, to make him feel good, the way she'd felt in the bath just minutes ago, as she did before the camera earlier today, and as she had for weeks being swaddled in his lap of luxury. She caressed the taut muscles in his shoulders, his back, and across his chest, eventually roaming past his robe to his nightshirt underneath, where she unfastened one button at a time, slowly seducing the man who'd given her everything. Her touch was at once tentative, inviting, electric, and forbidden.

Nonetheless, uninvited thoughts intruded, though she held them at bay. Were her attentions an outward expression of gratitude for all that he'd done for her? Or were they simply a callous quid pro quo, an exchange of favors, one for the other? Was she more like her mother than she'd ever allowed herself to believe? Or even cut from the same cloth as Reese? The term *gold digger* bounced around the back of her subconscious, but for the moment she convinced herself that it could not possibly apply to her.

She saw herself as a director might have, standing up from her perch on his chair's arm, playfully pulling away his pajama pants before straddling his lap, leaving nothing between them but her flimsy lace G-string. Her face brightened at the sight of him and she enjoyed the radiant heat that filled her clenched fist. She held him as a race car driver might clutch the throttle of a powerful car, knowing that one thrust would send it speeding recklessly into space. She had that kind of control over him, and she could see it in his eyes. Gillian held his gaze, daring him to look away.

Lifting up, she slid a condom from the pocket of her robe, slid it on him, and positioned herself, daring him to look away as she pulled her G-string aside and descended onto him, taking him in inch by inch. Soon he was swallowed whole, and his eyes were glazed orbs of lust. His orgasm was metaphysical, a spiritual experience, connecting them on an even higher plane.

Afterward, she was sure of one thing: She never wanted to lose him, or the sight of what she represented in his eyes. Gillian's need for Brandon wasn't just a function of material things, but of everything. She saw and appreciated herself more fully through his eyes. He fulfilled her and offered her a sense of stability and security that had been missing throughout her entire life. Because Gillian grew up without roots, she lacked foundation. A stable childhood was like a compass: No matter how far life took you from that origin, if you wanted to, you could always find your way back to the time and place that had helped shape the very essence of who you were. As a result of the many moves, men, and machinations that Imelda used to try to alter her own compass during Gillian's child-

hood such a foundation was nonexistent for her. There was no stability; there were no cousins, grandparents, or cherished holiday
traditions. Most important to Gillian, there was no father. Things
might have been better had there been one who had died in an accident, or been a deserting louse or an impossible drunk. But not to
know anything about him left a gaping hole in her identity, one
that had been beautifully camouflaged over the years with looks,
money, and prestige.

Afterward, she lay draped over Brandon like an expensive cloak,
soaking up the heat emanating from his body, basking in his love
for her. It was such an incredible feeling to be cherished by a man.
Early on she'd tried to chase Brandon away, to ignore him and give
him every reason to give up hope that she'd ever return his affection. But he didn't give up, convincing Gillian that he would be
around, and could offer her the security that she'd always needed,
but never even knew she wanted.

"Are you okay, baby?" he asked, stroking her back the way one
might a beloved pet.

"I've never been better," she purred. She kissed him sweetly before shifting a little to curl up in his lap, contented. "How about
you?" she asked softly. "I've been worried about you lately."

He took a deep breath. "Well, there is something I need to talk
to you about."

TWENTY-SEVEN

There is nothing romantic about poverty. Having no money meant no weekly spa facials at Mario Badescu in Midtown to ward off telltale wrinkles, no familiar greetings at four-star restaurants, no exquisite one-of-a-kind jewelry from Ethos. In general, being poor was hard on a girl, and downright devastating to a legendary glamour-puss like Reese, who was now forced to witness the dimming of her bright light in real time.

The mirror was no longer her trusted friend. The two-faced bitch was betraying her with sad images of dark shadows lurking beneath her eyes, lackluster skin with overenlarged pores, and hair as limp as two-day-old, overcooked spaghetti. Not to mention the ten extra pounds that a couch, no trainer, and comfort food had added in all the wrong places, or the haunting memory of her six-pack, which she'd proudly sported with midriffs and low-riding hip-huggers. The sour cherry atop these layers of tragedy was walking up Madison Avenue and not having one single head turn. It was sadly sobering not to have one person admire, envy, or lust

after her for the entire ten blocks it took to walk—as opposed to being chauffeured—from the subway to her lawyer's office.

When Justin was finished explaining the terms of her measly
settlement in his monotone legalese, Reese was one blink away
from an onslaught of tears. How much more humiliation would
she be forced to endure?

"If you'll just sign here, here, and here," he said, flipping
through the pages of the document, "that should do it." By the
time he took his unfair cut, and Uncle Sam grabbed his, Reese
would be lucky to have enough to start her life again in, say, Kansas
City, let alone in Manhattan. There was a time when she would
have scoffed at two hundred thousand dollars—she was fully capable of blowing through that during a long weekend in Saint Barts.
But with a sum total of $47.73 left in her checking account, she
was relieved to get anything.

Reese sucked it up, put her ego and emotions in check, and focused on survival. "When do I get the money?" As it was, she
barely had enough to make it through the day, and her cell phone
had just been cut off for nonpayment. She'd called her family for
help, but of course they regurgitated every snotty and condescending remark she'd ever fed them during her days of riding high. Her
mother wouldn't even let her come home to live, and her slacker
brother started bitching about the basketball tickets she never gave
him, and parties she didn't invite him to, blah, blah, blah.

"As soon as you sign, I'll have the contract couriered over to
Chris's attorney. He promised to have the money wired immediately. So, let's say first thing in the morning."

She was picking up the pen to sign her life away when Paul's assistant barged into the room.

"I'm sorry to interrupt, Mrs. Nolan, but Paulette Dolliver is on
the phone for you."

"Tell her I'll call her back later." As bad as things were, the last thing she needed was a conversation with Paulette. Besides, she couldn't imagine what Paulette could possibly want that would be urgent enough for her to track Reese down all the way from California—in her attorney's office, no less.

"But she says it's urgent."

Agitated, Reese picked up the phone, which sat on the credenza behind her. "What's up?" she answered.

"Have you signed the contract yet?" Paulette asked, sounding breathless.

"If you'll let me off the phone, maybe I can."

"Whatever you do, don't sign those papers!"

"Are you crazy? You know I don't have any money."

"Listen to me and you'll have a lot more than what you're about to get."

Still aggravated, Reese planted a hand on her hip. "Paulette, what the hell are you talking about?"

"If you had your cell phone on you'd know already."

"Are you suggesting that I've intentionally not paid my cell phone bill? Remember, I have no money!" she shouted.

"Which is exactly why I'm calling you," Paulette bitched.

"Would you get to the point?" Reese and Paulette had the strangest love/hate relationship. Since they were both hustlers, they were also thick as two thieves, but knowing each other so well, one didn't really trust the other. Neither of them identified with Lauren, who was way too Goody Two-shoes, nor with Gillian, who was too esoteric. Reese and Paulette had both grown up having to scrape for every crumb, and didn't know how to operate otherwise, even when bread was plentiful.

"Chris was arrested last night!" she finally announced. There was glee in her voice. Paulette was the kind of person who took delight in other people's misery; it always made her feel so much better about herself.

"What?! You're kidding!" Bewildered, Reese shifted the phone from one ear to the other. Her soon-to-be ex-husband was one of the straightest arrows she knew, so it was hard to imagine what he could possibly have been arrested for. He wasn't a drinker or a partyer, and he didn't do drugs. It would be easier to image Mother Teresa in cuffs.

"Listen, honey, I wouldn't kid about anything this important. This is the break we've been waiting for." She'd been trying to reach Reese since she heard the news from her private investigator early this morning.

"What happened?"

"He was stopped in Beverly Hills at four this morning. They charged him with auto theft and drug possession."

"Auto theft? That makes no sense; Chris can afford any car he wants. Why would he bother stealing one? And the man barely takes a drink, so I can't believe he was doing drugs, especially the night before a big game."

"I'm hearing that it was a mistake. Apparently he rented an Escalade and had valet-parked it at the Peninsula, and when he got ready to leave he just didn't recognize that the one he drove off in was the wrong Escalade. And, of course, an LAPD cop, seeing a black man driving an expensive car at four in the morning, that had been reported stolen, wasn't hearing any of that."

"What about the drug charges?"

"Apparently his passenger had Ecstasy and coke, and some meth was found hidden in the car."

"That's what he gets for fucking around with Kira!"

"It wasn't Kira, Reese. It was a guy."

Reese ignored the instant swell of relief that she felt at knowing Chris hadn't been with Kira. "This is all very interesting, but what does it have to do with me and my empty pockets?" For Reese, the only urgent matter was the near-zero balance in her bank account.

Paulette was never happier than when she was dishing or stirring hot gossip. "There's more," she teased.

"I'm listening."

"Try this on for size. Chris and his mysterious male passenger had just left a get-together at the Peninsula Hotel."

"And?"

"It was a down-low party, Reese. Your soon-to-be ex-husband is a bona fide bisexual. He's been on the DL for years." Had there only been time, Paulette would have flown back to New York to drop this bombshell in person, just to witness the look of shock on Reese's face.

She looked as though someone had told her that Mrs. Saint Nick was a dyke. "Wait a minute! I don't believe that for a minute. Hell, he's a baller!"

"In more ways than one." Paulette laughed. "I know this is hard to believe, especially since you were married to the guy, but trust me. Besides, this is just the ammunition we need to get you a bigger check."

The mention of cha-ching put things back into perspective for Reese, so she pushed aside her shock and got back down to business. "Do you have proof?" She dropped the pen she'd picked up as though it were suddenly poisonous. To think she had been this close to signing a settlement for a measly two hundred thousand dollars.

"How's this? My detective, who fortunately was still tailing him, was able to use a high-powered lens and got a good shot of him getting a blow job—by someone who obviously isn't a girl— through the hotel room window."

"I'll be damned." Reese had to sit down. The thought of the man she'd slept with for five years having sex with another man was earth-shattering. And what about AIDS? *Oh, my God*, she thought, *I could be infected!*

Paulette was oblivious to Reese's mental repercussions, and was still in story mode. "Apparently this down-low sex party is a monthly event for a group of like-minded high rollers. That's how they keep it so discreet. They all have a lot to lose: reputations, wives, girl-friends, kids, and the picket fence. It's some shit, girl!"

Reese was beginning to feel physically sick. The more she thought about it, the more she was determined to make him pay for what he'd done to her. "Bottom line, how much is it worth?"

"This shit is priceless! But for starters, tear up that ridiculous contract that you have there, and have Justin reopen the negotia-tions, starting at twenty million. He can afford it, and more impor-tant, he can't afford not to. I'm sure his Nike contract is already in peril, but if we add this to it, he's doomed—not only with Nike, but with any potential sponsors. He'd even lose his negotiating clout with the NBA, so I say we go for the jugular."

This was the best news Reese had had in months. Suddenly her future didn't look quite so bleak. Two hundred thousand was one thing, but $20 million . . . *Now we're talking!*

She hung up the phone, picked up the contract, tore it in half, and turned to a bewildered Justin. "We need to talk," she said, as visions of shopping sprees danced in her head.

TWENTY-EIGHT

"What a difference a couple of months make," Paulette quipped, as she and Reese strolled past Brandon's formal butler into the foyer of the impressive twenty-room estate that Gillian now called home. She looked every bit the madam of the house, draped in a burgundy silk Valentino kimono and crystal-encrusted house mules. Her skin was flawlessly effervescent, thanks to lazy afternoons by the pool, weekly spa facials, and the other trappings of the good life. As striking as Gillian had always been, she'd never looked better.

"I could say the same thing about you," Gillian replied to Paulette. The pregnancy had brought about change for Paulette, wrecking havoc on her appearance, which had always been marginal at best. Some women glowed with the light of life when pregnant; Paulette, at six months, was not one of them. Generally, she looked tired, run-down, and swollen. Her prepregnancy main attractions—her boobs—were now as large as vine-ripened watermelons. It was not attractive, particularly when coupled with a double chin, a spreading nose, and an extra thirty-five pounds.

"The last time I saw you, you didn't even have a boyfriend, let alone a baby and a baby daddy," Gillian continued.

The three women embraced one another, scattering a succession of double air kisses among them.

"Where's Lauren?" Paulette asked. She was looking forward to seeing her cousin. Even though Lauren still didn't know the bombshell news about her baby's paternity, Paulette nonetheless enjoyed a twisted glee at carrying Lauren's husband's child—something Lauren couldn't give him herself. To Paulette, her pregnancy was a physical confirmation of her superiority over Lauren. When she wasn't miserable, she was conversely ecstatic with nearly orgasmic joy. Her only regret was having to wait to break the blessed news to Lauren and the rest of the world about herself, Max, and their child.

Regretably, she hadn't heard from Max since she told him about his impending paternity. Of course, she'd called him almost daily, left a slew of messages, and even shown up at his office unannounced twice. She figured he just needed a little time to get used to the idea of their being a family, and soon it would all be good, especially once she told him that they were having a son: Maximillian Neuman IV. Her first order of business was to get him back in pocket; then she'd tell the world about their relationship. In fact, she'd already put the plan in motion to help get him there.

He simply needed a little extra motivation to extract himself from Lauren and embrace his new family. Paulette, of all people, realized that doing the right thing wasn't always so easy; therefore it was necessary for her to add a bit of pressure. It came in the form of a letter containing the barely veiled threat that if he failed to "acknowledge his responsibilities" she would force an investigation into his handling of her grandmother's will. For legal reasons she would rather have applied this pressure in person, but since he wouldn't talk to her, she was forced to put it in writing instead. She was a master of positioning and spin, and was very capable of getting her point across without implicating herself, especially since there was no evidence against her. Thank God she had had the foresight to record a conversation that clearly implicated him. If his forgery of the will were discovered, not only would it cost Max his career and reputation, but he could also go to jail for quite a long time. So Paulette was sure that he would fall in line quickly, though it was a damned shame that she had to give him such a hard push to get him there.

The three girls were settled in the cozy garden room, which overlooked the Hollywood Hills, sipping champagne—sparkling apple juice for Paulette—and watching the sun set, when Lauren walked in carrying gifts up to her eyebrows. "Hey, girls," she sang.

When the gifts were lowered onto a coffee table, the women all looked at Lauren with their mouths open; she looked incredible! Not at all like the calm, reserved girl they all knew. Of course, physically she had always been beautiful and exquisitely dressed, but what they saw today went way beyond that. Lauren looked like a woman who was in love and getting sexed really well, on the regular. Of course, this wasn't something she was necessarily aware of, but anyone with half a brain and a little intuition could see it clearly.

Paulette wanted to scratch her eyes out, since she automatically assumed that Max must have made up with her, and maybe they were back in love and fucking like bunnies. It never occurred to her that Lauren might have taken a lover of her own.

Reese was under the impression that *Paulette* and Max had kissed and made up, since that was the delusional portrait that Paulette had painted for her, so she automatically assumed that Lauren must be getting some on the side, and consequently wanted to give her a high five.

Gillian gave it less thought than the other two, and simply said, "Lauren, girl, you look awesome! What have you been doing?"

"Yes, please share your secret," Reese said, hoping to stir something up. She was definitely in a better mood these days after getting the goods on Chris, and had already had two glasses of champagne to celebrate.

Since Chris was caught with his pants down, literally, their attorneys had been negotiating back and forth at a furious pace. They were up to $15 million, and Justin had successfully negotiated a goodwill interim settlement of one hundred thousand dollars that had already been wired into her previously empty bank account. The first thing she did was to march into Barneys on a shopping spree, drop in at Joseph's hair salon for a haircut and conditioning to take care of the atrocious split ends that poverty had caused, and scoot by Mario Badescu for a series of intense treatments that included everything from glycolic acid to sea salt. After she'd been spit-polished and was back in fighting form, she sauntered into Nobu to eat a decent meal, and see and be seen. It felt good to be back on the fast track. She dreamed day and night of getting her millions from Chris, and finally being a free and single woman with all that money at her disposal—enough money to lure an even bigger catch than the one she'd thrown back, someone with class, style, and money. Maybe someone like Brandon?

Now, he was a catch! One that Gillian certainly didn't deserve. Reese had been secretly hoping he'd be here today, so that she could test the waters with him. Reese ran her fingers through her silky hair as she imagined lording over a house like this one, complete with a butler and chauffeur-driven Maybachs and Bentleys. She started, almost yanking out a fistful of hair when she heard her name called and realized that all eyes were upon her. Thank God they couldn't read her thoughts.

"What are you daydreaming about?" Paulette demanded. "We've been trying to get your attention, and you're sitting over there looking like you're miles away." By now they were on the third bottle of champagne, chasing it down with caviar, pâté, and an assortment of French cheeses.

"Not at all." Which was true; Reese was right there, all right, plotting to replace Gillian. "I'm sorry; what were you guys talking about?" She took another long sip of the delicious rosé Champagne Paul Goerg, savoring the crisp, effervescent bubbles. It was her favorite, and having just emerged from poverty she had a lot of champagne drinking to make up for.

"Well, *I* was just thinking about how much has changed, at least for you guys, since we were last all together. Gillian is about to be a big-time actress out here in L.A., and Paulette is going to have a baby!" Lauren hugged her cousin, and was genuinely happy for her.

Yeah, with your husband, you ditzy broad, Reese thought. She took another sip and shook her head. The whole silly affair was too stupid for her to comprehend. How could Lauren not know that her cousin has been screwing her husband for over a year now? Instead of taking care of business and figuring the shit out, she threw the bitch a baby shower! Reese had never found Max terribly sexy, especially after she got to know him; otherwise, friendship aside, she'd probably be the one taking him from Lauren. But what woman wanted a man who was as pretty as she was? She liked her men to have some edge. In fact, she didn't even mind a little roughneck action from time to time.

"So, who's the lucky man?" Gillian asked Paulette. "You've still not told us." Her catlike sixth sense told her there was something fishy going on with Paulette. She'd been evasive and coy whenever she was asked about the father of her child. As big a blabbermouth as that girl was, there had to be a really good—or really bad—reason that she hadn't publicized her baby daddy's identity to the whole world.

"You'll all find out soon enough."

"Since when did you, a premier publicist, become tight-lipped?" Lauren asked, amused by the change in her cousin.

These days it took little to amuse Lauren. Life was beautiful.

She saw Gideon at least a couple of times a week, and lived for those stolen hours when they would lie in bed, talking, kissing, and making love; in fact, she realized that she was *in* love. At first she didn't know what that light-headed, heart-palpitating ailment was, since she'd never had it before. She thought about him every waking hour; Max barely existed for her anymore. She was vaguely aware of his feeble attempts to gain her favor lately. He'd even shown up one night with flowers and a diamond bracelet. When she asked him what the occasion was, he answered, "Because I love you." There was a time when she would have melted in his arms like heated butter at such a sappy gesture, but now it hardly even mattered. What did matter to her was getting out of the marriage. She'd already consulted an attorney and was preparing for battle. Thanks to her grandmother they did not have kids, so it should be a relatively easy one to win.

On her wedding day, Priscilla had counseled Lauren not to have his child, no matter what he or her mother said, until she was 110 percent sure that she was the most important thing in his life. Morning after morning she'd woken up and asked herself that question, and when the answer wasn't a resounding yes, she'd take another birth control pill. Originally she felt deceptive for doing it, as if she were cheating Max out of a child and her mother out of a grandchild, but as time wore on she became convinced that she was doing the right thing. When Reese had Rowe and pawned him off on a staff of nannies right after the umbilical cord was cut, Lauren reaffirmed her vow never to have a child for the wrong reasons. That was one mistake she wasn't prepared to make. It was one thing to mess up your own life, but why start fresh by messing up a child's?

"Don't worry; you'll all meet him soon enough. He's a little shy, that's all."

Reese laughed out loud. "And a little married," she let slip. Four consecutive glasses of champagne had gone straight to her head.

"You're pregnant by a married man?" Gillian asked.

Paulette shot Reese a dirty look that didn't stick. "He's getting a divorce soon," she lied. Though to her it was only a partial lie; she knew that in time he would be getting a divorce, even if he didn't know it. He had to! As happy as she was to be having his baby and to have some real money, in the darkest hours of the day she didn't feel any worthier of happiness than her mother had all these years. Maybe even worse—at least her mother did marry, however badly, while she'd be just another statistic: a baby mama.

"That's what they all say," Reese slurred. Some women were such damned fools, she thought. It was laughable. Oblivious Lauren didn't have enough sense to know that Paulette had put a butcher knife in her back and was slowly twisting it in deeper, and Paulette was stupid enough to believe that Max would leave perfect little Lauren and her precious family name in exchange for her tired, soon-to-be-stretched-out punany. The only one who warranted a measure of her respect was Madam Gillian, who Reese never would have thought to have enough cunning to land a big fish like Brandon. She'd better enjoy it while she could. Reese took another sip.

"Reese, I think you've had too much to drink. Why would you say that to Paulette? We should all be happy for her," Lauren lectured.

"I may have had too much to drink, but I'd still have enough sense to know if my husband was fucking my cousin."

The air in the room froze solid. No one moved or even dared to breathe as the meaning of the words that had dribbled from Reese's loose lips sank in. They made a bizarre tableau, each stuck in her own sphere of disbelief. Lauren, who had been raising her glass to her lips, stood with her mouth open, though her brows had risen in slow recognition, and her eyes moved from Reese to Paulette. Instantly months of lies, innuendo, and funny feelings fit together snugly like a very simple jigsaw puzzle.

Paulette, who was normally adept at covering up deceit, was

caught so off guard that her expression was that of a kid with both hands caught deep in the cookie jar and crumbs around her mouth; her lips were moving as if she wanted to say something, but the words were inaccessible. Gillian's hand flew to her mouth, as if to stop the gasp that crept up her throat. She knew that Paulette could be a scurrilous bitch, but she never considered that she'd have an affair with her own cousin's husband—and then to have his baby, and worse, to let her cousin give her a baby shower! She was the worst kind of trollop imaginable.

Reese's reaction was delayed, slowed down as it was by alcohol. It wasn't until she saw Gillian, Paulette, and Lauren all looking mortified that she realized that the words she'd thought in her head had actually come out of her mouth. "I'm sorry," she blurted out.

"You cheatin', lyin' bitch!" Lauren yelled at Paulette. She thought of the countless times she'd stood up for Paulette to her mother, and how she'd always made sure that Paulette had money when they were growing up, so that she wouldn't feel bad when she got the newest toys and Paulette didn't. And how she had considered her a confidante when she had problems with Max—only to find out that Paulette was fucking him behind her back!

"Listen, Lauren—" Paulette began.

"No, you listen. How dare you sleep with my husband after all I've done for you?" Lauren screamed. "And then you're so low and despicable that you'd let *me* give you a baby shower!"

"All you've done for me? You make it sound like I'm some charity case." Paulette stood up to face Lauren. "Just because your family had the money doesn't make you better than me."

"No, what makes me better than you is that I'm not a whoring slut!" Lauren hissed, inching closer to her cousin. The calm demeanor that she usually wore was replaced by cold fury. Oddly enough, she wasn't mad at Max. Knowing him as she did now, she would expect him to stoop that low. But it really hurt that her cousin—her own flesh and blood—would betray her.

Paulette looked as if she'd been slapped hard in the face. "You can call me what you want to, but at least I know how to please a man, which is more than I can say for you."

Lauren stared at her hard, never letting her eyes waver, and in a calm voice that was barely audible, but steely and steady, said, "Like mother, like daughter." She regretted the words the moment they left her mouth, but it was too late to take them back. It was one thing to insult Paulette, who certainly deserved it, but far below the belt for her to attack her aunt's character.

This was the ultimate insult to Paulette. She looked around the room and saw disgust—definitely from Gillian, who was visibly appalled, and even from Reese, who was certainly not above what Paulette had done. She turned, grabbed her bag and ran out the door with tears stinging her lids. She had to get away from everything—the disgrace, the rejection, and the disgust, emotions that she had dealt with all of her life. They had little to do with Lauren, money, or Max, but were pieces carefully packed away in her private set of baggage. She was out the door before the other three could collect themselves.

Realizing that she wouldn't have a ride back to Paulette's house, where she was staying, and ever self-centered, Reese jumped up, gathered her things, and ran after her, feigning concern. "I need to stop her; she's in no condition to drive."

Gillian came over and put her hand on Lauren's shoulder, not knowing what else to do.

By the time Reese caught up with Paulette, she was in her car, had started the engine, and was about to drive off. Reese managed to hop in and buckle up before Paulette sped out of the driveway, headed down Mulholland Drive, which now bore a coat of March rain, made slick by the cold caused by the high elevation.

"Paulette, let me drive; you are in no condition," Reese said, as if she were suddenly sober herself.

"And you are? You're so fuckin' drunk you can't even keep your damn mouth shut," she spit.

"I'm sorry, Paulette. I didn't mean to do that; you know it," Reese pleaded.

By now Paulette's tears—which should have been shed decades ago—flooded her eyes, as they came upon a sharp curve that hugged the mountain over the steep canyon. Paulette turned the wheel to maneuver the car, but nothing happened. As the cliff approached, she applied the brakes: Again, nothing happened. In those few seconds, the realization that they were going over the cliff hit her in bold print. When the car broke through the guardrail, she and Reese both screamed. Her hands released the wheel and went flying to her face, as though she might be able to shield herself from the massive wreck that was now imminent. Her last thought was *Damn, now Lauren will end up with Max.*

Then everything faded to black.

TWENTY-NINE

Paulette's untimely death made news in papers and gossip rags from Los Angeles to New York. As a publicist who loved the limelight, so she would have been proud of the splashy headlines that heralded the bright New Yorker whose promising life had ended tragically in the Hollywood Hills. This normally would have been covered only in New York, but since it happened in L.A., the other media capital of the country, the story's appeal was broadened and made even sexier. As details emerged on a daily basis, it "grew legs," as Paulette would have said. In death, Paulette had what she'd always wanted in life: fame and notoriety.

The story's first growth spurt began when the badly injured but still alive passenger was identified as Reese Nolan, soon-to-be ex-wife of star New York Knicks forward, Chris Nolan, who, incidentally, just two months ago had had his own vehicular mishap on Mulholland Drive. Of course, every detail of that well-documented episode was dusted off, dressed up, and trotted back across newspaper pages. The articles recounted every scintillating detail, ending with a line or two about the auto-theft charges being dropped, but how drug charges were still pending.

Pictures ran of Reese stepping out of limos in thousand-dollar Blahniks, and up red carpets wearing the latest designer couture. The sideshow would not have been complete without including the infamous photo of Reese caught looking like a disheveled whore with her illicit lover in front of the Four Seasons hotel. Prominent doctors were interviewed and pontificated ad nauseam about how hideously disfigured the once beautiful woman would now be. One of the seedier gossip sheets even ran a headline: "Once Beauty, Now a Beast," showing a "before" shot, along with a doctored-up "after" shot.

Days later the story became even more salacious as it was discovered that the fuel and steering lines of the BMW appeared to have been tampered with, so perhaps this was no accident. Now it was murder! News anchors drooled over the scintillating story of the murder of a savvy New York publicist, and the sad disfigurement of one of the country's premier it girls.

As was to be expected, Paulette's pregnancy, once discovered, added even more chunks of fodder to the grinding rumor mill. The press began speculating wildly on the paternity of her unborn child, thus drawing a link, they surmised, to a potential murder suspect, and opening a fresh, new can of worms from which to bait an ever-eager audience. The Mulholland whodunnit became a grotesque but entertaining pastime as reporters dug around like pigs in slop, coming up with a growing list of unsavory suspects.

By now the TV gossip shows had elbowed their way into the trough, joining the wild feeding frenzy. The story was too scandalous to ignore as the list of suspects grew to include choice names like socialite Lauren Neuman, who'd had a blistering argument with her cousin mere seconds before the fatal crash, and whose husband, it was learned, had fathered the publicist's six-month fetus. Just as likely was the notion that said husband, noted New York attorney, Maximillian Neuman III, had murdered Paulette himself after she refused to have an abortion, thus threatening to ruin his marriage and his reputation. Lauren's mother was even bandied about as a suspect, once the family's feud over the deceased matriarch Priscilla Baines-Reynold's multimillion-dollar estate was unearthed.

The next suspect was even juicier to swallow: Chris Nolan. It was discovered that Paulette was somehow involved in his nasty divorce settlement, and had assisted his wife, the tragically disfigured passenger, in her negotiations by hiring a private detective.

No one knew exactly what, if anything, the detective had discovered, but since his involvement it was rumored that settlement talks had escalated into the tens of millions of dollars. By all accounts Chris had the qualifications of an excellent suspect: He was a high-profile celebrity, and he had infallible motives to kill *both* women.

The story had it all: glitzy celebrities, upper-crust socialites, an unwanted pregnancy, and an illicit affair. If this brewing concoction wasn't titillating enough, gossips and speculators added additional spice to the simmering pot, and rumors swirled like locusts on a prairie. Online chat rooms got into the act, creating a scintillating but totally fictitious story about a hot lesbian affair between soon-to-be superstar actress Gillian Tillman and the tragic figure Poor Paulette. They reported that the two had lived together in L.A. until Gillian took up with music mogul Brandon Russell, the man responsible for her starring role in her upcoming film release, *Gold Diggers*, as though this were irrefutable proof of wrongdoing, hence murder! According to HotGossip4U.com, once spurned, Poor Paulette threatened to divulge their lesbian affair to the press, giving Gillian and Brandon both compelling motives for murder. As preposterous as this unlikely scenario was, it added a strong element to the lethal cocktail. It became an explosive mixture of record and movie business executives, athletes, actresses, and socialites, all caught up in a juicy, possibly sapphic murder scandal.

By now the story had grown so monstrous that Poor Paulette became a bit player in her own death saga. She was often referred to as "that publicist" who was killed by Chris Nolan, Gillian Tillman, Lauren or Max Neuman, or fill in the blank with another celebrity name. In death, as in life, eventually Poor Paulette soon became second fiddle, a bit player, which surely was enough to make her roll over in the very expensive casket in which she lay.

There had been quite a debate among the family about whether or not an open casket was appropriate under the horrific circumstances. Mildred, ever concerned about family appearances—even in death—threatened to take over the ceremony and insist on a closed casket, but her sister, June, finally grew a set of balls and told her what she could do with her prissy "appearances." June and Lauren both knew that Poor Paulette would have wanted to be front and center during her final curtain call, so Lauren hired a Hollywood special-effects makeup artist and her cousin's favorite hairstylist to make Poor Paulette look her absolute best. It was no small feat.

Nevertheless, on the day of the funeral, Poor Paulette lay in a highly polished Italian mahogany casket with fourteen-karat-gold trimmings, in front of the pulpit at Abyssinian Baptist Church, turned out in Chanel couture. Considering her extensive injuries, she looked great, and the turnout was very impressive. The only things missing were a VIP list, a velvet rope, and an after-party.

Meanwhile, Reese was still laid up in Cedars-Sinai. Though she'd survived the horrific crash, she didn't look much better than Poor Paulette. Unlike her friend, who never wore a seat belt, Reese had worn one, which saved her life. Even so, her face looked as if Barry Bonds had taken a bat to it. She also had an assortment of broken ribs, a broken arm, and a shattered pelvis. Most would say that she was lucky to be alive, though once she got her first glimpse in the mirror, she would beg to differ.

Lauren sat in the first pew with her aunt, her mother, and Max, racked with the unrelenting weight of enormous grief and tremendous guilt. If she hadn't lost her temper over her cousin's affair with Max, whom she now cared nothing about, Poor Paulette would still be here. Lauren's eyes were nearly swollen shut, and she was physically drained by the flood of tears she'd shed since that awful night. Her mother sat on one side of her, looking as stiff as a double shot of Jack Daniel's, quietly praying that the whole sordid mess would be buried along with Poor Paulette. She had been appalled to learn that her niece had been sleeping with Max—*her* Max, whom she'd handpicked for her Lauren. And to think the little harlot was actually going to have his baby! To Mildred, the hussy was probably better off dead, saving them all from the enormous burden of a bastard child. But the worst atrocity was the disgrace of having all of her family's dirty laundry hung end to end across the pages of newspapers from coast to coast.

June sat to Lauren's left in a fixed state of shock. The stress of the last week had desecrated what little remained of the woman's spirit. Next to her sat Max, looking every bit as guilty and complicit as he was.

In the pew behind them sat Gillian, who'd just flown in from L.A. She wore an air of tragedy that suited her well. She'd received a call from her mother, who was now in France, hot on the heels of an eighty-year-old shipping tycoon whose wheelchair she was trying to push down the aisle. Her first comment was to congratulate Gillian on making the papers. It seemed that the story of Poor Paulette's death and the cast of celebrity suspects had also grown wings and landed in Europe. In Imelda's excitement, it was inconsequential that the reason for her daughter's publicity was her friend's death. Importantly, she'd advised Gillian to wear Valentino to the funeral. As tasteless as Imelda's comments were, Gillian followed her advice, and looked every bit the movie star in mourning, wearing a tailored black Valentino skirt suit and hat.

The rest of the audience was a strange combination of assorted celebrities, business professionals, and plain old ordinary people, most of whom had never met Poor Paulette, or even heard of her, prior to her untimely death. Of course, the press hung around like hungry buzzards waiting to pick apart what was left of her carcass, including *People* magazine, *Extra*, *Access Hollywood*, Page Six, and dozens of others.

After the funeral service, Lauren and Gillian managed to catch a few moments alone.

"How is Reese?" Lauren asked.

"Aside from looking like shit, being in excruciating pain, and mourning herself more than Paulette, she's fine." Gillian had visited her every day in the hospital, and Reese's eyes hadn't even misted over when she was told of Poor Paulette's death. But she'd wailed like a newborn baby upon seeing her own disfigured face. The hospital was forced to sedate her, and then put her on suicide watch.

"How are you?" Gillian asked Lauren, though she knew the answer. Lauren looked as traumatized as she had that night when they'd rushed to the scene of the crash, after Brandon, who'd just driven by on the way home, saw the accident and, not knowing who was involved, mentioned it to Gillian. Lauren heard him, and immediately had a sinking feeling in the pit of her stomach. By the looks of her, it was still settled there.

"I'm in shock. I can't believe she's really dead." The tears started fresh again. Lauren reached into her bag and pulled out a lace-trimmed handkerchief to dab away the tears.

Gillian put her arms around Lauren. "Remember, it's not your fault."

Between sobs, Lauren said, "If I hadn't made that nasty comment about her mother, she wouldn't have run off so upset." Lauren shook her head, hoping to stave off another flood of tears. "I feel so guilty."

"Remember, it wasn't an accident, so it had nothing to do with Paulette's being upset."

Lauren frowned, highlighting the fresh set of wrinkles that grief had settled into her brow. "But who could have wanted Paulette dead?" She shook her head.

"According to the rumors, at least, the list is very long. And I'm sure you know it even includes you."

"So I've heard, but why would I want to kill Paulette? I loved her."

"Yes, but *she* loved your husband, and was about to have his baby."

"But that's no reason to kill her," Lauren reasoned.

Gillian touched Lauren's arm to soften her words. "I know, but for a lot of people it's a really good reason."

Lauren pulled away, visibly upset. "I did not kill Paulette!"

"Listen, Lauren, I know you didn't." Gillian put her arm over her friend's shoulder. "I'm just playing devil's advocate so that you'll take this seriously and get a good lawyer, just in case. But don't worry—you have lots of company on the list, including your own husband."

"So I hear, but I seriously doubt that he'd be capable of it. He's a lot of things, but he isn't a murderer." Lauren had barely spoken two words to Max since returning from L.A. with Poor Paulette's body. He'd tried to apologize for the affair and console her, but she could barely stand the sight of him.

"Look at it this way: They were probably more like fuck buddies than lovers, so imagine how he felt when she ended up pregnant. It would have ruined his reputation and his career, not to mention his marriage."

"The marriage was already ruined," Lauren said sadly.

"Then there's Chris," Gillian tossed out.

"Chris? Why would he want to kill Paulette?" Lauren asked.

"Apparently Paulette hired a private detective to help Reese in her divorce settlement. Rumor has it that something was discovered that would have crippled his career, so maybe he was trying to kill both of them."

"This is so crazy."

"And it'll probably get even crazier. If I were you I'd hire a good attorney. I already have mine lined up."

"You?"

"Oh, yes. Though it's preposterous, according to the rumor mill I had a lesbian affair with Paulette. She became jealous of me and Brandon, and planned to blackmail me when my movie came out." Gillian rolled her eyes at the absurdity of it all.

Mildred came over, still wearing a stiff upper lip and not one hint of a tear. "We need to get going. I have a car waiting, and hopefully we can avoid the press."

Lauren was about to turn and leave when Gillian held on to her arm and slipped an envelope into her hand. "This is for you. I found it when I went back to Paulette's house the day after the crash to get a few things for Reese."

Later that night, in her suite at the Plaza, where she'd recently moved, Lauren had undressed and was about to pull her cell phone from her bag to call Gideon when she came across the envelope that Gillian had given her. She'd almost forgotten about it with all of the drama of the day. She opened it and read a copy of the letter that Paulette had written to Max, essentially blackmailing him.

It seemed to imply that Max had forged her grandmother's will. Lauren couldn't believe that Max would have done something like that. He seemed to love her family. For the first time she figured out that what he really loved about them was their money. Lauren suddenly realized that she really didn't know the man that she'd been married to for the last four years.

THIRTY

Gillian went directly from Paulette's funeral to JFK, where she promptly boarded Delta's evening flight back to L.A. With no luggage, she had arrived on one flight, attended the service, and immediately left on another. The last thing she wanted was to hang around New York to be hounded by the press and continually reminded of the spiraling tragedy in which she found herself embroiled. Even though Paulette could be challenging under the best of circumstances, her loss was deeply felt, and a piece of Gillian had died along with her, that carefree spirit that thrived those first exciting years when they met in New York, when they were all young, ambitious, and beautiful.

At least in L.A. Gillian would be safely tucked away behind the security of Brandon's money. With a sigh, she settled into the deep, comfortable leather seat, and accepted a glass of chardonnay from the perky stewardess.

It was a little over a year ago that she had taken this same journey from New York to L.A., but now she was flying first-class rather than hunkered down like a sardine in coach. At that time, she had had barely ten thousand dollars to her name, and no prospects for more; her future was about as uncertain as her shaky bank account. Today, thanks to Brandon, her bank account was flush with cash, and her career was set to explode. She also had a friend who was six feet under, and another lying badly injured in a California hospital.

Thoughts of Paulette took her back to that bright, sunny day when Gillian had first arrived in L.A. and somehow managed to claim the wrong bag at LAX, which was the beginning of a domino effect that brought her to exactly where she'd started: on board a Delta transcontinental flight, running from New York. She couldn't help but think that if she hadn't met Brandon, they would not have had the shower in L.A. at his house, and things might not have ended so tragically. But there were a million what-ifs.

When the plane landed, Gillian was the first passenger down the gangway. She made her way through the crowded airport, happy not to be bothered with bags. Her only concern was to find Charles so that she'd be driven home and tucked back into her sprawling oasis. Over the crowd of travelers she saw him standing rigidly in his formal driver's uniform, looking about for her, so she headed in his direction, anxious to get home.

"Miss Tillman?" a deep voice said.

She turned, startled, and came face-to-face with a tall, broad-shouldered black man in a shabby suit and a nondesigner tie. "Excuse me?" she said. She had no idea who this man was, but she tried to inject some degree of pleasantness into her voice; after all, lately she'd been approached by fans who were recognizing her from the publicity blitz that Brandon had orchestrated. Thanks to his clout, she'd been on every red carpet in Hollywood, not to mention every entertainment TV show.

But this was no fan. "I'm Detective Harris, LAPD. I'd like to talk to you, if you have a moment." He flashed his badge in one smooth move. Though he'd requested her time, it was clear by his stern demeanor that he didn't plan to take no for an answer.

Every B movie she'd ever seen ran through Gillian's mind: the tough cop in the bad suit with the shiny badge, and the rich, well-dressed murderess whom he's forced to bring down, even though thoughts of ravishing her run through his mind. She gathered her wits as best she could. "Yes, I'm Gillian Tillman. How can I help you?" She kept walking, hoping he would follow her right out of the airport, to keep from making a scene. He didn't. Instead he held his ground, and a few people who'd seen the beginning of the exchange paused to witness the rest of it.

"I need to talk to you about the murder of Paulette Dolliver." Unfortunately—and probably deliberately—his voice carried, and Gillian sensed a small crowd gathering, wanting to know exactly what the attractive woman had done wrong.

"I would love to talk to you," she said with a disarming smile, "but now is not a good time." Gillian looked around self-consciously.

No one ever wanted to talk to a cop; besides, Detective Harris was one of those officers who seem pissed off at their salary in comparison to others whom they deem not as worthy. "We can do this here and now, or I can bring you into the station." He raised his brow. "And, I don't think you'd like that very much." He seemed to be toying with her, amused by her polished veneer.

Her heart lurched in her chest. "Can we talk in my car? My driver is right here." By now Charles was at her side, looking quite concerned.

He shrugged. "Sure, no problem." The detective's sudden appearance at the airport had had its desired effect on her. She was definitely shaken up; now it was just a matter of time before he loosened her lips.

They stood curbside, not saying a word, until Charles pulled the

Bentley up. The sight of it further pissed the detective off. The fact that Gillian was black and so was he also pissed him off. She probably thought she was better than he was; he was sure of it. After getting into the back, Gillian raised the soundproof privacy barrier behind the front seat, then turned to face the detective. "So, how can I help you?" she asked. She suddenly regretted the cool crispness of the Valentino suit. The lines were hard and edgy, intimidating even, and the hat looked more mysterious than she'd care to appear at the moment. But this wasn't the set of a movie, so there would be no wardrobe or set change.

She's a pretty cool customer, the detective thought. She was as calm and composed as Marlene Dietrich in *Witness for the Prosecution*. She was, after all, an actress, he reminded himself. "I need you to tell me about the night of Miss Dolliver's death. I understand she was at the home you share with Brandon Russell."

"Y-yes," she began. "We'd planned a baby shower for her."

"Who is 'we'?" he asked, never taking his eyes from hers. He was always careful to observe the exact moment when the subject looked away from his penetrating gaze. It was usually very telling.

"Lauren, Reese, and me," Gillian answered.

"Just the three of you for a baby shower?" He looked skeptical. Those events usually included at least fifteen or twenty cackling women, he thought.

"It was a reunion of sorts, as well as a celebration."

"I can't imagine that all of you found Miss Dolliver's pregnancy cause for celebration."

She knew where this was headed, but decided to elude the implication. "We were all very good friends."

"Do good friends usually sleep with one another's husbands?" he asked. It was a good question, which—not for the first time—made Gillian wonder about the true value of their relationships. They were four women who came together at a time when none of them knew exactly who they really were, but found a semblance of recognition in one another. At the end of the day they all wanted—whether for themselves or their image of themselves—the finer things in life.

She shifted and lowered her eyes. "I had no idea that Paulette and Max were having an affair." And this was true; she was just as stunned as Lauren to find out that Paulette had been sleeping with Max. It was unimaginable. How could Paulette do that to her own cousin? It was the ultimate treachery.

"But Lauren knew; isn't that right, Miss Tillman?" His voice took on an accusatory tone.

"Not until that night." Lauren would have had to be a better actress than Gillian to have pulled that scene off. The girl was genuinely shocked by Reese's slip. Gillian had never seen Lauren that angry before in all of the years they'd known each other.

"How can you be sure of that?"

"Because that's what started it all."

"Started what?"

She took a deep breath. "Reese had had a little too much to drink, and let it slip that Lauren's husband was the father of Paulette's baby." She'd wondered on more than one occasion if it was truly a slip, or if Reese told the secret just to get a dig in at Lauren, which she would certainly be capable of.

"And the two, Lauren and Paulette, got into a fight?" he asked.

"Not a fight, just an argument."

"Did your lover, Brandon Russell, know Paulette?"

The statement about Brandon and the question about Paulette were both tossed out the way a pitcher might lob a changeup, but she quickly adjusted to the new rhythm. "Not really. They've met before, but that's all." She shrugged lightly.

"What do you know about Mr. Russell's business problems?"

Again, her gaze shifted from his. "I don't know what you are talking about."

"About the ongoing federal investigation into the financing of Mr. Russell's record label."

It was obvious to Gillian that the detective was simply fishing around, and there was no way that she would take his bait. "I'm sorry, but I know nothing of it," she answered defiantly.

This was not altogether true. In fact, Brandon had finally confided his legal troubles to her. According to the feds, his label was built on illegal gains. They alleged that it was financed by profits from the prostitution and drug trade of a Southern gangster called Crazy Joe. After Sunset Records took off, Crazy Joe kept Brandon's feet to the fire with a campaign of blackmail, and insisted that he continue their relationship by cleaning up the gangster's money. Brandon swore that none of this was true, and that video proof that he was being set up was on the missing flash drive.

Brandon told Gillian that the authorities—one agent in particular—were on a witch hunt to bring down a successful black man any way they could, and money laundering was a nice catchall category, kind of like tax evasion.

Agent Wimbley, a redneck agent from Arkansas who was driving the investigation, was pursuing a personal vendetta, and had told Brandon to his face, when he thought they were alone and that the conversation was off the record, that he hated arrogant niggers, and he considered it his duty to help keep them in their place. Brandon explained to Gillian that the missing flash drive contained the secretly taped video from the meeting when these racist remarks were made. He was sure that if a prosecutor or jury, should it come to that, heard those damaging statements, the flimsy case against him would collapse like a house of cards. But unfortunately, after the meeting, which was held in New York, he was in such a hurry to get to the airport that he tossed the flash drive with the incriminating footage into his checked luggage instead of his carry-on.

After Gillian admitted that Paulette had been alone with his bag, Brandon became convinced that Paulette must have taken it, so immediately after the car accident, when Gillian went by Paulette's place to get clothes for Reese, he'd insisted that she also search for the missing flash drive. He told her that if the authorities were to find the video while investigating Paulette's death, they would surely erase it to protect a fellow law enforcement agent, which could be the end of his company, and *her* film career, since *Gold Diggers* was partially financed with his money. So, while Paulette's body was still warm in the morgue, Gillian had driven to the apartment and gone searching inch by inch through Paulette's things. Though she didn't find the flash drive, she did find a copy of Paulette's letter to Max, which she later gave to Lauren.

Detective Harris reached for the door handle. "I'll be back in touch," he warned Gillian. He turned to get out of the car, but stopped and faced her again. "Just how close were you and Miss Dolliver, anyway?" he asked with a lewd grin.

"We were friends, as I said before." She gave him a steely glare. She was offended that he would go there, but not surprised. He was a contemptuous little bastard.

"I'll bet you were," he said, smiling slyly. Then he was gone, leaving Gillian with a sheen of perspiration.

The whole thing was actually amusing to Detective Harris. He didn't really buy the idea of a crazy lesbian love affair leading to murder, or that Brandon's investigation had anything to do with the car crash. There just wasn't enough of a motive. But it did make for compelling press. Besides, he had a long list of other very intriguing suspects that he was just about to sink his teeth into.

THIRTY-ONE

Every muscle, nerve ending, tendon, and blood vessel in Reese's battered body throbbed with pain. It was two weeks after the accident, and she still felt as if she'd had a head-on collision with an immovable object, which in fact she had. The painkillers administered by the hospital only dulled the constant, searing jolts. If her leg wasn't hurting, her pelvis was; if that wasn't inflamed, then her arm was killing her; and if that was soothed, then her ribs throbbed with every breath, though usually everything ached all at once. But the biggest pain of all was the mental anguish she suffered every time she took a look in the mirror. Her once-beautiful face was an ugly mess of stitches, black-and-blue bruising, grotesque swelling, and semihealed gashes; in other words, she looked like shit.

Fortunately she remembered nothing of the actual crash, only the terrifying seconds beforehand when she realized what was about to happen, and that nothing could stop the inevitability of Paulette's car's careening off the hillside. Her next moment of consciousness was when she woke up screaming in the hospital, surrounded by grim-faced doctors and tight-lipped nurses. They were all uttering nonsense among themselves about how lucky she was to be alive. It was easy for them to say.

A few days later she woke up again to find Gillian at her bedside, looking down at her with such pity. Reese despised that look, knowing what it foretold. It wasn't until the next day, when she felt a bit stronger and she asked the nurse to hold a mirror up to her face, that she knew the full extent of her facial injuries. She was unprepared for the gruesome sight that greeted her, and screamed with fright at what was left of her once beautiful face. Gillian tried to soothe her, to tell her that it would be all right, but those words were empty; they meant nothing to Reese, who'd spent her entire life trading on the now-depleted currency of her good looks. For her, there was no other reality. She was nothing without her Cover Girl appearance.

She vaguely remembered Gillian breaking the news to her that Paulette had died in the car crash, and even that didn't register; the only thing she could think about was her own pain. She would rather have been dead herself, than lying in a hospital bed, the object of such pity.

When Chris brought Rowe to visit, she heard her soon-to-be ex's audible gasp, the quick intake of breath, and she burst into tears. Even the thought of his $15 million settlement offer did nothing to ease her anguish. If she'd been strong enough to physically get out of bed and kill herself, she would have done it without a second thought. She saw no point in living—until she saw her son.

She hadn't seen Rowe in a month, and was surprised by how much he'd grown. He was bigger, taller, and quite the handsome little boy. When he saw her, he put his small hands on hers and said, "Don't worry, Mommy; everything'll be okay. The boo-boos will go 'way; you'll see." And he nodded his head very confidently for a five-year-old. Rowe seemed instinctively to know that she needed him now, and he was determined to be a big boy for his mother. She was mesmerized by her son, who seemed to radiate such hope. For the first time, her thoughts were centered on something, or someone, other than herself.

When he was born, Rowe was simply a necessary inconvenience to assure her cash flow. She'd never really viewed him as a part of herself. Perhaps for the first time, lying in bed with nothing else to hold on to, she felt pangs of true maternal love for her child, and tears rolled down her face. He dabbed her tears away with the sleeve of his shirt, and said, "You're still beautiful, Mommy, and I still love you." And she could tell that he really meant it. Here was a person who loved her, despite the fact that she wasn't perfect, beautiful, or glamorous. Maybe that was what people meant by unconditional love. After he left, she cherished the memory of his cute face, and lived for the sound of his sweet words when he called her every day.

Two days before her scheduled release, she had another unexpected visitor. This one wasn't nearly as pleasant. She opened her eyes to find a tall, dark-skinned man at her bedside, staring at her as though he could read her thoughts, even as she slept.

"Mrs. Nolan—or is that Miss yet?" he asked a bit sarcastically.

"Who are you?"

"I'm Detective Harris," he answered, flipping open his badge. When she didn't respond, he said, "I'm investigating the murder of Paulette Dolliver."

"Murder? But it was a car accident."

"I see you've not been told."

Gillian had insisted that the hospital remove the television from Reese's room, fearing that news of the tragedy would only deepen her depression. "Told what?" If she could have sat up in bed she would have, but because of the broken ribs she needed help just pulling herself upright.

"The brake and steering lines were deliberately tampered with. It was murder, Mrs. Nolan, and, I suppose in your case, attempted murder." He seemed to enjoy watching the repercussions after dropping the bomb.

A shudder of fear ran through her body, amplifying the pain. Reese was shocked; she had no idea that the accident was the result of anything other than Paulette's bad driving and her being too upset to be behind the wheel of a car. She remembered thinking that Paulette needed to pull over, and seconds later she had lost control. They were barely a mile from Gillian and Brandon's home when it happened.

"But why?" she asked. More than most people, she knew that Paulette could be a deceiving bitch, but hell, so could she; that was no reason to kill someone.

"That's exactly what I was hoping you could tell me." He sat down in the chair at her bedside, uninvited, and gave Reese an accusatory look, as though she had killed Paulette and nearly taken herself out in the process.

"How would I know?"

"From what I understand, Miss Dolliver had quite a few enemies, and since you two were so close, I imagine that you *would* know. You two did live together, didn't you?"

"Temporarily."

"While you were waiting for your big settlement from your husband?"

"That's correct."

"A settlement that Miss Dolliver was involved in securing for you, isn't that right?"

"She gave me referrals," Reese skirted.

"And paid for their services," he added, pulling out a copy of the contract and payment to the private detective.

"So?"

"So, I imagine that your husband might not be so happy with either one of you, especially having to cough up fifteen million dollars, when you were close to settling the week before for two hundred thousand. For lots of people that's a damned good motive for murder."

Reese had never once considered the idea that Chris would do anything other than write the check and pout about it, but on the other hand, those pictures had hit below the belt, and maybe they had also pushed him over the edge. After all, she never thought he'd have the wits to set her up with Shaun either, so maybe he was full of even more surprises.

"I don't know," she said, weighing her options. What if Chris was convicted of murder—what would happen? Well first off, she'd get full custody of Rowe, which would also mean more money, and possibly control over the rest of his estate. Maybe Chris did do it.

"What did the private detective find out, Mrs. Nolan?"

She knew that if she told him about the pictures they could build a pretty good case against Chris, and if it got out to the press, he'd be as much as convicted. "Pictures. He took some pictures of Chris."

The detective raised his eyebrow. "Pictures of Chris doing what?"

Reese thought about the luxurious home she'd been unfairly forced to leave, and of her son, who'd been taken away from her, and how she'd need every possible luxury and security possible now that she'd most likely be disfigured for the rest of her life, unable to make it on her looks alone. "He was in a compromising position."

The detective sighed impatiently, "With a woman?"

"No, with a man." There, she'd said it.

Detective Harris looked like he'd just won the lottery. This case was getting freakier by the minute. Talk about a motive—this was almost too good to be true. Even though Chris had an alibi on the day of the accident, it was common knowledge, since his prior arrest, that he hung around a rough, drug-dealing crowd, so he could have easily paid someone a lot less than $15 million to do the job. Detective Harris was nearly salivating at the career boost he'd get for bagging a superstar NBA player for murder. "I need to see those pictures."

"They're in New York," she said to stall him. Since Paulette had handled things with the private detective, she actually had no idea where they were. She did remember her saying something about their being put away for safekeeping, but she had no idea where that was.

"Tell me where and I'll send an officer." Now, this was good! Even if Chris Nolan didn't have anything to do with the murder, it would be quite a coup to have pictures of him getting it on with another man. The guys at the precinct would go nuts! He could probably make a fortune selling them to one of those gossip rags. Then he could be rich and fucked-up himself.

"No, I don't know exactly where they are. Paulette put them away for me, so I'll have to find them first." Finding them would be her first order of business once she got out of the hospital. They had to be either in Paulette's L.A. bungalow or in her New York apartment.

He didn't like that answer, but couldn't force her. Besides, she seemed motivated enough. He could almost see the dollar signs flashing behind her swollen and blackened eyes. "When do you get out?"

"In a couple of days." She would be discharged tomorrow and would stay with Gillian overnight, and the next day they would both fly to New York to get her settled in.

The detective pulled his card from a breast pocket and wrote his private cell number on it. "Call me the minute you have those pictures in hand." He laid the card on her tray and stood up.

"Certainly," she said, happy for him to be leaving. On top of her other aches and pains, a massive headache was now looming.

"Before I leave, tell me about Lauren Neuman, Paulette's cousin, whose husband she was having an affair with." He chuckled. He seemed to be genuinely amused by the crazy antics of these black people who obviously had too much money and time on their hands, and not enough good sense. There was one cousin fucking the husband of the other, best friends telling on each other, and now an NBA player caught with some guy. Worst case, he could sell the movie rights for this one, but it was so crazy that even Hollywood wouldn't believe it.

"Lauren is a nice person, and would never do such a thing." She was really thinking that Lauren didn't have the balls to do such a thing.

"What about her husband?"

Reese hadn't had time to consider that possibility. She had to admit it wasn't a bad one, either, since the accident would have gotten rid of Paulette and the bastard child.

Two birds, one stone. Just as in Chris's case.

THIRTY-TWO

Lauren's grief over Paulette's death was very complicated, and its complexity increased tenfold when combined with the anger and feelings of betrayal she also felt toward her cousin for starting her ill-fated relationship with Max. It was topped off by the deeply ingrained feelings of guilt she still harbored for the tough hand her cousin had been dealt all of her life.

Their relationship had always been unbalanced, and Lauren had worked hard to level it, feeling somehow responsible for Paulette's lot in life, as though she had to make up for the wrongdoings of her mother and grandmother. At the same time Paulette routinely sabotaged their relationship to prove that her cousin was indeed a selfish person, just like her mother, and was therefore deserving of her scorn. It was strangely ironic and symbolic that a man would be the final undoing between them—like mothers, like daughters.

Remembering snatches of the story that drove Mildred and June apart, Lauren wondered whether its final chapter also drove Paulette to take Max from her, to, in some sick, twisted way, avenge her mother. In any case it was all a very tragic affair, for which

Max was squarely to blame. She hated him for using Paulette, and couldn't wait for her divorce to become final. Then she could openly date Gideon, who'd been an incredible support to her during this awful time.

Predictably, the day after Gideon's SoHo gallery exhibition, her mother's phone line lit up like the space shuttle, with unrecognizably embellished rumors about Lauren with some photographer whom no one in their set knew. Why would she risk her marriage to handsome and successful Maximillian Neuman III to sneak around seeing some unknown photographer? Even after Paulette's death, when news of Max's affair and pending paternity got out, Mildred was still prepared to weather the storm and give her son-in-law clemency; after all, she knew what harm a harlot like Paulette was capable of doing to a guileless and unsuspecting man like Maximillian. As far as she was concerned, the whole sordid mess was Paulette's fault—again, like mother, like daughter.

Mildred was having breakfast outside in her garden room when Lauren showed up. It was a beautiful early spring day, with just the right amount of crispness in the air.

"Mother," Lauren said sternly, "I just wanted you to know that I'm divorcing Max." She picked up a croissant, pulled it apart, and popped it into her mouth. Though she'd been planning this for months now, she hadn't bothered to tell her mother.

Mildred had never heard such a defiant tone from her daughter before; it was quite alarming. She slammed her coffee cup into the saucer, sloshing the liquid over its edges. "What do you mean, you're divorcing Max? Have you lost your mind?" It was one thing for Lauren to move out, separating for a time to give him some space, but quite another for a Baines woman to actually get a divorce!

"No, in fact, I've finally found it," she said. "I let you push me into marrying a worthless, egotistical excuse for a man, and see where it got me? Or should I say, where it got us all? Especially Paulette."

"Paulette got what she asked for. If you swim with sharks, there's always a chance that you'll be eaten alive," Mildred said smugly, without a hint of remorse. She was confident that Paulette's dealings with those unsavory entertainment-business types were what had led to her demise.

Lauren was shocked. "How could you say that about your own niece? No one deserves that!"

"That's your problem, Lauren: You are *way* too naive. While you've got your pretty little head stuck in the sand, that slippery bitch was busy fucking your husband. Then she was planning to have a bastard child by him, and what do you do? You give her a baby shower!" She gave Lauren an incredulous look. "Maybe if you'd bothered to fuck him yourself occasionally, you would have been the one having his baby." Mildred didn't normally curse, but under the circumstances she felt that she was justified in saying just about anything that she wanted to.

Lauren was livid. "So that's what this is all about. Everything always has to come back to you, doesn't it? You're just pissed off because I didn't give *you* a grandchild by the *monster* you made me marry."

"Max is an adulterer, but I wouldn't call him a monster. Men cheat, especially when they're not getting what they need at home." She sipped her coffee, with her perfectly chiseled nose wedged firmly in the air.

"Men have also been known to kill their mistresses when a bastard child is involved."

"There is no way Max had anything to do with that woman's murder."

So typical, Lauren thought, that her mother would turn the affair all around and blame it on her or Paulette, rather than leveling it where it belonged—squarely on the shoulders of her no-good, handpicked son-in-law. Then she had the nerve to totally ignore the possibility that he might have been involved with Paulette's death. "So you want to defend Max? Try this on for size." She reached into her purse and tossed into her mother's lap a copy of the papers Gillian had given her.

Mildred picked it up as though it might bite. As she read the damning words the color drained from her face. It was one thing for Max to cheat on her daughter and knock up her niece, but quite another for him to steal her money. Some things were simply not forgivable. "Where did you get this?" Her hands shook with rage.

"That's not important. What is important is that Max defrauded this family out of millions of dollars, and probably would have done anything to keep Paulette's mouth shut and himself out of jail."

"So, what do we have here?" a deep voice asked. They turned to find a tall black man in a blue suit strolling toward the patio, which was located at the side of the house. He halfheartedly gestured toward the front of the house. "No one answered the door, so I thought I'd come on around back."

"Who are you?" Mildred demanded.

"Mrs. Baines-Dawson?" She nodded. "I'm Detective Harris, LAPD. Do continue," he said. Obviously he'd heard some of their conversation, and wanted to hear more.

"I did not invite you onto my property, and would ask that you leave," Mildred said in the snottiest tone she could manage under the circumstances.

"Ma'am, the police don't typically work by invitation. If we did all murderers would get away, so you can either answer my questions here, on your beautiful property," he said, looking around at the manicured landscaping appreciatively, "or we can go to a local precinct. After that we can call the media. It's your choice." Arrogantly, he sat down right next to Mildred.

She shifted in her seat and fixed him with a cold, hard stare. "So, how can I help you, Detective?" She folded her arms tightly across her chest, not looking the least bit as though she planned to be helpful.

"You can start by telling me what it is that you have there," he said, nodding toward the letter she still held.

"It's personal," she said. Though she had finally moved beyond wanting to protect Max, she did not want her family's name to continue being dragged through a police investigation, or the press. Since Paulette's unseemly death, she'd already noticed a dropoff in her own popularity. Of course, people had been calling her, trying to pry the latest information about the murder from her, so they could pass it along with the rest of their gossip, but there had been two intimate, key dinner parties since last week that she had not been invited to. Normally, she and her husband were aggressively sought after for dinner parties—they were the kind of couple who made the hostess look good—but what reputable hostess wanted to deal with the discomfort of an embarrassing scandal over canapés?

"I don't think you understand. Based on what I heard, that letter contains critical information that could be important in a murder investigation, so you can hand it to me willingly, or I can get a court order—again, your choice."

Lauren took the paper from her mother and handed it to the detective. "Detective Harris, I'm Lauren—Lauren Neuman."

"So, you're Maximillian's wife?"

Lauren simply nodded.

"My condolences," he said. After reading the letter and the attached documentation, he shook his head slowly. "So, your husband and his lover, your cousin, conspired to forge your grandmother's will, and she was blackmailing him with this information?"

"It would appear that way," Lauren said. Mildred shot a harsh look at her daughter. This was something that should be dealt with privately, not hung alongside the rest of the family's dirty laundry.

"Mrs. Neuman, when did you learn that your cousin's child belonged to your husband?"

"Right before the accident." Lauren lowered her head, desperately wanting to forget that fateful night.

"How did you find out?"

"My friend Reese Nolan had had too much to drink, and she let it slip."

"Then what happened?"

"Paulette and I had a fight. We both said some pretty ugly things. She got angry and ran out. That was the last time I saw her." Lauren broke down into tears, unable to stave off the flood of devastating memories—from going to the crash site, to later identifying her cousin's mangled body at the morgue.

After Lauren composed herself, Detective Harris asked, "How long had Paulette been in the house before she left?" Detective Harris noted that these were the first tears he'd seen shed by anyone for Paulette. For that and other reasons, he believed that Lauren had just found out about the affair, and therefore wouldn't have had time to arrange a convenient accident.

"I'm not really sure. I was the last to arrive."

"How long after you arrived did this fight occur?"

Lauren thought for a moment. "I don't know, about forty-five minutes, maybe."

"Did you see Paulette's car when you pulled up?"

"I didn't pay attention, but I don't think so."

"What did you see outside the house?"

"Nothing out of the ordinary, though this was my first time there, so I wouldn't know what was ordinary. Brandon has a lot of staff around, and the grounds are enormous. Why?"

Detective Harris had the impression that Lauren was the only witness so far who was telling him the whole truth. "It seems that Miss Dolliver's car was tampered with while it was parked on the estate grounds. Did someone park your car?"

"Yes."

"Do you know where it was parked?"

"No, once I handed the keys over, that was the last I saw of it until I left."

He'd interviewed Brandon's staff, who confirmed this account. Apparently they'd parked Paulette's and Gillian's cars around the back of the house near the garage where Brandon's cars were also kept, with the doors unlocked and keys in the ignitions. This was the perfect place and opportunity for someone to sneak in unseen and tamper with it.

"Does your husband have friends, family, or contacts in L.A.?"

"Yes, a few distant relatives."

"When was the last time he was there, to your knowledge?"

"Last month he had a meeting with a potential client." She remembered, because she was thrilled that he'd be out of town for a few days, giving her precious time to spend with Gideon.

"What if I told you that your husband hasn't had a business meeting in L.A. in over four months?" He'd had a very successful interview with Max's secretary that morning, who, like Neuman's wife, seemed anxious to slip the knife deeper into his back.

"Detective Harris, at this point very little would surprise me."

"Even the thought of your husband as a murderer?" He raised his brow, awaiting her answer. This Max guy was proving to be a scurrilous son of a bitch, so in that regard he and Paulette seemed to have been perfectly matched.

Lauren didn't bat an eye. "Yes, even the thought of my soon-to-be ex-husband as a murderer," she answered.

"Mrs. Neuman, if you don't mind, I'd like to keep this document. It could be very important to the investigation."

"You're welcome to it," she said. She'd already made copies, and she didn't give a damn what happened to Max, as long as he got what he deserved.

She glanced over at her mother, who looked like someone had driven a stake right through her heart. Her head was hung low and her face was drained of color. It wasn't clear whether her head was hung in shame, remorse, or embarrassment, though Lauren would have bet her money on the latter.

THIRTY-THREE

Over the course of two weeks, Reese had spent countless hours on her back in the hospital, alone with her thoughts. After the shock of her disfiguring injuries was dulled by the inevitable passing of time, she'd discovered a reservoir of feelings she'd never known existed. Perhaps they had been there all along, buried deeply beneath her polished surface, but she'd deftly avoided them, too busy being fabulous to tune into her own emotions.

In quiet moments, she felt an unfamiliar sense of gratitude for all that she did have, rather than remorse for that which she didn't. Before the accident she was always too busy scheming to get more, to enjoy what she'd already attained, like a rabid hamster on an ever-accelerating treadmill that was going nowhere very fast. She also came to understand the meaning of friendship; before it was a vague concept she'd never truly appreciated. To her, friends were simply people with whom she could exchange favors, rather than people who were there for one another, without regard to reciprocity.

Though she and Gillian had never been truly close before now, Reese was profoundly grateful for her friend's unwavering support during this crisis. She understood also that the almighty dollar could not buy the kind of emotional comfort that Gillian's caring presence provided; nor could it say the right things at the right time, or anticipate her needs and fears. At best money was a means, not an end. With the exception of the time Gillian was away for Paulette's funeral, she'd been to the hospital to visit Reese just about every day, bringing with her everything from silk pajamas to juicy novels and gourmet foods. She'd even hired a private nurse to accompany them back to Paulette's to gather her things, then on to Brandon's on the day of her discharge, and the same woman was scheduled to accompany them to New York and remain for at least a month. As much as Gillian didn't care to be in New York these days, she'd also insisted on staying a week to help get Reese settled, and since the filming was complete it was perfect timing.

During her recovery, Reese also came to know the meaning of true love, which was another concept that had been foreign to her. When she closed her eyes, she could clearly see her son's beautiful smiling face, and hear his sweet voice saying, "I love you, Mommy." He'd called her every day since his visit, always managing to cheer her up. She realized that the intense feeling that warmed her soul and lightened her heart was love. It hurt when she thought about how she'd dismissed him in the past, denying him—and herself— the power of that love. She prayed to God that she could make it up to him in the future.

Immediately following the accident, she repeatedly questioned, "Why me? Why must I suffer?" She now knew the answer: This tragic event was God's way of allowing her to see the beauty in His world, rather than only the beauty in herself. Sure, it still hurt to look in the mirror, but the cuts and bruises were healing, just as the self-inflicted wounds to her heart and soul would.

When she and Gillian boarded the flight from L.A. to New York, Reese was still covered in bandages. With a cast on one arm and a crutch under the other, she was unrecognizable as the glamorous It Girl often shown on Page Six.

"Gillian, thank you so much. I really appreciate what you've done for me," Reese said after they were both buckled into their first-class seats. It felt strange to be going back to New York, very different from the way she was when she left such a short time ago. What a difference a month could make.

"Don't mention it, really," Gillian said, touching Reese's arm, with a warm smile on her face. "I just hope someone would do the same thing for me." Like herself, she knew that Reese wasn't close to any family who might have looked out for her under the circumstances.

Reese immediately thought about Brandon. "I don't think you have to worry about that." She immediately felt embarrassed by the treacherous thoughts she'd had on the night of the accident. She distinctly remembered thinking that she should be the one to have him, not Gillian, and given the opportunity she would have gone for it, too, just as Paulette had gone for Max. "By the way, please thank Brandon for me." She realized that it was his money that allowed Gillian to help her.

"He's glad to be able to do it."

"How are things going with you two? Any wedding bells in the future?"

Gillian shrugged. "I'm taking it one day at a time, but things are good." Actually, aside from the federal investigation, things were great. For the first time in her life, Gillian felt there was someone really looking out for her—someone unlike her mother, who'd made a career out of looking out only for herself.

Now Gillian just had to help Brandon find that flash drive to clear his name, which was actually one of the other reasons she had insisted on going back to New York with Reese. So far Brandon's people had managed to keep the money-laundering controversy out of the media, but he feared that if he didn't resolve things be-fore next week's meeting with his attorneys and the FBI bureau chief, all bets were off. Once that happened, win, lose, or draw, he'd be finished: tried and convicted on the pages of the press. She fig-ured that if Paulette had the flash drive—and by all indications she probably did—and if it wasn't in the Los Angeles apartment, then it had to be in her New York loft.

"How is your settlement with Chris going?" she asked.

"We had pretty much agreed on everything, but things have changed, so I think it's time for us to renegotiate." Reese had a hard, intent look on her face that superseded the pain and heartache that had become a fixture. She seemed to have aged ten years in those few weeks.

Gillian nodded her head in understanding. Reese might be all banged up now, but she was still the same cutthroat girl Gillian had always known. *Some things never change*, she thought. Now that Chris was a prime suspect in Paulette's murder, she figured that Reese was preparing to up the ante, especially if the private inves-tigator whom she and Paulette had hired really had come up with some dirt, as the tabloids suggested.

When they arrived at JFK, Lauren was there to meet them. The three women hugged as if they hadn't seen one another in years, and in some ways it felt much longer. A limo, hired by Lauren, drove the three of them, plus the hired nurse, into the city. Minus Paulette, it was strangely reminiscent of the night the four of them were out on the town, swilling champagne in the back of a chauf-feured limo, ready to take on the world; in fact, it was the night that they all met Max. It seemed like so long ago, yet also like only yes-terday. Now Paulette was no longer among them, maybe even as a result of the handsome man whose attention they'd vied for on that fateful night. As they'd walked into the club that night, a bystander had referred to them as gold diggers, and then it had seemed very clear who among them was in fact a gold digger, and who wasn't. But, over time, things proved to be not as black-and-white as they appeared, since all that glittered wasn't gold, and one never knew conclusively what compromises might be made under the right set of circumstances.

"How are you holding up?" Lauren asked Reese. She couldn't help but stare at the scars that ran like chicken scratches across Reese's face. In a strange way they made her seem more real, whereas before she'd always appeared doll-like, plastic, too intentionally perfect.

"I've been better," Reese said, managing a very weak smile. "What about you? Are you okay?" She'd been so focused on her own pain that she'd forgotten that not only had Lauren lost a friend and cousin, but also her husband, on top of being betrayed by both.

"It's been tough," Lauren admitted. "I really miss Paulette, even though lately, of course, we hadn't been as close."

Lauren wore a sad expression, one of deep regret. She was sad that they'd let decades-old events affect their relationship. It had been as much her fault that they weren't closer as it was Paulette's. Lauren knew the family history, and could have done a better job of healing the injuries from the past, rather than ignoring them and continuing to straddle the fence between Paulette and her mother, and essentially letting her mother dictate her course. Looking back, she also realized that they should have talked about things, rather than pretending that they didn't exist. Their family history was like a big pink elephant squatting in the middle of the room, only in this case it turned out to be large enough to suffocate them all.

Reese reached over and covered Lauren's hand with her own. "You really can't blame yourself." She could see the pain clearly in Lauren's eyes, and knew that, regardless of what the police reports said, she'd remember only the nasty fight they'd had before the car crash. She thought about her son, and how important it was for her to try to make good memories for him and for herself, since she never knew which one would be the last.

"I just regret that our relationship wasn't better." She took a deep breath and smiled wanly.

"I know." Reese was coming to understand quite a bit about regrets these days. They rode in silence for the next few minutes as the driver expertly maneuvered the limo through the thick traffic on the Long Island Expressway.

Lauren was still staring out the window, lost in her thoughts, when she quietly asked, "How long had it been going on?"

Reese knew precisely what she meant. "At least six months that I knew of, but I'm sure it was much longer." She turned to face Lauren, putting her hand on her forearm. "I really don't think that Paulette did it so much to hurt you, as to try to make herself feel better. Does that make any sense?" Reese knew that she and Paulette were a lot alike, and what they were both really looking for all that time was much more elusive than gold, or Mr. Right; they were both in search of self-love. It was something that, regrettably, Paulette never found, but that Reese, at least, was beginning to realize existed.

Lauren nodded her head. "It does. And I don't blame her as much as I blame Max for taking advantage of her."

"It seems that he'll get what's coming to him," Gillian said. She been following all of the press, both legitimate and scandalous, surrounding the case. As much as she hated to admit it, her mother was right. In a twisted way all of the publicity about the celebrity murder case had actually helped her and the film. It was sure to increase the box-office receipts, especially after some of the more salacious journalists began to draw a line between the movie's title and the victims.

"He may already have. I just got word before your plane landed that he was brought in for questioning an hour ago." Detective Harris had called Lauren personally to let her know.

"Really?" Gillian and Reese said in unison.

"Yeah, and it doesn't look good for him. At the very least he'll go down for fraud." Whether or not he arranged to kill Paulette, Lauren really couldn't say, but it was very clear that between the affair, the pregnancy, and the forgery, he had some very powerful motives.

"It serves him right," Gillian said.

"If he did it," Reese interjected. "Don't forget, Chris had just as much of a motive."

"But Chris always seemed so . . ." Lauren searched for the word. "Innocent."

"One thing I've learned is that looks are not always what they appear," Reese said. She turned to look out the window as the car entered the Midtown Tunnel. Minutes later they emerged, back in the city where their journey together had begun.

THIRTY-FOUR

Walking into the loft she'd shared with Paulette was like stepping back in time for Reese, a warped, unsettling convergence of the past and present. Things were almost exactly the way she'd left them weeks ago, when she'd rushed to the airport, headed to L.A., except for the telltale signs that the police had searched the apartment at the start of the investigation. Paulette's half-empty coffee cup still sat on the dining room table, the liquid turning to brown, petrified sludge; dirty dishes were still scattered about the sink.

The three women, with the nurse behind them, paused in the doorway, absorbing the fact that Paulette would never again walk through these doors. They all felt like trespassers who were about to desecrate sacred ground. "I'll straighten things up out in here, while Ann gets you set up in your room," Gillian said to Reese, breaking the spell of awkward energy that hung in the air. She dropped her bag, took off her coat, and began clearing the dishes.

While Gillian tackled the kitchen, Lauren wandered around

the apartment lost in a daze, picking up photos and mementos as if they might provide a clue as to what exactly had gone wrong between her and Paulette. Lauren had never even been here to the new loft, which was a glaring testament to just how distant their relationship had become. She eventually ended up in Paulette's bedroom, where she was stopped dead in her tracks by a framed photograph of Max that Paulette had lovingly perched on her bedside table. It was tangible proof of their illicit affair. Slowly Lauren picked up the picture and carefully studied the face that stared out at her. It was now the face of a total stranger. The picture had been taken at some public event by a professional photographer, so it wasn't even an intimate shot taken during his and Paulette's private time. Max would have been too selfish to give her that kind of intimacy. Instead it was a stock picture, one that anyone could have gotten from a PR kit—sad, really. Without words, its existence spoke clearly of the fact that Max was simply using Paulette, and surely had no intention of ever having a real relationship with her, contrary to what Paulette seemed to want so desperately.

These thoughts forced Lauren to really consider the possibility that the reality of losing his marriage—for whatever it was worth—coupled with the humiliation of a pregnancy by his wife's cousin, and the devastating revelation of his criminal forgery, *were* enough to drive Max to murder. She looked closely at his face, his eyes, and the set of his chin, as though his features might provide some answers, but the only thing she saw there was arrogance, no substance and no soul.

A while later, after settling Gillian and Reese in, Lauren left to go back to her hotel, but she decided to stop by her old apartment instead. She'd had the foresight to park her car at the garage near Paulette's and meet the limo driver there before heading to the airport, since the four of them and the luggage would never have fit in her Jaguar. She was glad now that she had, since Max's detour into police custody gave her the perfect opportunity to drive by and pick up a few things she'd left in her haste to move out—including her passport.

Gideon had invited her to come with him to Senegal at the end of the week. Without thought she'd first said no, immediately feeling incapable of picking up and going almost halfway around the world to a place that didn't have even a Ritz-Carlton, but fortunately she'd listened to him and at least gotten her shots, just in case. She decided to call him with the good news.

"Hey, baby," she cooed into the phone. She'd never cooed before meeting Gideon; in fact, there were many things that she'd never done before meeting Gideon, things that were now second nature, and quite addictive.

"Hey, gorgeous." She loved it when he called her that. Not because she believed it to be true, but because he said it as if he truly did. "How are you?"

"I'll be better in a few days," she answered, pouting.

"What's happened now?" Concern registered in his voice. With all of the recent drama he constantly worried about her, which was one of the reasons he'd invited her on the trip—to get away from it all.

"The question is, What's *going* to happen?" She laughed at his confusion. "I'm being swept away to Africa by my prince."

Now he laughed. It was a beautiful sound. "He must be some guy."

"Trust me, he is the best. But listen, I've gotta run. I just wanted to let you know that I've changed my mind; I am going with you."

"Where are you? Wanna stop by for a little preflight instruction? I'm in Midtown; I could be at the Plaza in fifteen minutes," he teased.

She smiled. "I wish I could, but I'm headed to the apartment to pick up my passport." Now that she had made the decision to go with him, she was giddy with excitement.

"Where's Max?" She could hear the concern in his voice again.

"He was brought in by the police for questioning." She still could hardly believe that the man she'd married was quite possibly a murderer.

He exhaled loudly. "I can't say that I'm sorry."

"Nor can I, but listen—gotta go; I'll call you later." She puckered her lips together, sending a kiss through the phone's receiver.

"All right, darling."

She hung up the phone and tossed it into her bag, wearing a sunbeam smile and flushed with lurid thoughts of fourteen days and nights with this man whom she loved. She got out of the car and dashed into the house, anxious to get in and get out as quickly as possible. The last thing she wanted was a confrontation with Max. She turned the key in the lock and slipped into the dark, empty house, feeling like a stranger breaking and entering. The house and everything in it felt foreign to her, as though it all belonged to another person. The beautifully decorated rooms and exquisite furnishings were tasteful and well selected, but bore no hint of her personality; they could have been picked out of a catalog. Her house, though expensive, was cookie-cutter, as was her life up until now— and she was intent on breaking that mold. She dropped her bag onto the foyer table and quickly headed upstairs to retrieve her passport and a few other personal effects.

Fifteen minutes later she was bounding down the stairs on the way out the door when it opened, and there stood Max.

"What are *you* doing here?" He looked like hell, and smelled like cheap vodka.

Lauren's breath caught in her throat. "I-I had to pick up a few things that I forgot."

"Oh, like your husband, maybe?" He slurred his words and

opened his arms wide, as though presenting himself. It was a sad sight.

She tried to walk around him. "I've gotta go." He widened his arms to block her exit.

"Home to your boyfriend, huh? Who knew that you were such a little slut? I thought I was marrying Westchester, and got Harlem instead."

She planted her hand on her hip and angled one foot outward. "Let me by," she insisted.

"Or what?" he asked, moving closer to her. His eyes were menacing and bloodshot, and his breath was hot and rancid.

Anxious to leave, she reached for her purse. He snatched it out of her hand and threw it across the room. "What are you doing?" she yelled.

"It's time you paid for ruining my life."

"How did I ruin your life? From what I see you've done a brilliant job of that all by yourself."

"You spoiled little bitch," he spit. "I wasn't good enough for you to have my baby, huh?"

Lauren was stunned. She had no idea that he knew her secret.

"All this time I thought that you were just a barren, frigid bitch. Little did I know that you were just a frigid bitch who thought she was too good to have my child."

"Obviously Paulette didn't have that problem, and look where it got her," Lauren retorted.

Rage gripped him, narrowing his eyes, and sending blood coursing to his brain through arteries that now pulsed, and his fists were clenched tight with anger. "I oughta——"

"What, kill me, too?"

He raised his hand high above his head, ready to strike down to crush the source of his anger and hatred. Lauren represented everything that he cherished and exalted, but didn't really feel worthy of. Likewise, she reflected the things about himself that he hated and despised. Lauren shrank away, and her arms flew up reflexively to protect herself.

"Don't you even think about it." Max looked over his shoulder, only to find Gideon, who'd just opened the door and was wearing a look that said, *I'd be very happy to kick your ass.* The muscles in Gideon's neck twitched in anticipation of it. After the call from Lauren he couldn't shake the unease he felt that she was walking into Max's house alone; after all, the man was a murder suspect, and just because he was brought in for questioning didn't mean that they would or could keep him. When Gideon couldn't reach her on her cell phone, which she'd left downstairs, he immediately raced to the apartment.

Lauren's eyes closed in relief, and she let out a breath that she didn't even realize she'd been holding.

"Who the hell are you?" Max asked, frowning.

"I'm the man who will kick your punk ass if you even think about touching her." He reached out to have Lauren come to him. She retrieved her bag and hurried out of the house that she'd somehow once called home.

When they were safely outside Lauren melted in his arms. "How did you know?"

"I didn't, but I wasn't going to take a chance." He held her close, kissing her forehead. "I love you, Lauren."

"I love you, too."

He followed her to her hotel, and spent the entire night there holding her in his arms.

THIRTY-FIVE

Gillian had been nothing short of a godsend to Reese. She'd cleaned the loft from top to bottom, and made sure that it was fully stocked with food and that Reese had the medicines and medical supplies she needed. She'd even found a real estate agent to help her start the search for a place of her own, and Reese was actually looking forward to the solitude she'd learned to value after hours lying alone in the hospital. For the first time she had really gotten to know herself, and she wasn't *all* bad. She felt ready to get on with her life.

To that end, later today she and Chris were meeting, without their attorneys, to have what she hoped would be their last conversation about the settlement. But there was one thing that she had to do first. When she was getting into bed that first night at the loft, she'd found an envelope with her name on it inside her pillowcase. It was from Paulette, and read:

Dear Reese,
In case you get back to New York before I do, here are the goods!

This is the key to the safe-deposit box where I've stored the photos and negatives of Chris for safekeeping. Use them in good health (and for lots of wealth!).

Ciao,
Paulette

Reese called a car service and made the trip to Paulette's bank, where her safe-deposit box was kept. After showing proper credentials, she was provided with the contents of the box. Sure enough, inside was an envelope containing the lurid eight-by-ten glossies of Chris having oral sex with another man, along with the only set of negatives, at least according to Paulette. Again she flipped through the photos, but this time a feeling of sadness came over her. She never really knew her own husband, but then again, he never really knew her either. She stuffed the envelope into her bag and picked up another one that lay in the box. It had Brandon Russell's name scrawled across it.

Puzzled, she looked around before opening it. She really felt like a trespasser now, but Paulette was dead, so what was the difference? Inside the envelope she found a computer flash drive and a copy of a letter that had been handwritten to Brandon. It read:

Dear Brandon,
It seems that I have something of yours that you will proba-bly be needing. Let's discuss what I should do about it. I would hate for something so important to get lost again....

Paulette

Reese turned the flash drive over in her hand, wondering what could possibly be on it. And why hadn't Paulette just given it to Gillian or Brandon when she went out to L.A. instead of hiding it away in a safe deposit box? Given how sneaky Paulette could be, there was no telling what she had been up to. Reese tossed the letter and drive back into the envelope and then into her bag. She had her own problems to solve.

ours later, Reese met Chris in the library bar at the Hudson Hotel. After hearing about Lauren's near-attack by Max, she decided that a public meeting was definitely in order; after all, maybe Chris did murder Paulette, and attempted to kill her. It was hard to believe that Chris would do something so brutal, but stranger things were happening.

"You're looking better," Chris said, taking a seat in one of the bar's club chairs. He, however, looked a little worse for wear himself. Chris appeared to have lost a good fifteen pounds, and looked like he had slept fitfully for weeks. Under the dire circumstances, it shouldn't have been surprising.

But it was. To Reese, Chris always seemed invincible, but a drug charge, threats of bisexual exposure, divorce, the loss of a multi-million-dollar deal, and rumors of a murder rap could strip the S from anyone's chest. "Thank you. I feel a little bit better every day." She could tell that he was studying the scars on her face, but trying not to. Everyone did. She was beginning to get used to it.

He sat back in his chair and clasped his fingers together in his lap. "So, Reese, what did you want to see me about?" Chris was anxious to get down to business and get out of here. It was hard to miss a six-foot-five-inch basketball player, especially one as popular—and now notorious—as Chris was. He was beginning to notice other customers peeping, pointing, and whispering.

"I wanted to talk to you about the settlement."

"That much I figured, but why not let our attorneys finish this up?" Before the car crash they'd come to a verbal agreement on the sum of $15 million. Knowing his conniving wife, she probably wanted to extort more money from him by threatening to turn the pictures over to the police, realizing that they would provide an even stronger motive for him to kill both Paulette and Reese.

"I want to renegotiate," she said. The light tone was gone, as was the air of vulnerability. Since her return to New York, Detective Harris had called her every day, insisting that she turn over the pictures and negatives of Chris.

He rolled his eyes. It was just as he thought. "Reese, we already had a deal. And if you'll remember, this will be the third time you've wanted to renegotiate." The muscles in his jaw tightened. "I'm really sick of you extorting money from me," he hissed, leaning forward, struggling to keep his voice down. People were openly looking now.

Reese reached into her bag and took out the envelope that she'd gotten from Paulette's safe-deposit box, and pulled out the pictures and negatives. "This is not about money," she said, lifting the pictures. "This is about my son." She tore the pictures in half, then tore the halves in half, before sliding them, along with the negatives, across the table to a stunned Chris. She'd just tell Detective Harris that she hadn't been able to find them.

"I'm not interested in hurting you or taking any more of your money," she said earnestly. "In fact, I'm sorry for a lot of the things I've done in the past. But what I'm most concerned about right now is the future. I want joint custody of Rowe." She sat back and folded her arms across her chest.

Chris sat back too, stunned. He'd never seen Reese do anything as selfless as giving up those negatives without a fight—or a check; nor had he ever seen her so sincere. Maybe her head injury was more severe than he thought, or maybe somehow she was different. "Why the sudden change?" he asked. She'd never expressed any real interest in Rowe before, not since he was born.

"I don't blame you for asking that; you have every right to. I know that I've not been the best mother—or wife, for that matter—but I have changed. As painful as all of this has been for me, it's taught me some very important lessons. I've learned the value of people—relationships and love—over money and material things."

Silent tears trekked down her cheeks. "Lying in that bed in such physical and mental pain, I realized that all of the money or medicine in the world could do nothing to make me feel as good as I did when I saw Rowe's smile or heard his voice. I promised God then that if I recovered, I would make it up to him and try hard to be a better mother. So, that's what I'm asking—that you give me that opportunity."

As much as he had grown to despise Reese in the past, Chris did sense a change in her, and even more important, he knew that being with his mother would only help his son, and he couldn't deprive Rowe of that. "I wouldn't dream of standing in the way," Chris said. "I'll have my attorney redraft the papers first thing tomorrow."

"Thank you."

He held up the negatives. "And thank you."

When she got back to the loft, Gillian was packed and ready to leave for the airport. "Are you going to be okay here by yourself?" she asked Reese.

"Absolutely," she answered. She was still giddy from the outcome of the meeting with Chris. "Gillian, how can I ever thank you for all that you've done for me?"

"Thanks aren't necessary; just get well soon." They hugged each other before Gillian turned to wheel her luggage out the door.

"I almost forgot," Reese said, reaching into her bag. "I think this belongs to you—or to Brandon." She handed Gillian the envelope she'd retrieved from Paulette's safe-deposit box.

Gillian turned the package over, and could feel the outline of the flash drive inside. Relief washed over her in waves, but being the good actress that she was, she never let it show. "It must be something I left in Paulette's apartment in L.A.," she said nonchalantly.

"Well, have a good trip, and call me when you get there." Reese gave her another big hug.

I certainly will have a good trip now, thought Gillian. This was exactly what she'd come hoping to find. She was so excited that she could have grown wings and flown herself back to Los Angeles.

THIRTY-SIX

Gillian could hardly wait to tell Brandon the good news. She'd finally found the flash drive that would save his company and his reputation! Anxiously, she called his cell phone on the way to the airport, but got voice mail. She was so excited she could hardly sit still. Finally she could relax and enjoy the huge success that was coming her way. In the back of her mind she'd been waiting for the other shoe to drop, fearful that Brandon would be indicted any day now, bringing her film career—and lifestyle—to a screeching halt. But now that she had evidence that the investigating agent was just a racist on a vendetta, she was as sure as Brandon was that it would be a thing of the past; after all, they had no hard evidence on him, only some loose connections and lots of speculation.

When the plane landed at LAX she headed straight to baggage claim, where she found Charles already waiting for her. In short order her luggage made its way around the carousel, but this time, as was her habit these days, she looked carefully at the name tags before having Charles load the bags up.

As she walked out of the airport doors, her thoughts also revisited the uncomfortable conversation she'd had with Detective Harris right after her last trip. She hadn't heard from him since then, so she supposed that he'd come to the sane conclusion that there was no way that she or Brandon was in any way involved in Paulette's death, for a very simple reason: They had no motive.

On the way home she again called Brandon's cell phone, and again she got his voice mail, so she decided to try his assistant, who informed her that he was in back-to-back meetings, and probably wouldn't be home until late. After arriving home herself, Gillian changed clothes and headed straight into his study. She wanted to pull up the video on the flash drive to make sure that it was still there and hadn't been accidentally erased somehow. She plugged the device into the back of the computer and waited for it to pop up. She was giddy with excitement, envisioning how happy Brandon would be to see it.

After a few keystrokes, the contents of the drive popped up on the computer screen. She expected to see a video file, but instead there were two Excel spreadsheets. She closed her eyes, shook her head, and sighed heavily. She was very disappointed that the drive didn't contain the evidence to clear Brandon's name. It was a good thing that she hadn't been able to get in touch with him. She would have hated to get his hopes up, only to be dashed. Gillian was about to pull the flash drive from the computer in defeat, when a voice told her that she should look to see what she *did* have. She opened the first spreadsheet and saw what appeared to be a routine accounting of Sunset Records' books. Nothing important there. Then she opened the second document and found another almost identical spreadsheet. It contained the same company name, same time frame, and same line items, but totally different numbers. That was when it dawned on her that Brandon had been keeping a double set of books. She wasn't an accounting or legal expert, but it was clear—even to her—that Brandon must have been laundering money. Why else would he need to keep two sets of records or concoct such a far-fetched story about a video to cover up the contents of the flash drive? Gillian dropped her head into her hands to keep the room from spinning. She saw her future going straight down the drain, right alongside his. She had to calm down and think about exactly what this meant. The first thought that came to mind was that Paulette had known about this, which explained why the note she'd written had had such a strange, cryptic tone.

A coat of perspiration covered her body as she also realized that this could have been reason enough for Brandon to murder Paulette. Not only would he have a really good motive, but he also had the opportunity, since her car was parked at his house when it was tampered with! Could Brandon have actually killed Paulette? Or maybe one of his gangster friends did it for him? At this moment she realized the explosive nature of the information she had.

She took the flash drive out of the computer and paced the floor, trying desperately to decide what she should do next. She wondered what Brandon would do to her if he realized that she knew about the double set of books and the note from Paulette. Obviously he hadn't wanted her to know about it, since he'd come up with the elaborate lie about a racist agent. He simply wanted her to help him get the flash drive back from Paulette, hoping that she wouldn't actually look at it. The big question was, Would he try to get rid of Gillian to protect himself?

Pacing wasn't helping, so she shut down the computer and left his study, tucking the flash drive into one pocket and the note in the other, careful to make sure that nothing in the room looked disturbed. As she was walking down the hall toward her suite, she heard the door open and the butler say, "Good evening, Mr. Russell."

Oh, shit, she thought, *he's home.*

THIRTY-SEVEN

Eight months later searchlights crossed the night sky, beckoning throngs of fans to Hollywood Boulevard's Grauman's Chinese Theatre. Along the red carpet photographers trained their zoom lenses and reporters were at the ready, pens poised and mikes queued; all were waiting anxiously to catch a glimpse, take a shot of, or grab a sound bite from Gillian Tillman, the latest Hollywood sensation.

"This gorgeous actress, the star of *Gold Diggers*, is the newest addition to Hollywood's elite A-list," a hyper, bone-thin blond reporter from *Extra* spoke into the camera. "Her role in this highly anticipated movie is nothing short of brilliant! There is already talk about an Oscar for the former Broadway actress, model, and New York native. She burst on the scene just this year after honing her craft on Broadway." She looked away from the camera, then back again. "Here she comes now! Let's see if we can get an interview."

When Gillian stepped out of the Silver Shadow inches away from the red carpet, she looked like several million dollars. Hundreds of fans burst into applause; some even had tears in their eyes as they clapped in unabashed glee. This maniacal support was surreal, something out of a bizarre Hollywood script, perhaps. The film had been screened to enthusiastic critical acclaim, but the masses had yet to even see it, though none of that mattered, because Brandon's publicity plan for Gillian had worked like a charm.

The whole concept was to have Gillian appear on the scene out of nowhere, looking amazing and as if people *should* know her, even if they didn't. For fickle, trend-following Hollywood types, this was a perfect scheme, because everyone wanted to be in the know and ahead of the curve. Everyone strove to be the first to know the hot new anything, so when the movie was released to fantastic reviews, everyone from studio heads and entertainment reporters to peers and fans immediately adopted Gillian; it would have been so "out of the loop" not to.

When she stepped onto the red carpet wearing custom-designed diamond-encrusted stilettos, it was clear to all that Gillian owned it. She looked like an exotic goddess as she glided up the red carpet with a poise way beyond her accomplishments. She strolled it as though she'd done it dozens of times, and this was simply another walk in the park. This was the premiere of *her* movie, and *she* was the star, a star who was definitely ready for her close-up. Gillian was celestial as flashes from photographers' cameras lit up the sky around her, as her fans orbited her galaxy. It was magical, and she deserved it after all of the suffering she'd endured.

"Gillian, Gillian, over here!" The *Extra* reporter was scrambling to get an interview ahead of her rival at *Entertainment Tonight*.

Gillian graciously paused and obliged the reporter with a dazzling but coy smile. It was important that it not be a beaming cheerleader's smile, which would show too much overeagerness, rather than supreme confidence. One would never guess that at this very moment Gillian craved a smoke in the worst way, a habit that had recently returned with a vengeance. "Yes, Donna." Her PR people were the best, and had prompted her on the names of all of the important reporters. And Gillian knew that she'd make a fan for life if she simply said the name; and it worked like magic. Everyone wanted to be her new best friend, and the entertainment reporters were no different.

"Gillian, first I must say that you look stupendous; you are absolutely glowing. What a night!"

"Thank you, Donna. This really isn't my night; it truly belongs to the brilliant writers, directors, and my fellow cast and the crew of *Gold Diggers*," Gillian lied. This was all about her. "I've been blessed to be surrounded by such incredible talent, and I thank each of them for helping me achieve any success that I have."

"Tell our viewers, in your own words, what *Gold Diggers* is about."

"It's a parable that broadens the concept of the gold digger as we know her. We've all heard the term before, often used to describe a cheap hoochie chasing a dollar, but this movie elevates it to include a wide range of women *and men*." Gillian looked into the camera. "And yes, men can be gold diggers, too," she teased the audience, and then turned back to Donna. "But also consider the C-list actress who scopes out and bags the A-list actor, or the college-educated woman who lands the star athlete, or, more simply, the tall, beautiful babe strolling along with the short nerd with the tall pockets. This film simply broadens the definition of the term *gold digger* by dramatizing the similarities between diverse people when it comes to the acquisition—or maintenance—of money and power."

"Speaking of men, will you be changing your name to Mrs. Gillian Russell?"

Gillian ignored the interesting transition, smiled, and raised her left ring finger to display fifteen-karats of Harry Winston engagement and wedding rings. Again she flashed the coy smile that would become her trademark. "Brandon and I thought it best that

I keep my maiden name, given the fans who've already gotten to know my work on Broadway."

Six months earlier they'd been married in a private ceremony aboard Brandon's new yacht, *The Sleeping Dog*, as it cruised the Mediterranean. Lauren and Gideon, who'd been traveling throughout Africa, joined them; and so did Reese, who had traveled alone from New York.

After discovering the contents of the flash drive, Gillian had run into Brandon as he entered the house, and shown him the device as though she'd just found the Holy Grail, giving him no indication that she'd looked at its contents, or that she'd ever seen a copy of the note written to him by Paulette. That performance was also Academy Award—worthy.

At first, she wasn't sure that she could live with him, knowing that he was at least a money launderer connected to gang members, and at worst possibly a murderer. But money and luxury had a funny way of soothing the conscience. She rarely ever thought about those pesky details anymore; she was too busy nestling deeper into the lap of luxury.

"It takes a very secure man not to insist that you change your name."

"My husband is nothing if not secure," Gillian said.

She stepped away from the mike, waved, and continued her stroll up the red carpet.

EPILOGUE

"He is soooooo fine," the blonde said as she watched Rowe dribble the basketball upcourt with all eyes centered on him. She had the look of a piranha set to eat him alive.

"Uhmmmm. Tell me about it," her friend purred. "I hear he'll be this year's first-round draft pick."

The two girls sat watching the game like two talent scouts. It wasn't the statistics on the court that they noted, but the numbers that were soon to come.

"Yeah, which means a very big contract." Though it was the dead of winter, they both wore tops that were skimpy enough to be considered bikini halves.

"So, how are we going to meet him?" Neither one of them took her eyes off of Rowe during their entire conversation with each other.

"A friend of mine promised he could get us into the team party later tonight."

"Cool." The blonde tossed her hair, getting in practice for tonight.

"May the best girl win," the brunette challenged.

Some things never changed, Reese thought, as she sat behind the two scheming hoochies, cringing while she listened to them plot to snag her son. The only difference was that these days there were more white chicks going after the black athletes than there were black girls, and somehow that made it even worse. She wanted to interrupt and tell them that they needed to go gold digging in another mine, but she knew that it wouldn't have made a difference. Even if it did for these two, there were hundreds, if not thousands, of others to replace them, each one hoping to be the lucky girl who struck gold. Yes, Reese knew this game all too well.

In the years since the accident and her divorce, Reese had devoted most of her time to her son, and then his career. They'd grown very close, and she guarded Rowe fiercely. In fact, she moved to California to be near him during his time at UCLA.

"What are you wearing tonight?" the brunette asked the blonde.

"The shortest, tightest, and smallest thing I can squeeze these into." She laughed, sticking out her augmented chest. "Trust me; I know exactly how to get his attention."

"Don't we all!" the brunette said slyly. They threw their heads back in laughter as they gave each other a big high five.

READING GROUP COMPANION

1. Which female character ended up being the most notorious
    gold digger? Why?

2. Which character experienced the most significant transforma-
    tion? Explain.

3. Does Paulette's family history explain and/or excuse her
    behavior?

4. Was Lauren to blame for her family's escalating problems by
    failing to address or acknowledge them?

5. Truth be told, aren't most people gold diggers to one extent or
    another? After all, who digs for dirt?

6. Is there a difference between gold diggers and people who
    simply want to marry well, or increase their lot in life? What is
    that difference?

7. How far did Gillian fall from Imelda's tree?

8. Was it wrong for Lauren to mislead Max about her fertility?

9. Can men be gold diggers? Is Max one?

10. Who do you think really tampered with Paulette's car?

Tracie Howard is the author or coauthor of five books: *Revenge Is Best Served Cold* (with Danita Carter), *Success Is the Best Revenge* (with Danita Carter), *Talk of the Town* (with Danita Carter), *Why Sleeping Dogs Lie*, and *Never Kiss and Tell*. She is a former columnist and lifestyle editor for *Savoy* magazine, and the owner of a fashion accessories company called Ethos (www.ExperienceEthos.com), whose products debuted in Barneys in fall of 2006. She lives with her husband on the East Coast.